"Thor, Baldacci, Flynn, Hamburg. Get ready as Banner fits right in!"

AMAZON REVIEW

"Move over Jack Reacher there's a new guy taking over."

AMAZON REVIEW

"Great stuff. Exciting and fast paced. On par with Flynn & Thor."

AMAZON REVIEW

"The writing was superior, the story line was compelling and the action was top-notch. Sorry I could only give this one a five star rating!"

AMAZON REVIEW

RIDING THE DEVIL

A HARRY BAUER THRILLER

BLAKE BANNER

RIGHTHOUSE

ISBN-13: 978-1-63696-324-2

ISBN-10: 1-63696-324-2

Cover design by: Damonza

Printed in the United States of America

www.righthouse.com

www.instagram.com/righthousebooks

www.facebook.com/righthousebooks

twitter.com/righthousebooks

ONE

I watched the white Jeep bearing the sheriff's badge turn in at the gate a quarter of a mile away, where the small bridge crossed the creek. It bounced and lurched on the uneven dirt track, but it didn't raise dust. It was too cold to raise dust. I put out a hand to stop the punch bag swinging. The sun was not long up over the Wind River Mountains to the east, though the smell of pine was already in the air, stained by the smell of my own sweat.

I walked the short distance from Ash's garage-cum-gym to the covered decking and sat on the wooden steps to wait. The white Jeep coiled up the track and crunched to a halt opposite me, beside my RAM. The door swung open and Sheriff Seth Levi swung down. He pressed his hat on his head and gave a nod.

"Mr. Bauer."

"Sheriff."

He studied his boots for a moment. They were dusty, scuffed and turned up at the toes. After considering them he looked up at the tops of the trees at the back of the house, then higher still at the very blue sky. I felt a hot stab of irritation in my gut.

"Sky looks the same up here as it does down in Pinedale, Sheriff."

He grunted a sigh. "Mr. Bauer, we need to talk."

"Have you found him?"

He shook his head, but still wouldn't look at me. He sucked his teeth and looked at the decking instead. "No, Mr. Bauer." Now he turned to look at me. "We've scoured the valley and there's no trace of him. But I have to level with you. I get the feeling you ain't telling me everything there is to tell. I can't help you, if you ain't gonna help me."

I looked down at my thumbs, weighing up how much to tell him.

"I knew Ash some years back, about ten years ago. He was in the Feds." I looked up at the sheriff's broad, honest face. "Did you know that?"

He shook his head. "Ash never talked much about hisself."

"He had some trouble with one of the Mexican cartels. I don't know the details—"

"You a Fed? Is that how you know him?"

"No. I'm military. At least I was back then. Special operations. Anyway, came a point where Ash had had enough. He resigned and he moved out here with his daughter. He was looking for a saner, healthier way of life."

The sheriff nodded slowly a few times at the decking. "He found it. Him and Sonia was happy here. They was private people, but we don't mind that, and Sonia was starting to make friends. Ash too, though slower."

"You want coffee?"

He sighed and nodded. "Yeah. Sure."

He followed me across the covered decking and into the Spartan living room. I moved behind the breakfast bar and set about grinding some fresh beans. The toasted bitter smell was strong.

When it was on the hob I said, "I can't tell you much more than I've told you already, Sheriff. Ash contacted me out of the blue and asked me to come and spend some time here. He said he was worried about Sonia." I smiled and held his eye. "She must have been six years old when I last saw her. He said she'd gone out with friends the night before and hadn't come back. Naturally I told him I was on my way, but I also told him to talk to you."

"Yeah," he said with a twist of bitterness. "He weren't none too keen on that idea. I think he figures we're a bunch of country bumpkins out here."

I shook my head. "It's not that, Sheriff. It's a question of resources. He worked out of the New York field office on Broadway. The resources they had at their disposal were simply the best in the world. However good you and your deputies are—and I am sure you're damn good—you haven't got the FBI's resources. Anyway, when I got here there was no sign of Ash or Sonia. That's when I called you."

The coffee started to gurgle. I turned off the gas and grabbed a couple of cups. "What you *have* got is a lot of space for bad things to happen in. She could have been mauled by a bear, bitten by a snake, fallen down a mountainside...," I looked at him and held his eye, "or she could have been drugged, raped and/or murdered."

He sighed and sagged, like the idea had deflated him. "Yeah, that don't happen much out here. What does happen here, like just about everywhere else, is kids reach sixteen and start doing things they didn't use to do when they was fifteen. I got five kids, three boys and two girls. Each one of them was once sixteen. They're all good kids. They all got good grades. They love their mom and respect their dad. And each-damn-one of them was a pain in the ass at sixteen."

I smiled, grabbed a bottle of Jameson's from the cupboard and a couple of shot glasses. "Get the coffee, will you, Sheriff?"

I led the way back out to the decking and we settled ourselves at a small round table, looking out at the Windies to the north and east. As he sat I poured him strong black coffee and a shot. As I helped myself he said:

"Teenagers need to rebel. They need to kick against their parents sometimes. Thing with Ash is, he wants to be his daughter's best friend. He told me a couple of days ago, 'We share everything, Seth. I'm her best friend.' That ain't healthy." He knocked back the whiskey, smacked his lips and picked up his coffee. "Parents cannot be their kids' best friends! Hell! What were *you* doin' when you was sixteen?"

"I plead the Fifth."

He chuckled. "Yeah, me too. But Ash don't get that. He don't see that if she does something he disapproves of, gets drunk, makes out with a boy, hell—puffs on a joint—she ain't just gonna get grounded, like any other parent would do, she is going to be crippled with guilt because she let her daddy down. This great daddy who was her best friend. That is one hell of a high standard he's holding her to."

I knocked back the whiskey and refilled our glasses. "I agree, Sheriff, but I am not sure what point you're making. You think Sonia has gone AWOL with a bunch of friends? That doesn't explain where Ash is. He's been gone three days and she's been gone two."

"And nobody between Cheyenne and Jackson, Evanston and Douglass, Yellowstone and the Devil's darn Tower has had sight or sound of them. Ain't it just possible, Mr. Bauer, that his daughter went off with friends, the way kids do sometimes at sixteen, he went looking for her and found her, and now they're talking things over?"

I nodded a few times, slowly, looking at the haze over the distant mountains. "Yup," I said, "it's possible, but he would have left me a note, or called me. But there's something else. Ash told me he was worried that there were some kids in town who were pushing drugs to young teenagers. So I ask you, is it possible that Sonia was hanging out with these kids, they got her stoned and raped her. That intentionally or by accident, Sonia was killed, and when her father found out he was killed too? Is that possible?"

He grunted, picked up his whiskey and stared at it. "Yeah, that's possible too. What about her mother? Maybe she went to stay with—"

"Her mother is dead."

"Shit."

"She was murdered. There is no one back East. It was just him and his daughter, and he was trying to give her a safer, healthier life." I sipped my coffee, and as I set down the cup I asked him, "Who were her friends, Sheriff? Had she started hanging around with a bad crowd?"

He shrugged. "They're just a bunch of kids, not what you'd call a bad crowd."

"What about his worries about drugs?"

"There's a gang of 'em. They ain't bad kids. I ain't never seen Sonia drunk or high or anything like that. From what I hear, they mainly seem to be into UFOs and that kind of..."

He hesitated. I said, "Crap?"

"I guess. So they do a lot of stargazing. They see a satellite or a shooting star and they think it's a spaceship from another planet. Her—" He cleared his throat and stared out at the empty acres. "The boy she hangs around with the most—my day we would have said her boyfriend—is Dave—"

"Dave Jorgensen? Ash mentioned a Dave Jorgensen." He nodded. I asked, "Have you spoken to him or his parents?"

"Course. I called when she hadn't come home. I spoke to his mother. She said Dave wasn't home either. We talked for a bit. She didn't seem too worried. I called again in the morning. Dave was back. He said he'd left Sonia at the gate, bottom of my lane. I told Ash, but he said Sonia hadn't showed up."

"Who else?"

"Sadie Cody, George Cody's daughter. The only other kid who's with them regular is a kid they call Slick, lives down by the brewery on Marilyn. He's a bit wild. Samuel Connolly. I've had words with him and his dad a few times. Then there's Marv. He's what they call a nerd. He knows a lot about computers, gets them pictures of Mars and the moon. They believe there's alien bases up there."

I studied his face a moment, wondering if he was real smart

and playing dumb, or if he had just grown lazy living in the cowboy version of the Island of the Lotus Eaters.

"So when Dave says he dropped her off at the gate, where had they been all night?"

He looked slightly embarrassed. "Watching UFOs. We gotta call 'em UAPs now. Unidentified Aerial Phenomena. They stayed out late at the lake. They say they saw some lights moving in a crazy way."

I repeated the question. "Where?"

"'Bout a mile past the Lakeside Lodge, on the 741. They had a couple of beers, watched the stars, and then Sonia saw how late it was and said she had to get home. That was about nine PM."

"About the time you called Dave's mother."

"They came back in Dave's truck, dropped her at the bottom of the lane—"

"That's what he says. He should have brought her to the door."

"Yeah, well—" He drank his coffee, which had gone cold, and chased it with the shot. He smacked his lips and said, "They said they were scared of how Ash'd be. He could be pretty intimidating. Plus he had to take the others home too."

I frowned. "He dropped Sonia first? That doesn't make much sense. He had to pass through town to get here to Ash's place. He could have dropped the gang at the Riddley's intersection and then brought Sonia home." I sighed and ran my fingers through my hair. "It's what any seventeen year-old boy would do. You get to spend a few minutes alone with your girl, and hope for a goodnight kiss."

"I know. It's what I thought too. But they all agree."

"You mean they all corroborate each other's stories. That doesn't prove shit." He gave me a queasy look. I asked, "So what now?"

"What now?" He looked at me with weary eyes that were a little bloodshot. "Now is where I decide whether to issue a BOLO on Ash Bauer, and get to wondering just exactly how mad he got when she arrived home late?"

I sighed and spoke quietly. "That's bullshit and you know it!"

"Yeah? Maybe so. But I've got five kids willing to swear they dropped Sonia off at that gate." He stabbed a finger down where the track led to the road. "Which means that Sonia disappeared somewhere between that gate and this house. And if I don't find her pretty damned soon, the State Police are going to be lookin' at Ash pretty damned close—whatever I may know or not know!"

"It's too much of a coincidence, Sheriff, them both disappearing like that—"

"*Unless* he's on the run!"

"-—*after* telling me he was worried about the rise in drugs-related crimes." I studied his face a moment. He looked away. "Was he wrong?" I pressed him. "Has drug-related crime risen? Are there pushers selling drugs to kids?"

He took a deep breath. "No, he wasn't wrong. We talked about it a couple of times. He was worried—"

He stopped himself. I said, "About what, Sheriff?"

He shrugged, shook his head and spread his hands. "About that, about the drugs, and Sonia..."

"About Slick? Was he worried about Slick, Sheriff?"

He puffed out his cheeks. "Yeah, you don't miss much, do you?"

"I pay attention. You said you'd had words with him and his dad. Was it about drugs?"

"Yeah." He glanced at me, like he was wondering what my attitude was to drugs. "If y'ask me he's developing a cocaine habit. Now, we got some of the strictest drug laws in the United States in Wyoming. You get caught with more than three ounces of marijuana, that's a felony, you can go down for five years. And Wyoming judges ain't known for being liberal, especially about drugs. Now, if a man is in his thirties, he beats his wife and he's always drunk or stoned or both, well maybe that's the wake-up call he needs. But if a kid's seventeen, and his biggest crime is bein' plain stupid..." He shrugged. "I'd rather take him aside, give him a taste of my belt and warn his dad to take him in hand."

If he was hoping for approval all he got from my face was a blank stare.

"You said Ash and Sonia were close. Did they go fishing or hunting together? That kind of stuff?"

He frowned. "Sure," then he smiled, "I guess you don't do that a lot in New York."

I returned the smile, but kept it on the side of my face, where it was ironic. "No, there it's a trip to the mall, or McDonald's, where the meat is already dead."

"If it *is* meat. And that's a moot point."

"Did they have a special place where they liked to go?"

The humor drained out of his face. "Yeah, there was a place, on Lake Freemont." He pointed toward the mountains. "Out along the 741, as it happens. Beyond where the kids said they went, six or seven miles past Lakeside Lodge. The ground begins to rise toward the Wind River Range, toward Gutierrez Peak."

I didn't say anything. He paused, thinking. He didn't look like he was enjoying what he was thinking.

"There's a couple of plateaus up there, and a bit of woodland. They used to go there a lot. You get a great view of the lake from on high..." He trailed off, eyeing me. "Sonia loved it up there. You think they might've...?"

"Sounds like a good place to look for UFOs. It also sounds like a great place to have a few beers and smoke a joint without the sheriff taking his belt to you. Might be why they were so late."

He rubbed his face, then lifted his hat and ran his fingers through his hair. "Jesus Christ!"

"Bunch of teenagers, way out there, drunk, maybe stoned. Something might have happened, Sheriff."

He stared at me. "What about Ash?"

"Well, maybe that's where he went to look for her."

He stood heavily and put his hat back on his head. "I'm going to take a look. You want to come along?"

TWO

He called his deputies on the way and we met them there.

We stood on the green plateau, jutting from the bluff out over the lake. The wind was cold and the air was rich with dry, green tangs under a very blue sky, with the copper sun a few inches above the mountain peaks behind us. Behind us also was a sprawl of dense forest that swarmed up the mountainside. It was dark in there. The ground was thick with brown needles and ferns that grew four and five feet in height.

In front of us the ground sloped steeply down to the black water of the lake. There, on the slopes, the ground was also thick with pine trees: lodgepole, white bark and limber. The dark was dense under the canopy, made impenetrable by bracken and sword fern.

Beyond the green slopes, maybe three and a half thousand feet below, the water lay like black glass, over a mile across and nine miles from northern tip to southern shore, chilling the air and causing cold, blustery winds to be drawn in from the valley. Those gusts now battered my face and pulled at my jacket where I stood at the edge, looking down. I heard the sheriff shout and turned. The wind stretched his jeans against his legs and flapped them behind him. It whipped his hair across his face and folded his hat brim back, making him clutch at his head.

"It's a hell of a lot of territory!"

I nodded and past him I saw the two deputies' vehicles pulling off the road to bounce and lurch their way up to where we were standing. I pointed over toward the tree line where I could see a dark smudge, maybe two hundred yards away.

"That a campfire?"

He looked, and after a moment shrugged. By then I'd started walking and he joined me. The deputies had seen me point and the lurching trucks turned, aiming to converge with us where we were headed. They got there first and by the time we arrived the deputies had already parked and swung down from their trucks.

Phil, two hundred and fifty pounds of walrus moustache and belly, was hunkered down by a ring of stones four feet across, full of black and gray ash.

"It's cold," he said.

Behind him Pete, Dave and Chavez had moved away and were stepping in among the trees, peering among the ferns and the needles.

Phil stood. "Don't look like they left any trash behind, beer cans or food wrappers or such."

The sheriff grunted. "They were careful to clean up when they left."

"What's that?" I hunkered down by the fire. A gust of wind trailed a fine cloud of cinders past me. I reached into the ring of rocks and pulled out a stick, maybe a foot long, a quarter to half an inch thick. It had been sharpened at one end, and most of the irregularities removed with a sharp knife. It was only partially singed.

The sheriff stared at the stick and then at me. "What? It's a stick."

I studied it a moment, then stood. "Look." He came closer. Phil stood at my shoulder. "See how the wood has been singed in stripes about half an inch apart?" They both said, "Huh." I went on. "That's because there were hunks of meat or vegetable on there, cooking. Don't you ever do that? You cut the meat into cubes, a chunk of onion, maybe some red pepper...?"

The sheriff shrugged again. "So what?"

I tried not to sigh. "So after whoever cooked it, he ate it."

"I guess so. I'd kind of got that far. What's your point, Mr. Bauer?"

"If he ate it from the stick, there's a chance there's saliva and fingerprints on it. Maybe the ash and the heat have contaminated it. Maybe they haven't. But it's worth a try, right? If we can place the kids here, it means they lied about where they were, and that would mean they lied about when they brought Sonia home. It's something."

He jerked his head at Phil. "Go get an evidence bag from your truck and bag the stick. We'll send it to Cheyenne."

Over by the trees Chavez raised his voice above the wind. *"Sheriff. We got some tire tracks here."*

We picked our way over shrubs and rocks, hunching our shoulders against the wind. When we got there, most of the tracks had been mashed up by the deputies' own tracks. But there was a section in the damp earth that was clearly not Chavez's RAM or Pete and Dave's Ford. The sheriff pushed his hat back and scratched his head. "Guess I better get a plaster cast of this. Phil, you got any plaster in your truck?" Phil shook his head. "You better get back to the office. Did you bring the camera?"

"Nope. Didn't think to, Sheriff."

"Well, you'd better bring out the camera and the plaster. And bring the tape, too." He turned to me and frowned. "Is this a crime scene?"

I felt my skin go cold and pasty, and a nauseating sadness in my gut. I nodded. "I guess it's a potential crime scene, Sheriff, yeah."

"Should you be here, Mr. Bauer?"

I nodded. "Yeah, I should be here." He scratched his head and sighed. He'd done a lot of that this morning. I added, "I've done a lot of hunting in these mountains, Sheriff. I know them like the back of my hand. I am also trained in search, rescue and extraction. Let me stay and give you a hand."

"OK, I guess we can use the help."

He turned away from me and started yelling at his deputies to go over every inch of the area. *"I wanna know who had made the fire, I want any trash they might have left behind. I want everything and anything that will tell me who was here and when!"*

The existence of the fire wasn't much on its own. But if it had been made by Sonia and Dave and their gang the night she disappeared, it meant they had lied about where they'd been. That had two knock-ons: it raised the question, as I had pointed out to Sheriff Seth Levi, if they lied about that, might they not also have lied about delivering her to her gate? But it also raised the potentially more important question: what made them lie about where they'd been?

There was a sick, uneasy feeling I knew we all shared. We were not only looking for beer cans, food wrappers and cigarette butts —something to show beyond a doubt that they had been here. We were looking for Sonia and her father, too. We were looking for the dead.

It was past eleven when I saw the sheriff talking to Phil. Seth was doing a lot of talking and Phil was doing a lot of nodding. The wind had died down, but I still couldn't hear what he was saying, so I headed back to where they were standing beside the circle of rocks. Seth saw me approaching, patted Phil on the shoulder and came toward me like he had something to say.

"I want you to come with me." He put his hand on my shoulder and guided me toward his Jeep. "We got a few bits and pieces. That stick was good thinking. We found a few more. We got some other things too: a disposable lighter, a piece of kitchen paper where somebody blew his nose. Can you believe that?"

I stopped and made him turn to face me. "Sheriff, I want to stay and look."

"Yeah, I know. But I need your help."

"With what?"

"Get in the truck."

He walked around the hood and climbed in behind the wheel. When he fired it up I got in beside him. He started talking again as I slammed the door and we moved off.

"I'm going to send the stuff to the lab. I don't know what they'll get. Maybe the lighter will give us something, the stick or the paper. I don't know if we can or not, but the kids don't know that, right?"

He glanced at me. I didn't say anything so he went on.

"I want to go and see Dave and I want you to come with me. I think he's a good kid. When he sees you," he shrugged as the Jeep bounced and jolted onto the road, "I tell him you're from New York, old friend of Ash's, and Ash was with the Feds. Let him draw his own conclusions, right?" He laughed. "When he sees you staring at him, and I tell him we're sending these things to the lab, it'll scare the bejaysus out of him. Might just jolt him into admitting something."

I looked out the window and spoke half to myself. "Admitting what?"

"If they only admit they were there that night, and not where they said they were, that gives us enough to take 'em in and question them separately. If we can do that, pretty soon one of them is going to tell us why they lied, and where Sonia is."

"Where Sonia is," I echoed, "and where Ash is."

The sheriff called ahead to say we were coming, then filled me in on the way. Dave Jorgensen lived with his parents on West Washington Street, on the east side of Pine Creek, where it flows beside the Boyd Skinner Park. They had a large, sprawling, one-story clapboard house set in half an acre of lawn, with a white picket fence and a double garage in back. His father, Ralph, was a vet and a strict Protestant. His mother, Ingrid, stayed at home and baked blueberry pies.

It was Ingrid who opened the door to us. She was pretty in a blonde, Scandinavian way, with plaits and blue eyes. She had a careful blend of smile and frown on her face that said we were always welcome, but what was this about? Sheriff Levi spoke.

"Ingrid, this here is Harry Bauer I mentioned to you on the phone. Is Dave here? I need to talk to him."

She glanced at me then back at Seth. "Sure, come on in." She spoke over her shoulder as we followed her into a large, comfortable living room. "Ralph is out at the MacDonald's Ranch. Will you have some coffee? I just made some pie..."

There was a potbelly stove burning logs, and a sofa and two armchairs drawn around it. There was a small TV in the corner that didn't look like it got much use. The sheriff was saying, "We won't stay long, Ingrid. We just want a quick word with Dave."

"Sit by the fire. I'll get him."

She pushed through a door and disappeared. Neither of us sat. Seth went and stood warming his ass by the stove. We stared at each other for a couple of seconds. Then the door opened and Ingrid appeared with Dave. He looked at me, swallowed and went pale.

Ingrid said, "Won't you sit down?"

The sheriff grunted and sat on the sofa. Ingrid sat beside him with her hands on her lap. I watched Dave sit in the armchair, right beside Seth, at right angles to him. When they were all settled I sat opposite Dave, holding his eyes with mine.

Seth rubbed his hands and hunched his shoulders. "Sure is cold. That wind comes down out of them mountains and *whoo-ee!* You know, on consideration, I would not say no to a cup of hot coffee if you was to offer it again!"

They both laughed and she turned to me, more guarded in her eyes. "And you, Mr...?"

I blinked once, slowly, before shifting my gaze to hers. "Bauer," I said, "Harry Bauer. Thank you, Mrs. Jorgensen. That would be nice."

She stood and went to the kitchen. Dave, alone suddenly, looked from the sheriff to me and back again. He spoke and tried to swallow at the same time. "How can I help you, Sheriff?"

"Well, Dave, this Mr. Harry Bauer here, he was a friend of Ash's. Now, I didn't know this, and I figure you didn't neither, but Ash was a special agent with the FBI. And that was where him and Mr. Bauer met. And he is here in Pinedale to try to find out what happened to him and Sonia."

He paused. Dave didn't move. Only his eyes moved as he swiveled them to look at me. And he swallowed three times. The sheriff went on.

"Now, thing is, Dave, me and my deputies went out along the 741 to where you said you'd been the other night with Sonia. We searched pretty thorough, but we didn't find any sign that you'd been there. No tire tracks, no fire pit, no nothin'." He paused but Dave didn't answer, so he went on. "But we did go on up somewhat farther, on Mr. Bauer's suggestion, to a spot, up near the White Pine ski resort, where Ash and Sonia liked to go hunting sometimes."

He paused and I saw Dave's face turn the color and texture of wax. He swallowed hard again and I could see his hands shaking where he was holding them in his lap.

The sheriff arched an eyebrow. "Now, up there we found a ring of stones where somebody had made a fire. It was cold, but there was still a lot of ash there. That tells me it wasn't made all that long ago, 'cause the wind had not blown it away. We found a few sticks, too, that somebody had sharpened to cook food over the flames. We found a disposable lighter, couple of cigarette butts, a tissue somebody used to blow his nose..." He spread his hands, shrugged. "Now, thing is, Dave, I am fixin' to send these items to the lab in Cheyenne for analysis. There will be DNA residue and prints on pretty much everything we've collected. So we'll know then who was at that party up there in the woods."

He paused again, leaned forward with his elbows on his knees, and looked hard at Dave.

"So I thought I'd give you the chance to tell me, before I send it off, if it was you and your friends up there, with Sonia, the night before last."

Dave's eyes strayed down to where his hands had clenched into a ball in his lap. The sound of his mother in the kitchen seemed suddenly very loud. He took a shaky breath, held it and said, "She—Sonia—had a feeling we might see some activity over the lake. She said she had an intuition. She'd been there last summer, with her dad," he glanced at me but looked quickly away, "she said she'd seen green orbs over the water during the night. She said she got up and went out by the fire 'coz she couldn't sleep, and there was three of them hovering a few hundred feet over the water, glowing green—"

I cut him short. "So what happened? Were you alone with her?"

"No, sir!" He shook his head. "There was me, Marvin, Sadie and Slick and Sonia."

"So what happened?"

"We made the fire and I'd brought some food which we cooked over the embers..."

"Cut to the chase, Dave."

The sheriff frowned at me but I ignored him. Dave went on.

"Slick had brought some beers. Him and Sadie was drinking, but me and Sonia didn't want to drink. Marv didn't either. We wanted clear heads in case we saw something." He glanced at me again like he was looking for approval. He didn't find any and went on. "So, Marv was telling us about a theory that the aliens weren't really aliens. They were like a parallel life form that inhabits this planet alongside us, in like a parallel dimension. And that was what all the elves and goblins and skinwalkers were in the past..."

I spoke quietly, deliberately, staring at the floor. "What happened to Sonia, Dave?"

"I am getting to that, sir. You see it's all connected."

I raised my eyes to look at him. "Are you going to try and tell me she was abducted by aliens?"

"No, sir. She was not abducted by aliens, sir. It was Slick who said that if these beings were like paranormal creatures, we should be able to contact them by hypnosis, or going into some kind of trance. Marv said that there were cases on record of people contacting aliens through hypnosis, and Slick and Sadie started saying we should try.”

“Jesus!” I sank back in my chair and ran my fingers through my hair. “Go on,” I said, “what happened next?”

“Well, Slick tried to hypnotize Sadie, but she kept laughing. Then Marv said that if Sonia had seen the lights last summer, then she was obviously in tune with them, and one of us should hypnotize her. I didn’t want them to. Marv said he could do it, but I wouldn’t let him, and in the end Sonia said she didn’t mind, but she wanted me to do it.”

I stared at him. “So you hypnotized Sonia?”

He swallowed hard. “Yes, sir.”

THREE

The door opened and Ingrid came in from the kitchen with a tray of coffee and four slices of blueberry pie. "It's blueberry compote from last year, I'm afraid, but I think you'll like it." She grinned at Seth and he made an "Mmm..." noise.

I watched as she handed out the coffee, poured the cream and then handed out the pie, with small forks and paper napkins. I was thinking that a man and his sixteen year-old daughter might be dead or dying out by the lake while we were drinking coffee and eating blueberry pie. When she was done I set the pie on the table and sat forward with my elbows on my knees, looking hard at Dave.

"Let me see if I can get a handle on this. You *hypnotized* Sonia?" I felt hot in my belly and I was getting mad. "What happened next? What did you do next?"

Ingrid stared at her son. "You did *what?*"

"Marv said there was no danger. He'd researched it. He said it was safe, just like being really relaxed. And, honest, sir, what I didn't want was Slick or Sadie doing it, 'cause they can be a bit crazy sometimes." He turned to the sheriff, appealing to him, "I would never do anything to hurt Sonia, Sheriff. You know that." He turned to his mother. "You know that, Mom." He turned back to me. I could see the tears in his eyes. "I mean, I'm sorry, sir, but I really cared for Sonia. I would never do anything to hurt her, and I really thought—" He started again. "She really wanted to see those orbs, and I was afraid if I didn't help her, she'd let Slick do it."

The room went silent. He stared at me and I stared back. Finally I said, "Cared?"

"What?"

"You said you really cared for her, in the past tense. What does that mean? You don't care anymore?"

"I mean, yes, of course I still care, but..." He trailed off.

"What happened, Dave?"

He covered his face with his hands, muttered, "Oh, Jesus!" then dropped his hands into his lap. It was a gesture of resignation, almost relief. "She lay down. I sat beside her and told her to relax. I told her what you see on TV, to listen to my voice and with every word I said she'd become more relaxed. I told her to go to a peaceful place inside and to call the orbs."

Ingrid went pale and closed her eyes, muttering, "O Heavenly Father forgive him, for he knew not what he was doing."

Dave glanced at her a moment and went on. "She went real still and she started breathing real slow, and I started to get scared. I told her to call on the orbs again, to ask them to show themselves. Next thing she just sat up. Sadie screamed, pointing behind me at the lake. I looked and there were three balls of phosphorescent green light just hanging over the water. Sonia got up and started running toward the lake. Slick ran after her and I ran too. I dunno." He looked down at the floor between his feet. "I guess I didn't want her to be alone with Slick. Sadie was screaming not to leave her alone and I think she and Marv ran back to the truck. But Sonia was running real fast, like she didn't care, she wasn't afraid of tripping or falling. And Slick runs real fast too. I couldn't keep up with them. I really tried my best, calling them to stop and wait. But they wouldn't.

"Next thing they were in the woods. I went in after them. I

was screaming at them by now, begging them to come back. I was really afraid. But I couldn't find them anywhere. They just seemed to have vanished. I scoured the woods from end to end, calling them.

"Next thing I seen Slick. He was just standing there, watching me. He had the lake behind him, kind of luminous. The lights had gone, and I could just see his silhouette. I asked him if it was him, 'cause I wasn't sure. I was really scared, and he said, of course it was. I asked him where Sonia was, and he said he didn't know. She was probably back at the camp. So we went back to the camp but she wasn't there either. That was when Slick said we should go home."

Ingrid screwed up her brow. "*What?*"

"I said we should call the sheriff and get Search and Rescue out to look for her. She might have fallen and hurt herself. But Slick said..." He faltered, staring at me with wide, terrified eyes. "He said, if anything really bad had happened to her, we could..." He faltered again. "Me and him, they could accuse us of murder and that would mean the death penalty. He said it could be the death penalty for all of us. We should just say we left her at the gate, and Search and Rescue would go look for her anyway."

I spoke quietly. "So Sonia has been lying out there, injured, maybe dead, in the cold, because you were too much of a coward to speak up."

He stared down at his hands. "...yes."

"What about Ash? What happened to him?"

He shook his head. His face was pleading. "I don't know anything about that. I swear..."

I stood. The sheriff was already on his phone.

"...I want a helicopter out there and a boat, and we need to call people in, we need to scour the hill and the woods between the White Pine Ski Resort and the lake shore. I want every inch of the area searched. We may be looking for Sonia, we may be looking for Ash too."

Dave had started to weep convulsively into his hands. Ingrid stepped up to me and placed her hands on my chest, staring into my face like she was searching for something.

"Mr. Bauer, I can't imagine what you are going through, or what your friend Ash must have gone through. I am so sorry, I am so sorry..."

I nodded, mumbled something and walked out of the house into the cold day. I stood at the white picket gate, staring at the dust. I don't know what I had expected when the Brigadier asked me to take the case. Ash had contacted him—I had never met the man—

But he'd told him he suspected the Gulf Cartel were moving in, and he suspected that the man known simply as Otropoco was behind it.

I'd told the Brigadier it was law enforcement's baby. Let the DEA and the FBI handle it. That was not our brief. Our brief was taking out the trash: assassinating people who committed crimes against humanity, and thought they'd got away with it.

That was when he told me that Otropoco had murdered Ash's wife to get him off his back, that he was responsible for well over a thousand deaths of women and children in the area of Tamaulipas. Their deaths had been purely for the purpose of terrorizing the villagers into growing and manufacturing his dope, and convincing local law enforcement to toe the line.

There had been more deaths, rival gang members, men he suspected of informing on him to the DEA, young girls unwilling to become prostitutes. Torture and murder with his own hands was estimated in the dozens, if not hundreds, and gang-related killings and torture by his men, on his orders, was impossible to calculate.

I had taken the job imagining it would be a case of tracking the bastard down and killing him. But in just a couple of days staying in Ash's house, talking with the sheriff about him and Sonia, it had become personal.

I heard the door close behind me and the sheriff's boots on the path. I pushed through the gate and moved to his truck.

"We're going back?"

"Yeah." He wrenched open the door and I climbed in beside him.

"Drop me at my place. I want to get my truck. I don't know how late I'm going to be out there."

He eyed me a moment, but didn't say anything.

By the time I arrived at the lake it was gone one o'clock and half of Pinedale seemed to be out there offering to help. They'd parked their cars and trucks in an improvised parking lot beside the road, overseen by a deputy, and over toward the slopes there was a swarm of people moving in irregular lines across the plateau, and in through the trees and the ferns. They were walking slowly, looking down at their feet.

There was also a chopper moving like a dragonfly in a grid pattern over the water: hovering, moving on, pausing, turning to the right and moving on a little, then swooping to one side. It was a hunt for the dead, or for clues to the whereabouts of the dead.

I climbed from behind the wheel and picked my way across the rocks, the shrubs and the grass toward the ragged line of people; the loose string of reds and blues and checkered creams, jeans and hats, all inching inch by inch toward the steep slope and the drop into the void.

I saw Seth leaning against his Jeep, talking into his radio, and made a detour. He watched me approach and put the radio away, slammed the door and came toward me.

"Mr. Bauer, Harry, I know you're taking this personal, and Ash was your friend. I want you to listen to me because I have to tell you something."

"Don't patronize me, Sheriff. I'm familiar with death. You got something to tell me, tell me."

"They found something in the water."

"Something?"

"They don't know what it is yet. It might be nothing, might be clothes. There's a couple of jetties down there. The boat found it. The chopper's bringing it up now."

My eyes went to the chopper where it was hovering. Now I could see there was a cable dangling from it, and as I watched I saw a bundle swinging slowly over the rim of the hill. The advancing people all stopped and stared. The bundle rose above their heads, an awkward, bulky shape, dark, inhuman, trailing water.

Seth said, "Just let me look at it first, will you?"

I stared down at his face. "That's not necessary."

I pushed past him and started walking toward the spot where the chopper was headed. The bundle was growing larger. I saw denim, hair, a boot, but a man's boot. The chopper hovered and the bundle began to slip and jerk toward the ground. I saw the hair closer. It was long, fine, darkened by water. A wave of nausea washed over me. They were both there, tangled together.

They touched the ground. Water spilled and gushed around them. Her face flopped to one side. She was ugly, inhuman, swollen and blue, a grotesque caricature. The man I took to be Ash was tangled up with her, bloated, a monster whose humanity had fled.

People were converging on them. Someone ran away to vomit. A woman started crying, clinging to her husband. The sheriff stood by my side. I said, "That's Ash? I haven't seen him for ten years..."

He looked at me curiously for a moment, then nodded. "Yeah, that's Ash and that's Sonia."

"He must have come to the same conclusion we did, and come here looking for her. When he found her, he couldn't let go..."

———

HE WOULDN'T LET me ride with him to the morgue. So I went home, made a fire and poured myself a generous measure of Jameson's. Then I sat looking at the flames remembering the Brigadier sitting beside the fire at Cobra HQ, in Pleasantville. He was holding a glass of whiskey and I could see the flames reflected in the deep amber. His eyes held mine and he spoke quietly.

"If Ash is right," he had said to me, "and Otropoco is moving into that area, find his scent, hunt him down...and kill him."

Then I thought about three kids running around, drunk and stoned in the woods, at night above the lake. About a kid called Slick, standing in the shadows of the trees, silhouetted against the luminous water of the lake, telling Dave they should go back to the camp, back to town, leave Sonia behind.

And I thought about Ash, the man I had never met, who had left everything he had, he knew, to protect his daughter; I thought about him looking at her dead, bloated form beneath the water, feeling his own life drain away through the hollow, unquenchable agony inside.

I would go tomorrow. I would talk to the sheriff. I would talk to the doc. I would find out what happened, who did this, and I would kill them.

———

I PUSHED through the door into the Sheriff's Department on South Tyler Avenue. Phil, the deputy looked up and said, "He's expecting you, Mr. Bauer. His in his office over yonder."

He pointed with his head and I crossed the floor to the door. It had gilt writing on the upper, frosted half that read: "Sheriff Seth Levi." I knocked and went in.

He watched me close the door and said, "Good morning, Harry. Will you have some coffee?" Before I could answer he pointed to the captain's chair opposite him and said, "Sit down."

As I sat he rose and poured me a large espresso from a machine in the corner. He smiled as he set it on the desk in front of me. "I know you like it strong."

I nodded my thanks, then said, "Sheriff—"

"Most folks round here call me Seth, unless I'm arresting them or about to shoot them."

He laughed. I made it as far as an unenthusiastic smile.

"Seth—"

"I know why you're here, Harry."

"Tell me."

"I don't want you getting involved in this."

"How did they die?"

He sighed noisily, "For cryin' out loud, Harry, I am tellin' you plain as plain—"

"Give me some closure, Seth. Let me return to New York with certainties. However ugly they may be, they are better than wondering."

Another sigh, heavier. It was a sigh of inevitable surrender. "We ain't got the full coroner's report yet."

"But you know. Tell me."

"She probably drowned," he half shrugged, his head on one side, "but there were wounds. Doc don't know yet what caused them. It could have been from falling against branches or rocks."

I examined the coffee. It was very black. "Do you know how many knife wounds I have seen in my life, Seth?"

"I know you're going to tell me."

"I've lost count. But I can tell you, and your doc, that a laceration from a branch or a rock resembles a knife wound in exactly no ways."

"Come on, Harry, drop it."

"Tell me."

His face flushed. "OK! I'll tell you. But I am also tellin' you I *do not* want you causin' trouble in my town! You understand?"

"I understand. I just want to know the facts."

"We got this!"

"You got it. I understand. How did they die, Seth?"

"The medical examiner said, on first inspection, the wounds looked too clean for branches. They looked…"

He trailed off, watching my face with something like despair. I felt sorry for him. I said:

"They look like knife wounds."

"Yeah, that's what they look like."

"To the forearms and hands and to the belly."

He scowled. "How in the *hell* do you know that?"

"Almost sixty percent of knife attacks start with the assailant reaching to grab the victim with his left hand. Then he stabs or slashes with the blade. The victim always tried to fend off the attack with their hands and forearms. They get cut, and then the assailant most often goes up and under for the belly."

"Sweet Jesus…"

"Who?"

Seth shook his head and wagged his index finger in the negative. "No, Harry. You leave that to me. I do not want you doing anything stupid."

"I am not a stupid man, Seth. I am a professional with eight years' experience in the British SAS. I don't do stupid things. I just want to know who did it."

"The British SAS? I heard those guys are crazy."

"Yeah, but we're smart crazy. Who did it, Seth?"

He sank back in his chair, trying to read my face, digesting the new information. Finally he said, "I don't know who did it. And neither do you. The only person who does know right now is whoever did it. And *you* are going to let *me* find out who that is."

I ignored him and said, "It was one of three people—"

In spite of himself he frowned. "Three? Who?"

"One: Dave ran down the hill after Sonia and Slick, found them in the woods kissing, became jealous and killed her." I took another sip of coffee. "Questions: why didn't he kill Slick too, and why is Slick protecting him." I held up two fingers. "Two: Slick went after her, like Dave said, he tried to come on to her, she rejected him and he killed her."

I drained my cup. He said, "And three?"

"A third, unknown person who was there. A crime of opportunity."

He shook his head. "I don't buy that."

"Have they found the knife?"

"Uh-uh," he said carefully. "Not so far."

"How many times?"

"Three times in the lower belly and once in the heart. There's no way on knowing which was first or which was fatal."

I nodded. "OK, I don't buy the mystery crazy guy in the woods either. That being the case it was either Dave or Slick."

"Assuming Dave's story is true."

I thought about that for a moment. "Yeah, assuming his story is true. If he's scared of Slick we might have got an edited version of the truth. So, who are you going to talk to next?" He looked away, didn't answer. I pressed him. "Are you going to pick up Slick?" He still didn't answer. "You have to talk to Slick before you talk to the others, and you have to bring in Slick, Sadie and Marv at the same time, so they can't talk to each other."

"Cut it out, Harry! I know how to do my damn job! Just leave it alone! I am going to find who did this. Go back to New York and I'll let you know when the trial is."

I chewed my lip for a moment, watching him. After a moment I stood. "Thanks for the coffee." At the door I stopped with my hand on the knob. "You spoken to the DA yet?"

He closed his eyes like he was counting to ten.

"Yes! He says we can't prosecute on the evidence we have. Now will you *drop it!*"

"Yeah. Let me see the bodies and talk to the doc. Then I give you my word, I will leave and I won't interfere anymore in your investigation. You have my word."

FOUR

It was a short walk through the cool, bright morning. My offer had been too good for him to refuse, so on the way I decided to see how far I could push it. I said:

"You think it was Slick."

I didn't frame it as a question. After a moment he shrugged. "That's where I'd lay my money right now. But quote me and I'll deny it. This is an open investigation."

"But…"

"But the kid's out of control. He snorts a lot of coke. Him and his dad. And there's something else." He paused, hesitated.

"What?"

"We flew in a DCI team from Afton. They went over the site and did a pretty thorough job. They found traces of cannabis around the fire." He shrugged. "Like you'd expect, I guess, but they also found traces of dried peyote."

I arched an eyebrow. "Peyote? Up here?"

"Yeah." He lifted his hat and scratched his head. He looked unhappy. "Slick's dad, Sean, he's originally from Sierra Blanca, in Texas. I know he goes down there couple of times a year and brings back dried buds. Either his son stole some from him, or Sean gave 'em to his son."

I nodded. "They're out there looking for flying saucers, talking about going into trance to contact the aliens, Slick gets high on peyote, has a psychotic break and kills Sonia."

"Maybe. Slick had traces of coke in his nose. Sonia showed positive for cannabis and for peyote, Harry. I'm sorry."

"Slick gave it to her."

We had stopped at the corner. A chill breeze dragged a couple of leaves across a broad lawn and crept down my back.

"He's just eighteen, Harry. Don't go doing anything crazy."

"Just eighteen? The girl he killed was just sixteen."

"We don't know that yet."

"You don't," I said quietly.

He shook his head and made for the plate-glass doors of the coroner's office. "I am going to regret this," he said. "I know I am."

Inside the white, tiled desolation of the morgue, an attractive woman in her thirties with blonde hair and dark blue eyes watched us approach. The sheriff said, "Doc, this is Harry Bauer, an old friend of Ash's. I think he's took Ash's death worse than he'll admit. He wants to see the bodies." He turned to me, "Harry, this is Doc. Claire Erickson. She's standing in for the ME. Maybe you should pay her a visit before you go back to New York."

I gave him the dead eye and told him, "Thanks for the advice. I'm just fine." To her I said, "May I see them, Doc?"

She arched a pretty eyebrow at me. "You sure you're OK?"

"I'm sure."

She slid open the steel drawer and pulled back the sheet. The bloating had gone, but her young skin, which should have been a vibrant, living pink-white, was a dead waxy gray-blue.

"We can't be absolutely certain what killed her—"

"She didn't drown."

She glanced at me. "No. She was already dead when she was submerged. It was one of the stab wounds—" She pulled the sheet down to her hips. There were three ugly gashes in her lower belly, and another in her left breast. "—but we have no way of telling in what order she received them, because she'd been too long in the water. However, I would say that the blow to the heart was probably, ultimately, the cause of death."

"She'd been smoking and drinking."

There was a trace of a smile. It was a sad smile. A compassionate smile. "She had probably had a beer, not much more than that. There are traces of cannabis. Again, barely enough to make her giggle. My guess is somebody persuaded her to take a couple of puffs."

"What about the mescaline?"

"There was a bit more of that. She had eaten a dried bud, and that would have induced hallucinations. Peyote is very unpredictable, and it does produce nightmarish hallucinations sometimes. In my opinion, if a couple of them took peyote, it could conceivably have triggered the attack."

"But that's not enough for the DA." Nobody answered. I said, "What about Ash?"

She closed the drawer and pulled open the one next to it.

Ash was about six-two, well-built and muscular. His hair was cut short. The bloating had gone from him too, and he had the same waxy blue-white color of death.

"He drowned," she said simply. He had blonde hairs entwined in his fingers. "We've sent them for DNA analysis, but I'm pretty sure we'll find they're hers."

She held my eye a moment. I said, "He went down to the jetty and found her. And instead of bringing her up, he clung to her."

She nodded, her eyes flicking over my face. "Extreme grief could have led to convulsions, and he drowned."

I looked at the two of them, cold, lifeless, a father and a daughter who had loved each other, and hurt no one, but had both been sentenced by fate to die in pain and grief. And in that moment it became personal.

. . .

Seth followed me out to my truck. I leaned on the hood and asked him, "Have you tried to get a confession out of the kids?"

"It's less than twenty-four hours since we found them, Harry. And if you'd stop trying to run this case and let me get on with my job, maybe I could start bringing them in and questioning them. You gave me your word, remember?"

I eyed him a moment, making rapid calculations in my mind. Finally I sighed. "I know. I appreciate it, Seth. Guess I'll head back to New York. You'll call me."

"I'll call you." As I pulled open the door he added, "Hey, Harry." I stopped and looked back. "I'm serious. The doc knows her stuff." He pointed a big finger at me. "I think Sonia and Ash have got to you. You should have a talk with her before you go."

I didn't answer. I watched him walk away, then climbed behind the wheel of my pickup and drove down Pine Street toward Marilyn Street. There I turned in and stopped halfway down the road. I killed the engine and sat with my arms on the steering wheel and my chin on my arms, looking down the street at the Connells' house. I could see them in my mind, Slick and Sean sitting in front of the TV, drinking beer from cans, smoking hash, laughing.

I swung down from the cab, walked slowly across the road to their front door and hammered on it with my fist. After a moment it opened inward into a shadowy kitchen. There was a man there, looking at me. He was about six foot tall, lean, in jeans and a sweatshirt. He jerked his chin at me. "What?"

"Did you give your son peyote and hash to give to Sonia and the other kids?"

The corner of his mouth curled into a small, insolent smile.

"Fuck you."

"Is that a yes?"

He took a step forward, one hand on each side of the jamb.

"No, it's just a fuck you. I don't need to tell you nothin'. I don't need to tell the sheriff nothin'. What I'm telling you is, you can all go and fuck yourselves."

"Your son killed a sixteen-year-old girl and her father."

His smile turned into a laugh. "You didn't hear me the first time? You want me to spell it for you? Fuck you." He took another step and pointed at me. It was a gesture, not like holding a gun, but like typing one-fingered, jabbing his index at me. "Fuck —you. I-do-not-give-a-shit!"

On the last word I took hold of his finger and bent it back. His eyes bulged with panic and pain, his neck went tense and his mouth opened in a silent scream. I stepped in close, gripped his wrist in my left hand and pulled the finger right back. When I spoke, it was barely a whisper.

"Do you give a shit now, Connell?" He was making a squeaking noise in his throat. "I think you are learning to care, Connell. Growing as a human being. So tell me, before I rip your finger out of its socket, did you provide your son with peyote and marijuana to give to the other kids?"

He nodded furiously, making small "Ah, ah, ah," noises. "Just, please! Please don't! It was just some coke an' shit—so they could have a ball! I didn't know! I didn't, *ah!*"

My face was an inch from his. "Know what, Connell? You didn't know what?"

"I didn't know what was going to happen! I swear! I just wanted them to have a good time!"

"And maybe pick up a few clients while you were at it?" He was whimpering too hard to answer. But I didn't need his answer so instead I asked, "Where is your son?"

"Inside! Inside! Please don't break my—"

"Call him."

His voice came like a sob. "Hey! Slick! C'm'ere, will ya!"

There was the sound of movement and Slick appeared in the doorway. He looked like he'd just fallen out of bed. He squinted at me and his dad and muttered, "'Sgoin' on?"

I let go of his father's finger and smashed my elbow into his jaw. And as he slid down the wall I reached out with my left hand, gripped Slick by the collar of his T-shirt and dragged him toward me.

"You got a knife, Slick?" He shook his head. His eyes said he was scared. "You don't fancy trying to stab me in the belly, or in the heart, Slick?"

He whispered, "No, sir."

"What is it, Slick? You only get your knife out with children and young girls?"

"No, sir, I didn't do that."

I got up close and stared hard into his eyes. "Did you kill Sonia, Slick?"

"No, no sir, I swear..."

"I think you killed her, and I swear to you, Slick, that the future holds one of two things for you. If you're lucky, it's a lethal injection. If you're not, I am going to beat you to death with my bare hands."

He was shaking his head and his dirty hair was flopping over his eyes.

"I didn't kill her, sir. I promise you I didn't."

"Where did you get the peyote?"

"Dad. He brought it from New Mexico. I heard it was a kind of spiritual experience. I thought it would be nice for the guys."

"The marijuana and the coke?"

"We bought that in San Francisco."

"What about the knife?"

"No, man! No!"

I snarled, "Well if it wasn't you, who?"

"I don't know. I swear I don't know. She ran! She was crazy. I ran after her, but I couldn't find her in the trees. I was tripping badly..." He trailed off. I let go of his collar.

"You'd better come up with a more convincing story, Slick. Because in the next few days I am going to kill you, and I can promise you it will not be quick."

I gave him a small shove. He staggered back and collided with the doorframe.

"I'll be coming back for you. When I do, you'd better have some useful information for me."

I turned and walked back toward my truck, leaving only silence behind me.

FIVE

When I got to Ash's place I climbed the wooden stairs to the bedroom, opened the closet and pulled out the bag I'd packed and brought with me. From the bottom of the bag I pulled out my Sig Sauer P226 with a twenty round extended magazine, a spare magazine and a box of 9mm rounds.

I took out also the Fairbairn and Sykes fighting knife, with the carbon steel blade and the ridged brass handle. It wasn't a hunting knife or a survival knife. I had several of those. This was a knife designed exclusively to kill, with a straight, razor-sharp, double-edged blade like a dagger; and a point like a needle.

I took the knife in its sheath and strapped it to my calf under my jeans.

The Sig Sauer I took downstairs, and cleaned it carefully and methodically. Then I loaded the magazine and rammed it in the butt.

After that I went out to the truck and took a drive down to Boulder, about twenty minutes south of Pinedale. There, at the intersection, I turned west onto Highway 351 and cut across to Big Piney. It was another thirty miles and there was a bitter cold wind coming out of the south across the plain. I had the windows open but I barely noticed the cold. My mind was focused on the plan I was putting together in my mind.

When I got to Big Piney I made my way to the Burney and Co superstore. There I bought two twelve packs of Rainier beer and two bottles of Jack Daniels. I also bought some essentials for myself, including six pairs of long bootlaces.

At the checkout a cute girl smiled at me and asked, "Party?"

"You bet."

"Any place nearby?"

I arched an eyebrow at her. "Your place?"

Her cheeks flushed and she giggled too much. I took my stuff out to the failing afternoon, where the sky was turning gunmetal cold and the wind was beginning to whistle in the trees. I took the 189 back, north, as the grainy dusk quickened toward night. At Daniel I turned right and entered Pinedale from the west. The streetlamps were on, and when I arrived at Pine Street there was a steady flow of traffic touching the blacktop with pools of amber. I crossed the bridge and turned right at the Rivera Lodge, then rolled slowly through the trees into Marilyn Road. It didn't take me long to reach the Connell house. I left the motor running, climbed out, pulled the beer and the whiskey from the trunk and I rang on the bell.

I heard some movement inside, then a muffled curse and after some scuffling the door opened. There was a woman there. She had probably been attractive five years earlier, before the drinking had started to tell. She had bleached hair, a Harvard University sweatshirt and a cigarette.

"What the hell do you want?" she said. "You just stay the hell away from..." She trailed off as her eyes came to rest on the beer and the whiskey.

"I came to apologize."

"Apologize?" Her eyes moved up to my face and she smiled. "No kidding?"

"I lost a close friend. I'm a passionate man and it's hard for me to think straight sometimes. But that ain't Slick's fault, or Sean's, and they shouldn't have to pay for my mistakes. I shouldn't have acted the way I did." I held up the drinks. "This is a peace offering. I hope you'll accept it."

"Accept it? You bet! Rainier, my favorite, and Jackie D. Can't go wrong with Jackie D. You, sir, are a gentleman!" She gave me a once-over. She was still smiling. "You wanna come inside?"

"Some other time."

"Well, sure. You're out on the Fayette Pole Creek Road, incha? The old Magnusson ranch?"

I nodded. "Yeah, that's me."

"OK." She gave me a sly wink and took the drinks from me. "I know where y'are now. A man who knows how to make a nice apology."

"You have a nice evening, and tell Sean and Slick I said I was sorry."

"I'll do that...uh...?"

She made a question with her face. I said, "Harry."

"Like Dirty Harry?"

I held her eye a moment and smiled. "Just like Dirty Harry."

"I'm Emma, Dirty Harry."

"Nice to meet you, Emma."

"Sure thing."

She went inside and closed the door with her ass. I heard her calling, "*Sean! Sean! Look what I got!*" and knew I had not made a mistake.

When I got home, as I pulled up the dark track toward the house, my headlamps picked out a white Toyota parked outside the porch, and as I came to a halt beside it I saw Dr. Erickson sitting on my steps with her elbows on her knees, watching me. I swung down from the cab and looked at her a moment.

"Doctor—"

"Harry. You don't look real happy to see me."

"I guess that depends why you're here."

I went to the back of the truck and pulled out my groceries. When I got to the stairs she was standing.

"I hope I'm not intruding."

There was a hint of a bristle to her voice which I decided to ignore. "You want to get the door? It's open."

She pushed open the door and switched on the light. I dumped my stuff in the kitchen.

"What can I do for you, Doc?"

"Seth asked me to look in on you. He said you'd been out today."

"He thinks he's my mother."

She shrugged and gave a cautious smile. "He thinks he's everybody's mother. I thought I'd drop in anyway. I have to agree with him, Harry. Their death seems to have hit you hard."

It was clearly an invitation to "talk about it." I ignored it and asked her, "How long have you been sitting on the steps?"

"Ten minutes, maybe fifteen. I was wondering where you were, and whether it was a good sign or a bad one."

"In this cold that is over and above the call of duty. I'm fine. I went for a drive, did some grocery shopping and came home." I leaned my arms on the kitchen doorjamb, looking down at her. "I apologized to Ash for not getting here on time. Now I'll head back to New York."

She eyed the groceries, calculating how long they would last, then looked me in the eye telling me she knew I was lying. "That easy, huh? I don't know how close you and Ash were, Harry, but I just wanted you to know it's OK to ask for help. And I am here to help if you need it."

"Thanks. I appreciate that."

She smiled, then combined a sigh and shrug. "Well, this is obviously not a good time for you. I can see you're busy."

She moved to the door and I took a couple of steps after her. I heard myself say, "Doc?" and wondered what the hell I was doing.

She stopped and turned back. "Yes?"

"I'm sorry." I was surprised to discover I meant it. "Forgive me if I am not very hospitable. I'm kind of tired, not really myself."

She smiled. "That's understandable."

"I'm not great at talking about..." I looked around, searching for a word that wasn't death. Finally I said, "Feelings, stuff like that. I was eight years in a special regiment." I smiled without much humor. "If we'd all talked about everything we experienced, we'd never have got any work done. So you learn to deal with it in other ways."

She nodded. "Sure," and after a moment, "You have my number. Just call."

I stood on the porch and watched her red taillights move unsteady into the dark.

Back inside I closed the door against the night, lit a fire and had a shot of whiskey. Then I set my alarm for four AM and lay down to sleep on the sofa. As I worked my way from my feet up toward my head, relaxing each muscle, allowing my thoughts to run in irrational sequences toward dreams, I was aware of a feeling inhabiting my body. A feeling I could only describe as a sense of troubled peace. It was going to get ugly, but I was doing the right thing.

I dreamed—it seemed to be for only a second—of silence and warm blood pooling in moss and mud, under the moon. Then the alarm woke me. I sat up, cold and rational, knowing exactly what I had to do. I stood, drank cold coffee, checked I had what I needed and went out under the frosted, declining moon. The cold air touched my skin and made me shudder. Two owls called to each other as I went down the wooden steps. I ignored them, as I ignored the silver light laid upon the canopy of the trees. My mind was not there.

I fired up the big truck, left the lights off and turned it around to roll silent down the hill, jolting over ruts and rocks beside the cold, silver creek. I rolled out onto the blacktop, turned right toward Pinedale and drove nice and easy. I had no choice but to approach along Pine Street but, at the Game and Fish Department, I slowed and turned into Mill Street to avoid the center of town.

The houses were all dark, with windows like dead eyes in the limpid glow of the streetlamps. I left my headlamps off and crossed Tyler Avenue. I moved on and left the courthouse and the sheriff's office behind me. There was not a soul on the streets but me; and I wasn't sure right then if I qualified as a soul.

Finally I crossed Franklin and took the dirt track between the Henderson's and the depot, to Lake Avenue. There I slowed, crossed over to Marilyn Street and parked outside thirty or forty feet from the Connells' house. I killed the engine, opened the rear door and moved silently to the front door. The lights were all off, and the house was silent. I took my Swiss Army knife from my pocket, selected the small screwdriver, fit it to the lock and gave it a firm thump with the heel of my hand. Then I turned and prayed they had not put a deadbolt on the door. That would complicate things.

As it was, they had one, but they'd been too drunk and stoned to slide it home. I eased the door open, stepped inside and closed it behind me. Then I hunkered down, closed my eyes and counted slow and steady to one hundred and twenty. As my eyes grew accustomed to the dark, so I listened carefully to every corner of the house. Pretty soon I had picked out Sean's snoring, Emma's lighter rasp and splutter, and Slick's heavy, slow breathing. He hadn't graduated to snoring yet, but he was on the right track.

When I opened my eyes I found I was in the kitchen. Moonlight was filtering through the glass in the door and through the window over the sink. I stood, took my knife from my boot, and moved quietly from the kitchen into a narrow, carpeted hall. An open door on my right gave on to a pitch-black living room that stank of marijuana and stale beer. There were heavy curtains at the end covering French doors onto a backyard. I couldn't see, but I could imagine what there was in the room: a threadbare sofa and a chair facing a giant TV, a coffee table littered with beer bottles, an empty bottle of Jack Daniels and a lot of silver foil.

I moved on down a short passage where there were two doors, both closed. I paused at the first and listened. That was where Sean's heavy snoring was coming from, and Emma's rasp and splutter. I moved on to the next door and took hold of the handle. I jabbed it down fast to avoid a squeak, and then pushed the door open.

I hunkered down among the shadows again and waited. Nothing happened. I could see the faint glow of the moon through his drapes, and in front of that, I could see the black bulk of his bed. That was where the breathing was coming from. I sheathed my knife, took the P226 from my belt behind my back and took one long, sliding step up to the bed.

He was lying on his back, with his left hand on his chest and his right dangling over the edge. I shook his shoulder gently with my left hand while holding the muzzle of the Sig in front of his eyes. I spoke softly, "Hey, Slick, wake up."

He frowned, sighed heavily and opened his eyes. That was when I smashed the butt of the gun into the tip of his jaw. His eyes rolled in his head and I knew now he would not wake up till I was ready for him.

Loading a hundred and fifty pounds of dead weight onto your shoulders from a bed is not easy. I managed it with difficulty and carried him, less than silently, down the passage and out of the kitchen. If I had not loaded them up with booze, and if they had not contributed the dope, they would have heard me. Fortunately I had covered those bases.

Out under the cold moon I carried Slick to my truck and dumped him on the back seat. I tied his ankles with a bootlace. Tied his wrists with another, and put a piece of masking tape over his mouth. Then I softly closed his kitchen door, got in behind the wheel of my truck and headed back the way I'd come.

Only instead of turning right at the intersection with Pine Street, I turned left and passed Riddley's onto the Freemont Lake Road. It took me about half an hour to get to the place where Sonia had been killed, by which time it was half past five and Slick was lying awake on the back seat of the truck, with large, terrified eyes.

I pulled off the road and found the cover of some trees near where the kids had made their fire. There I killed the engine and swung out of the truck. The air was icy and the moon was high and bright, laying liquid silver on the black surface of the lake, the dark water under which Sonia had lain dead.

I reached in the back and dragged Slick out, then shoved him, hobbling toward the cold fire. When we were there I kicked him hard in the back of his knee and let him fall facedown on the frosted soil. With my boot I rolled him on his back. His face was creased and he was crying like a child. I hunkered down beside him.

"I'm going to make this easy for you, Slick. You can die here in the next fifteen minutes, without ever seeing the dawn—" He began to convulse, shaking his head with bulging eyes. "Shut up and listen to me. Or you can go home to your family, and start a new life. I think it's a simple choice."

I reached down and ripped the tape from his mouth. He took big, rasping gulps of air.

"All you need to do, Slick, is answer my questions, and tell the truth." I pointed at his face. "You understand something, Slick, I do not want to take the law into my own hands. I do not want to kill an innocent man. I want my daughter's killer to face justice, to stand trial and to be convicted. Do you understand that?"

He nodded furiously.

"It is no use to me if the wrong man goes to trial. It's no good to me if the wrong man dies. You understand that?"

He nodded again. I was quiet for a while, staring into his face.

"Now, if you killed her, that puts you in a predicament, doesn't it? Because if you lie I will know you are lying and I will kill you. But if you tell the truth and confess to her murder, then you fear I will kill you also. A double bind."

He swallowed hard, then tried to speak, but no sound would come out.

"So let me explain this in a way that you will understand. I just want the *truth*, Slick. I just want to know what happened. I can understand two young people, experimenting with altered states of consciousness, doing crazy things, not knowing what it is they *are* doing. And then the crazy nightmare of waking up and realizing you killed the girl you wanted to make out with. That is almost punishment in itself.

"But what I can't handle is the thought of never knowing, of not being able to lay her soul to rest in my own heart." Again I asked, "Do you understand that?"

His breathing had slowed. He nodded.

"Yes, sir, I do understand. If I tell you everything that happened, will you let me go?"

"I'll do more than that. I'll let you go, and I will testify in your favor in court, as having helped me to ease my agony."

"Please don't hurt me, Mr. Bauer. I will tell you the truth, just like it happened, but please don't hurt me."

I grabbed him and hauled him into a sitting position, leaning his back against a rock. I sat opposite him and put the P226 away, behind my back.

"I don't want to hurt you, Slick. I am not looking for revenge. I am looking for justice, and above all understanding. I need to know what happened, so I can find peace."

"OK," he said, "I'll tell you."

SIX

THE MOON WAS IN HIS EYES. I COULD SEE IT CLEARLY, IN a dark yet translucent sky. He was shivering, and clouds of condensation issued from his mouth.

"I'm real cold."

"Tell me what you've got to tell me, and I'll take you home. I'll put the heater on. It'll be warm in the truck."

He nodded, but he was shivering so hard he couldn't talk. I figured shock was setting in, so I took off my jacket and put it around his shoulders.

"I really liked Sonia, sir." He was talking in an odd, jerky, stopping and starting rhythm because of his shaking. "She was always nice to me. She used to tell me I could do and be much more than I believed. That night Dave, he's a real dick, he was being like real possessive. Like she was his chick. Like he owned her. An' she was really into the whole hypnosis thing, like experiencing different kinds of consciousness, to, like, contact the aliens. But Dave was just kinda like, 'No man, it's not safe, we don't know what can happen,' and all that shit."

"You gave her a joint?"

"She was into it, man. She had like two puffs, but she couldn't hold it down. 'Cause, y'know, she didn't smoke, right? So I said why didn't she take some peyote. And Dave was all like, 'no man, it ain't safe,' and I'm like 'peyote is totally cool and natural, man. It's like, shamans use it, right? To open their third eye and shit. So she says, OK, she's gonna try it and see if she can contact the orbs. 'Cause all this time, man, dude, there are like five green orbs over the lake and we were like freaking out."

"So you gave her the peyote?"

"She wasn't even sick, man. But after a minute she gets up—"

"You took peyote too?"

"Oh, yeah, man, like, I was crazy. I was just tripping and I wanted to talk to them, man. Like, you know, where are you *from?* Why don't you just land where we can all see you? Do you have warp drive like the Federation? And me and Sonia, we were on the same vibe. Dave was getting mad because she was like ignoring him and we had this kind of telepathy thing going."

"What about Marv and Sadie?"

"They were just smokin' a joint and chillin'. To be honest, sir, truth is I don't know. Because I was just into the lights and the thing me and Sonia had goin'. Dave tried to hypnotize her, but she just jumps up and says, 'They're calling me!' and she ran. And I was right on her heels. We were both running down toward the trees and the lake. She went in among the trees, in the shadows. And suddenly, I swear man, I was like hyperaware, and I knew there was a Reptilian in among the trees."

"A Reptilian?"

"Yeah, man. Like, David Icke? He says there are a whole bunch of different species that visit the Earth, man. Like the grays, the Nordics, the Insectoids and the Draconians. The Draconians are also called the Reptilians. I know this sounds crazy, but I swear it's true, man. And the Reptilians are bad news, man. Real aggressive, and they will just, like, tear you apart and eat you. They are real savage. And I just *knew* there was one in the forest, and I was calling to Sonia, trying to be quiet so she'd hear me, but the Reptilian wouldn't. Maybe that was stupid but I didn't know what to do.

"So I am movin' through the trees like a Ninja, but all the fuckin' trees are moving, writhing like snakes, sliding and slithering against each other. And in among the trees, man, I can see naked women, dancing. And I am getting pretty wild inside. My head is going crazy. And next thing the trees part and there is this huge reptile, standing on its hind legs, with a crest on its neck splayed out. It was all crazy colors, and hissing, 'bout eight or ten feet tall, and I could see its teeth and its claws, and crazy red eyes. I didn't think. I was terrified and I had this roaring in my ears and in my head. And I just lunged at it. I went crazy, sir. I was hallucinating. I truly believe they made me do it. I would never in a million years have hurt Sonia. I just went out of my…"

I cut him short. "What about the knife?"

"What—the knife?" He swallowed hard again. "Well, I was so scared, I lied about that."

"You always carry a knife."

He nodded. "How'd you know?"

"You're the kind of guy who always carries a knife."

"I do. I always carry a knife. But when I saw it wasn't a Reptilian. When I came to my senses and saw what I'd done, I ran and threw the knife out into the lake. Then I panicked. I knew I could be facin' the death penalty. So I dragged Sonia by her heels to the edge of the drop and rolled her over. When I was comin' back I saw Dave. He was looking for Sonia in the forest. He asked me where she was an' I told him I couldn't find her either."

He went quiet. He'd stopped trembling so bad, but he gave the occasional shiver. I asked him, "What about the others?"

"They were convinced she'd been abducted. At first they said we should wait for her to be returned. But then I convinced them, if she wasn't returned, Sheriff Levi was going to hang her death on us. Best thing we could do is say we delivered her to her gate, and went home."

"Then the state police could frame her father instead."

He said, "I didn't," three times in rapid succession and wound up, "I didn't think of it that way."

I sat looking at the moon for a while. She was a liar and a deceiver. She cast a beautiful silver path across the black water, but if you once trusted her, if you once placed your foot on her path, you were swallowed by the clammy darkness, and you died, screaming for air in silence.

"You sell drugs?"

"Nothing hard, some marijuana, little bit of coke..."

Heroin?"

"Ain't much demand. Housewives mainly, few kids. Mainly it's marijuana and coke. A bit of 'e.'"

"You ever sell to Sonia?"

"No, man! No, she was not into that, at all. I mean like, *at all!* She just wanted to make contact with the aliens, man. You can believe that."

"Now, I want you to understand. What goes down here tonight, Slick, will stay forever between you and me. Nobody else will ever know. So I am going to ask you, who's your supplier?"

"Seriously? No, man..." He gave a nervous laugh.

I sighed and reached into my boot, under my jeans and pulled out the Fairbairn and Sykes. I let him look at it a moment, then asked him, "You want to go home tonight, Slick?"

"Hey, c'mon..."

"Who is your supplier? One."

"What, you want to cut in on our operation? What are you doing, sir?"

"Who is your supplier? Two."

"Come on, man! I told you everything you wanted to know! I told you everything, man! You said you'd let me go!"

"Who is your supplier? Three..."

"No wait! I'll tell you! I'll tell you! Wait! Wait!"

"Name and address, and telephone."

"Jamie, Jim, de La Fontaine. Corner of Van Buren and Lenox, in Oakland."

"The Bay?"

"Yeah, Frisco, San Francisco Bay."

He told me the address and the man's contact number. I took a moment to memorize the information and removed my jacket from his shoulders. Then I leaned forward and plunged the fighting knife three times into his lower belly. His screams sounded like the screams of a fox in the night, under the moon.

I paused a moment to look into his eyes. They were full of terror, and incomprehension. I didn't say anything. I didn't explain. Just like nobody had explained to Ash why his daughter had been taken from him. I pushed the razor-sharp, seven-inch blade through his ribs and deep into his heart, leaning all my bodyweight on the hilt to drive it home. He went into spasm, his heart clenched the knife. He twitched violently for a few seconds, staring into my eyes, and then his life went out.

After a moment I withdrew the blade and cleaned it on his shirt. I cut his bonds, collected them and put them in my pocket.

Then I sat for a while, looking at the body, telling myself I had found her killer and punished him. But his punishment had not brought resolution. It had not brought justice. It had not made sense of anything or given meaning to what had happened. It had merely brought another death.

I pulled on my jacket, ensured I had left nothing that could identify me, and returned to my truck.

I returned to my home by back routes and country roads among vast, flat fields, making sure the tires picked up plenty of mud to conceal the mud and grass from the lake. It was unlikely anyone was going to do that kind of forensic analysis out here, but it paid to be careful. I kept my headlamps off and my speed down, navigating by the light of the moon. If any of these good people saw a truck out at this time, I wanted to be sure they wouldn't know it was mine.

I finally pulled through my gate at six AM. I parked by the porch, opened the hood to let the engine cool faster, and went inside to make coffee and breakfast. While the coffee was brewing I put my clothes in the washing machine, showered and changed into fresh jeans, a shirt, socks and a clean pair of boots. The ones

I'd used that night I cleaned thoroughly and put away in my wardrobe.

At seven thirty I closed the hood of the truck, placed the leather case with the Sig and the knife under a floorboard in one of my barns out back, and finally went inside to stretch out on the sofa and catch up on some sleep.

At nine thirty I awoke and went out to feel the truck. It was cold. I went to the barn and collected my leather case, wrapped it in brown paper and addressed it to myself. I dropped it on the passenger seat and drove down to Highway 191, but instead of turning into Pinedale, I turned south. It was an hour and a half's drive, through Boulder, Farson and Eden, as far as Rock Springs, in Sweetwater County.

I got there just after eleven and my first stop was the post office, where I posted myself the Sig and the knife. After that I drove half a mile down Foothill Boulevard to the White Mountain Mall and took my time stocking up on just about everything I was likely to need for the next week. Finally, at one PM, I was on my way home again. I figured I had given them time to find the body and for the sheriff to get a search warrant.

I arrived at two thirty and found two Sheriff's Department Jeeps parked outside the house. Seth was on the porch with Phil. Out back, around the barns, I could see Pete, Dave and Chavez.

I parked beside Seth's truck and climbed out looking mad.

"What the hell's going on, Sheriff?"

He didn't answer for a moment. He just scowled at me. When I was at the foot of the steps he asked the question.

"What the hell have you done, Harry?"

"What are you talking about? You practically have a confession from Slick! What the hell are you doing searching Ash's house?"

Suddenly his face was crimson and he was shouting. *"Don't bullshit me, Harry! Where were you last night?"*

I screwed up my eyes, climbed the steps and stood scowling down at him. "What are you talking about? I was where I've been every goddamn night since I got here, sitting in this house! Where do you think I was, out celebrating? You had better tell me what in hell you are doing here, Seth. Because in five minutes you are going to have every damned attorney from New York to Cheyenne headed for your office."

"I have a warrant." He slapped it against my chest. "I have a warrant to search this house and this property!"

"For *what?*" A rage I knew was irrational welled up in my head and suddenly I was yelling at him, pointing out across the valley toward Pinedale and the Connell house. "*What in hell do you think you're going to find, Seth? The murder weapon? The man is dead, for crying out loud! He died hugging his dead daughter! Can't you at least respect his fucking memory? Why don't you search the Connell house? Why don't you get a goddamn warrant to search Slick's room?*"

His eyes didn't waver from mine. When he answered his voice was quiet and cold.

"I'm not looking for the knife that killed Sonia, Harry. Where have you been this morning?"

I screwed up my face. "*What?*"

"Don't make this any harder than it has to be. Where have you been this morning?"

"I've been shopping, for crying out loud!"

He looked at Phil and jerked his head at my truck. Phil went to have a look. Meanwhile Seth pointed his thumb at the front door. "You want to open up?"

I shouldered past him, shoved the key in the lock and pushed the door open. I turned to him and snarled, "You know the way."

A piercing whistle from Phil called the other deputies to the house. They climbed the stairs and filed in, avoiding my eye. When they were inside, Seth came up close.

"Where were you last night, Harry?"

"I already told you, I was here. Why don't you quit being cute and tell me what this is about, Seth?"

"You didn't go and see Slick?"

"Seriously?" I sighed noisily and sat in the rocking chair. "You bring four deputies to search my house because I got mad and went to lean on Sean and Slick?" I held his eye. He didn't answer, just stared at me. "Did they also tell you that I went back to apologize?"

"After you went to apologize, what did you do?"

"I came home. I drank some whiskey and I fell asleep on the sofa. *Why*, Seth?"

"It's on the warrant." He pointed at the paper in my hand. "Slick Connell has been murdered."

I didn't react. A voice in my head kept telling me I should react, but I couldn't. I sagged back in my chair and stared away, through the open door, down at the gate. Eventually I said, "And you think I killed him."

"Did you?"

I gave a small, ironic laugh. "Sheriff, I knew Ash ten years ago. We had the kind of camaraderie that comes from doing a couple of operations together. I liked and respected the guy. It made me mad. Like it would make anyone mad, that he and his daughter died the way they did. But you have to understand there is one hell of a stretch from that to committing murder to avenge a man I hadn't seen for *ten years*." We stared at each other for five long seconds before I asked him, "Are you sure it was murder?"

He frowned. "What do you mean?"

"Maybe it was suicide. Maybe the little shit had some humanity after all and he had a guilty conscience. How was he killed?"

He grunted and lowered himself laboriously into the chair opposite me.

"He was stabbed three times in the lower belly, and then once in the heart, with a razor-sharp, double-sided knife."

"Holy shit. Same MO as Sonia."

"Revenge, Harry."

I snorted, thought for a moment. "And you only have two candidates for revenge, me and Dave. Dave won't wash. He wasn't crazy enough about her to kill for her, and he isn't made of that kind of stuff."

He nodded. "But you're a trained, professional killer."

I shook my head. "I was. But Sonia was practically a baby when I last saw her, and me and Ash just weren't that close."

"If that's true, why'd he call you?"

It was a good question, but I was ready for it. "Anyone else he might have called would have been a Fed. That would have meant not only red tape and an official investigation, it would also have meant attracting unwanted attention. Remember, he suspected the Gulf Cartel was moving in here. That was what worried him. He wanted some discrete help, not the full might of the Bureau swarming all over Pinedale."

He was watching me, assessing my answer. Before he could reach the wrong conclusion I moved him on.

"Last time I saw Slick was when I went to lean on him and his dad to come clean." I eyed Seth a moment and offered him the ghost of a smile. "I scared the shit out of him. I actually felt sorry for the little bastard. Made me wonder if he was telling the truth."

Seth's face screwed up like a fist trying to squeeze sense out of the impossible. "You *what?*"

"Hell, I don't know!" I looked out at the sun and the woods and shook my head. "How many people take peyote every year in the Southwest, and Mexico?"

"I have no idea."

"Must be thousands. How many kill each other?"

"I don't know, Harry. What's your point?"

"As far as I am aware, peyote has never led anyone to kill another person."

He leaned forward. "So now you're saying you don't believe Slick killed Sonia? This is a pretty sudden turnaround."

"No, I am not saying that, Seth. I'm saying I don't know. To me, last night, he didn't look like a killer."

"What does a killer look like?"

I eyed him a moment. "Dead. Ruthless." Unconsciously I

looked away so he wouldn't see my eyes. Watching the breeze move the trees outside, I asked him, "Has it occurred to you that the same person who killed Sonia, might have killed Slick?"

"No," he said, "not really."

He stood and climbed the stairs.

They searched the house and the barns, and my truck. They turned everything upside down but, after an hour, found nothing that could connect me to Slick's murder. When they were leaving, Seth paused on the steps.

"Did you kill him, Harry?"

I gave a tired smile and shook my head. "I was pretty good at what I did, Seth. But it's not like the movies. I am no Ninja. I don't know what the Connell house is like on the inside, but I'm guessing it's small and cramped, and a big guy like me creeping through a house like that in the middle of the night..." I shook my head some more. "I'd probably wake the whole damn household."

He watched me with hooded eyes, gave a small snort of a laugh and took one step down toward his truck. There he stopped and turned back to face me.

"You're a dark horse, Harry. My gut tells me you're a good man, but I think you are also smart." He gestured at me. "Big guy like you stumbling around in a cramped, dark house? You're right, you'd wake the whole damn household. Unless, that is, they were passed out from two dozen bottles of beer and a bottle of Jack Daniels, plus an ounce or two of marijuana you can be sure they smoked."

"I wasn't there. I didn't kill him."

He turned away and looked at my truck, eying the tires as he spoke.

"Where, Harry? You weren't where?"

I frowned like his question didn't make sense. "At his house, Seth."

"Yeah, but he wasn't killed at his house."

"And how in hell am I supposed to know that? The last time I saw him he was at his house. And when I went back later to make the peace offering, they were settling down to have a party. If he wasn't killed there, where the hell was he killed?"

He stared at me long and hard. "I'm not sure I should tell you."

"For crying out loud, Seth! What's the matter with you? Get real! What motive do I have? That I knew the guy ten years ago?"

He sighed, raised his hat and ran his fingers through his thinning hair.

"I'm not accusing you of anything, Harry. Maybe you ain't got much of a motive, but I don't know anybody has a better motive." He shook his head. "And the way he was killed, the place he was killed... For all I know you're a damn vigilante, or an equalizer or something."

I stared at him. "Out in the woods, where Sonia was killed..."

"You're either innocent or real smart. He was not killed in the woods, no. He was killed by the campfire."

"I'm sorry, Seth." I took a step down and sat on the steps. "If I'd got a hold of him when we found the body, I might have beaten him to death, but knives are not my scene, and as for motive, I just don't have one. Ash just didn't mean anything to me beyond being a colleague." I shrugged. "Maybe you have a killer on your hands who has struck twice using the same MO. I don't know much about the Connells, but you know as well as I do Slick and his dad are both mixed up in drugs. That's a scene that can get pretty ugly."

He turned and walked away. I watched him climb in his truck and slam the door. When the engine was idling he lowered the window and leaned out.

"That's a lot of groceries for a guy who's going back to New York."

I smiled. "I thought I'd hang around a few days and take Doc Erickson out to dinner."

He sighed, turned around and drove away, lurching and bumping down the track.

SEVEN

That afternoon I called Dr. Erickson.

"Harry, I'm glad to hear from you. How are you feeling?"

There was a smile in her voice and I put one in my own.

"I'm alive, which is something, I think. Ash and I weren't that close. Seth is making too much of it."

"Still, it must be tough. How are you sleeping?"

"I have dreams, but I sleep."

"You need something to help? Help you sleep I mean."

I put the smile back in my voice. "What can you suggest?"

"Pills."

"No, thanks. I don't do pills."

"There are other options we could discuss."

"Will they affect our doctor-patient relationship?"

"No. I'm talking about counseling, some form of therapy, meditation—"

"I don't need therapy, Doc. Sometimes life sucks. There is no therapy for that."

"Tough guy." She was gently taunting, but it wasn't a put-down.

"I'm not woke, Doc, if that's what you mean. I'm awake, but I'm not woke."

"Meaning?"

"Meaning, just because I don't like something, I am not entitled to pretend it's not real, or demand its removal. Bad things happen, and when they do you have a choice: go under, or keep going. That's all there is."

"That's a pretty bleak view."

I gave a small laugh. "Again, just because I don't like it, doesn't mean I can pretend it's not so."

"OK, Harry, enough with the existential philosophy. I'd like you to come in and see me. Speaking as your doctor, however tough you are, you just lost a friend and his young daughter in pretty violent circumstances. We need to take care not to slide into depression. Depression is a medical condition, Harry, and it can happen to anyone, however hard they are. I want to make sure that doesn't happen to you. That's my job."

"OK, I'll make a deal with you."

"A deal..." She sighed. "OK, shoot."

"I will explain to you, in detail, what I am doing to avoid falling into a depression, and you can give me your professional judgment, keep tabs on me and prescribe medication if you think it is necessary."

"OK, when do you want to come in?"

"No, see? That's the condition. I tell you over dinner."

She didn't sound amused. "Harry, I need you to take this seriously."

"I'm taking it seriously. Deal or not?"

"Harry, I don't see my patients in restaurants!"

"Are you married?"

"No, I am not. But that is not the point."

"Seeing someone?"

"Harry, stop trying to hit on me. It is completely inappropriate."

"Last time I was in a doctor's surgery I was twelve years old. I don't get sick and I don't plan to waste the taxpayers' money,

Claire. I am not hitting on you. I'd just rather tell you what my plans are over a meal than in a surgery."

There was a protracted silence. Finally she said, "You are one serious pain in the ass, Harry Bauer."

For some reason I had the feeling that the fact she insulted me using my surname was a good sign. Go figure. I smiled. "I can't deny that, Doc. So are you seeing anyone serious?"

"No, Harry, I am not."

"In that case, you can have dinner with me, and I can tell you my plans."

"Fine!"

"You're welcome."

"Thank you."

"Tomorrow night? Pick you up at seven?"

"Are you like this all the time? I feel completely exhausted."

"You could try counseling, therapy or meditation, but I would not recommend pills."

She thanked me, with more than a little irony, and hung up. I climbed the stairs to Ash's den upstairs, removed a couple of dumbbells from his chair, a Viking sword and a katana from his desk, and switched on my laptop.

I opened Google Earth and homed in on Oakland, Van Buren Avenue and Lenox Avenue. It wasn't hard to identify the place. There were several apartment blocks and one detached house. The house was set back from the road among trees and lawns, behind a high fence. I spent some time studying the area from ground level and from above. It was in Adams Point. Oakland as a whole had one of the highest crimes rates in the States, but within Oakland, Adams Point had virtually no crime. It was hard to tell without physically being there, but it didn't look like the kind of place where you would have a roaring trade selling drugs. It wasn't bad enough, and it wasn't high class enough. It just looked like a pleasant middle-class neighborhood.

That seemed to confirm what I had gathered from Slick. La Fontaine provided pushers with produce, but he didn't sell direct.

He kept his hands clean, probably had means of laundering his money, and let schmucks like Slick and Sean Connell do all the cutting, pushing and dealing with junkies.

I thought about Slick and his father. They were schmucks. That was true. But La Fontaine would have a lot of other boys— in Oakland, in San Francisco, in the Bay Area as a whole—doing ugly work. They would not be schmucks. They would be psychopaths and sociopaths.

They were the people Ash had come to Pinedale to get away from. It was the world he had come to Pinedale to protect his daughter from. But it was a sickness, a cancer, that was metastasizing, stretching tentacles to every corner of the world. There was no place where you could get away from it, no place where you could keep your family safe. It was a dark, sick world that belonged to them.

I memorized the area, made mental notes, switched off the computer and went downstairs to the kitchen where I made myself a steak, put it between two slices of rye and went out to the porch to eat it sitting on the steps.

I wasn't surprised, half an hour later, to see a red Toyota pickup turn in at my gate and lurch its way too fast up the track beside the river. It skidded to a halt in front of me, the door swung open and Sean Connell staggered out on unsteady feet. He had a bottle of beer in his hand and his face was wet with tears.

He pointed at me, holding the bottle by the neck with three fingers, and aiming at me with his index.

"You fuckin' son of a bitch." He said it in a crying voice, like a kid who's been denied his promised candy. "You *fuckin'* son of a *bitch!*"

I didn't answer. I watched his wet mouth sag open, like wet washing on a line. He was hurting bad inside. I searched for compassion inside myself but didn't find any. I didn't care about him.

"You killed my son." He whined, and then again, "You killed my *fuckin' son!*"

"He killed Sonia, and Ash died because of it."

His face flushed red and he shook his finger, spilling beer. "You don't know that! *You don't know that!*"

"He told me, Sean. He told me he killed her by mistake."

"It was an accident," he said more quietly, frowning, like he wasn't sure it made sense. "You can't blame him for an accident."

"I said it was a mistake, not an accident. He meant to kill, he just thought she was somebody else."

That was too much information for his sodden brain. He made a face of contempt and spat in the dirt. "Fuck you," he said. "I don't give a good goddamn! Screw you, and Ash and his whoring daughter! You killed my son…" He swayed a moment and then screamed, "*You killed my fuckin' son!*" He pointed at me again. "Now I am going to kill you."

"That's not a good idea, Sean."

He hammered the bottle against the hood of his truck. It bounced off and he tried it again, four times. It didn't break, but he spilled all the beer over his jeans, so it looked like he'd pissed in his pants. Finally he threw the bottle on the ground, wrenched open the truck door and pulled a hunting knife from inside.

I didn't get up. I didn't react. I stayed with my elbows on my knees, eating my steak and watching him.

"Don't do that, Sean. You're hurting and you're drunk. Go home, call Doctor Erickson. Get her to give you a sedative. We'll talk when you sober up."

"Screw you," he said again, and sounded sleepy. "You killed my son. Now I am going to kill you, the same goddamn way you killed him. Get on your feet and face me like a man."

"Go home, Sean."

He lurched two steps toward me, holding the knife out in front of him. He was about five paces away and becoming dangerous. He spoke quietly. "I am going to cut you."

He lurched another step forward and I stood up. Suddenly his eyes were alive and he was smiling.

"I am going to hurt you, Bauer."

I took one step up so I was on the porch. If he wanted me he'd have to climb the stairs, and the state he was in that was going to require some serious multitasking.

"Chicken shit," he said. "What's the matter? You're not so brave when you're facing a man, huh?"

"Is that what you are, Sean? You don't look much like a man from where I'm standing. You're drunk and you're crying like a girl."

It had the desired effect. He lunged up the stairs, unstable on his feet and not sure whether to look at my face or the stairs in front of him.

I lashed out with my right foot and smashed my heel into his nose. Blood spewed over his mouth. He made a strange, squeaking noise, his legs buckled and he sprawled back in the dirt. I went after him but he was tougher than I thought. He was still holding the knife. He scrambled to his feet with blood smeared all over his lips and chin. His eyes were wild and his neck was swollen. He spat blood and lunged at me.

I stepped back and the blade flashed a few inches in front of my face. I stepped to the right and he lunged at me again, slashing at my chest now. I kept my right side forward, with my hands high and open, drawing his attack. He telegraphed his third lunge. He was going for my right arm. I beat him to it with a small skip and smashed my right heel into his knee.

His bloody mouth sagged open. He kept saying, "Oh, shit! Oh, shit!" as he hobbled away. He still had the knife in his hand. I said, "Drop it."

His voice was shrill. "I'm going to kill you! I swear I'm gonna fuckin' kill you."

He limped toward me, holding the knife out in front of him. I could see his temples pulsing in his head.

"Drop the knife, Sean."

"*I'm gonna kill you!*"

I turned and walked away toward the garage, which doubled as a gym. I could hear Sean screaming at me to come back. I ignored him and entered the gym. There I had a large wicker basket with a variety of *bokken* in it. A *bokken* is a Japanese wooden sword used for practice. I selected a forty-eight-inch *bokken* I'd carved myself out of almond wood. Almond wood is really dense and really hard.

I took it by the handle and made my way back toward Sean, where he was limping and sobbing toward the garage.

"Drop the knife, Sean."

His voice was a whimper. "I'm gonna kill you."

I had told him three times. I didn't plan to tell him again. I took the sword in both hands, took a long step forward and slightly to the right, raising the sword above my head as I did so, and as my foot touched the ground I brought the hard wooden blade down on his wrist. He dropped the knife. I dropped the sword, stepped in close, twisted my right heel out on the ball of my foot, flicked my hip and drove a right hook right through his jaw. He did the wobble dance for a couple of seconds and fell to the dust.

I checked his pulse to make sure he wasn't dead, then went and got the hose. The water was cold and he came round after a second or two spluttering and gasping. I turned off the hose and he slithered back away from me in the mud. His knee had swollen and was stretching his jeans.

"Pick up your knife and get the hell out of here, Connell. Just remember, I could have killed you. You came here threatening to kill me. I had the right to defend myself. Now, I can call Sheriff Levi and get him to take you away, with your prints all over that knife, or you can get on your feet, take yourself to Doc Erickson for that knee, and stay the hell out of my way from now on."

He grabbed his knife, struggled to his feet and pulled himself painfully into his truck. I stepped up close to his window and spoke quietly.

"Your son killed Sonia because he was out of his mind on the peyote that you got for him. Whatever happened to your son, he had it coming. Now you had better stay out of my way, Connell. You don't want me thinking you are as responsible as he was."

He turned the truck around and rattled away down the path. The bumping and lurching over the rocks and potholes must have been painful for his knee. For a moment I thought I should feel pity, or compassion, but I didn't feel anything. I picked up the *bokken* and carried it to the gym. There I changed my boots for trainers and spent the next five hours training until my muscles and my joints were screaming with pain.

EIGHT

The next day I was up at six and spent two hours training. At eight I showered, alternating hot and cold for fifteen minutes. Then I breakfasted on eight rashers of bacon and four eggs. All the while I was thinking about James La Fontaine. Jamie. He had called him Jamie La Fontaine. If there was a link with Otropoco, he was it.

At ten AM I went outside and spent two hours practicing with Ash's bow. It was an Osage orange longbow with a sixty-five-pound draw weight. Shooting at sixty feet I got most of the arrows in the red and a few in the yellow, but after two hours my shoulders were aching and my fingertips were raw.

I went inside, pulled a steak from the fridge and threw it in a pan. As I watched it sizzle and singe, I thought about the house. The corner of Lenox and Van Buren, protected by all its trees, lawns and fences. And inside, Jamie La Fontaine.

He was as responsible for Sonia's death as Slick had been. In some ways more so. Because he was the power behind what had happened. And behind him...

The voice made me start. I put the steak on a plate and went out to the porch. The postman, Mike, was climbing into his van.

He slammed the door, leaned out his window and pointed at my table.

"You got a parcel! Left it there for ya! Y'have a good one!"

I waved as he backed up, turned around and headed down the track.

I glanced at the parcel on the table. I knew the writing. It was my writing. It was the parcel I had sent myself. I carried the box inside, opened it and burned the carton and the paper in the fireplace.

I spent the next while sharpening the Fairbairn and Sykes and cleaning and oiling the Sig. I left them both handy, in a drawer beside the TV.

The steak had gone cold. I ate it with my hands, hosed down the truck and put in another four hours of training before I shaved, showered and pulled a pair of chinos, a clean shirt and a jacket from my bag. They needed ironing, but I figured that would make the doc want to mother me, which was fine. Finally, at a little after six thirty, as the dark was closing in, I set off to collect Dr. Erickson.

I rolled into the parking lot of the Pinedale Medical Center at three minutes to seven and pulled up where the plate-glass doors were spilling warm light onto the paved path that led from the entrance to the blacktop. She'd obviously been waiting for me because she pushed out before I had a chance to swing down. I came around the hood to open the door for her and she raised her eyebrows at me and gave me a once-over.

"OK," she said as she climbed in. "What have you done with the *real* Harry Bauer?"

I didn't answer but climbed in behind the wheel beside her and slammed the door.

"Well, Dr. Erickson, we have the Wrangler Café, the Cowboy Bar, the Patio Grill Authentic Mexican Restaurant or the China Gourmet, where I believe they serve deep-fried Chinese Gourmets."

She arched a single eyebrow. "You know that could be construed as very racist."

"Yeah, but I am kind of hoping that you're as smart as you look and you realize that really racist is gassing six million people because of their race, rather than poking fun at their cuisine. So, Dr. Erickson, what is your fancy?"

She started to say three different things in succession, but finally settled on, "I think authentic Mexican Patio Grill sounds pretty good. And frankly, I am about ready for a margarita."

We drove in silence down Freemont Lake Road and joined Pine Street at the Riddley's intersection.

"It's a long time since I went out to dinner with a woman. You'll have to help me out." I glanced at her and smiled, to show I was joking. "Do I ask you about your day to show I am interested, which I am? Or should I be sensitive to the fact you've had it up to your eyeballs with your job and you only want to think about margaritas and fajitas?"

There was humor in her eyes, but she said, "Boy, it has been a long time, hasn't it? What do you do in New York?"

"I'm not kidding. Most of the time I hide in my house and try not to get shot by liberals."

She gave her head a little twist. "Are you deliberately provocative, or are you just trying to sound me out?"

I grinned. "Maybe I'm just nervous because it's my first date in a while. A margarita for you and a bottle of tequila for me."

She laughed. Then after a moment of silence she said, "Sean Connell came in."

I pulled into the lot outside the Patio Grill and killed the engine.

"Did he tell you how he hurt his knee?"

I climbed down and she didn't answer until we were inside, sitting down, the waitress had given us our menus and taken an order for one margarita and a cold beer. Then she said, "No."

"No?"

"He said he had tripped and fallen. He was pretty drunk, so

that part of it was credible. But his kneecap was almost dislodged, the bruise was the shape and size of a cowboy boot heel, he had an equilateral bruise running diagonally across his right wrist, his nose had been ruptured and his jaw had been fractured on the left side, leaving a very clearly marked fist."

I smiled. "Boys will be boys."

"You're trained in martial arts, right? You were in special operations?"

"Mm-hmm."

"Did you train in Jeet Kune Do?"

"Yup."

"Correct me if I'm wrong, but in boxing, in a hook, the fist is held facedown, right? Like so..."

She demonstrated, bending and raising her elbow, making a fist so that the back of her hand was raised toward the ceiling.

"I'm impressed, not many people know that."

She ignored me and went on. "But in Jeet Kune Do, the hook is shorter, and the fist is held upright, like so." She demonstrated, holding her fist with the back facing me. "Thus engaging the biceps and triceps and giving the punch more force."

I laid down the menu and smiled at her. "I think I may be in love."

"Am I right?"

The waitress brought us our drinks and left.

"You are. And now you are going to tell me the fist imprint on Sean's jaw was consistent with a Jeet Kune Do right hook. I have nothing to hide, Dr. Erickson. Sean came to my house intending to kill me. Because he says I killed his son. He pulled a knife on me, he refused to put it down, so I was forced to defend myself. When he had dropped the knife I asked him if he wanted me to call Seth. He said he didn't. So I advised him to go and see you."

She sipped her margarita and gave a small sigh of pleasure. "Is that how you deal with things in the Bronx?"

I laughed. "You're kidding, right? In the Bronx they would have cut his throat and thrown him in the East River."

"He told me about his son."

I took a pull on my beer and nodded as I wiped my mouth. "Seth told me about it. Obviously I am the prime suspect."

"Did you do it?"

"Hey, don't beat about the bush. Come straight to the point."

She spread her hands and shrugged. "It's the obvious question."

I sighed. "Look, Dr. Erickson—"

"Will you please stop calling me that? This is practically a date."

"Practically?"

"If I didn't suspect you of homicide, it would be a date. You might as well call me Claire."

"OK, Doc, in my past life I was in the British SAS for eight years. Seth knows that and that makes me the prime suspect in every act of violence that goes down in Pinedale. But the fact is I got enough of all that in Afghanistan, Iraq, South America and various parts of Africa to last me a lifetime."

I took a pull on my beer and she watched me without saying anything. As I set down the glass I said, "Another way of looking at it, Claire, is that I spared Sean today. I could have finished it a lot quicker in legitimate self-defense. But I didn't."

She made an "I guess so" face and I added:

"Besides which, I know enough about police procedure and forensics, and how a prosecution works, not to do something as plain stupid as killing the prime suspect in my friend's murder, using exactly the same MO, in virtually the same place and without giving myself an alibi."

She sipped her margarita and looked at me in a way that suggested I was making sense. I gave a small laugh.

"I am not saying I didn't want to kill him. There were moments when I did, after I saw Sonia's body. Hell, I went to his house and told him so. But if I'd killed him it would have been then, in hot blood."

"You went to his house to tell him you wanted to kill him? Does Seth know that?"

"Yeah." I nodded. "He also knows I went back to apologize."

Now she looked incredulous. "You *apologized*, to *Slick Connell?*"

"I actually apologized to his mother. But I asked her to pass it on. It was intended for the whole family."

She frowned at her glass. "You're a very unusual man, Harry."

"I came here to help a friend who was in need, and asked me for support." I paused a moment for thought, conscious of her watching me. "I got here too late, and seeing Sonia like that... That hurt and made me mad. But that doesn't entitle me to go around killing everyone and anyone I suspect. Slick was entitled to the benefit of doubt, like everybody else. So I apologized. Now, seeing how he was killed, it seems to me maybe he was telling the truth."

When she eventually smiled at me, gave her head a little tilt to the side and said, "Well, we may be on a date after all, Harry Bauer," I felt no compunction, no shame and no guilt. Instead I smiled at her and said, "That's good to hear. There are just two people in this town I want to know me for who I am, and to like me."

"Oh?"

"One of them is Sheriff Seth Levi. He is a good man and I believe he was a good friend to Ash. I have a lot of respect for Seth."

"And the other?" She asked it with two spots of color on her cheeks.

"You. I like you. I look at you and I see a beautiful, intelligent young woman who hasn't forgotten how to give a damn."

"That's probably the nicest, and the strangest, compliment I have ever received."

"Maybe you should get used to nice, strange compliments."

She gave me a look that said I was doing OK and picked up her menu. When the waitress had left with our order, Claire laid both her hands flat on the table and spoke like she was scolding them both.

"You were going to tell me your plans. You are a hard man, I can see that, and tough as old boot leather, granted. But you have had a bad experience that would have traumatized anyone, let alone a friend, and what we can't do is pretend it didn't happen. Denial is not an option, Harry."

I nodded a while, looking at her hands. "I get that and I agree. So let me outline my plan. For starters I am going to take a few days, maybe a couple of weeks, in San Francisco. I like San Francisco, always have. I'll be lazy, I'll eat a lot of seafood, go for walks, take in some concerts, relax..."

"That's excellent, Harry, but it's not enough."

"Wait, hear me out. During that time, while I am convalescing, if you like, I will meditate, in the most flexible sense of the word, on my friendship with Ash, on his daughter. I know I can never make sense of what's happened. There *is* no sense, no why and no because for their deaths. But what I *can* do is find a way to...," I spread my hands, "I can find a way to give meaning to their lives."

She sagged back in her chair, drumming her fingers on the table. "Wow," she said at last. "That's deep."

"Better than pills."

She smiled without humor, then snorted. "If you can do it, yeah. Not many people can do that, Harry. Not in a couple of weeks. Most people can't do it in a lifetime. Accept there is no reason for death, but give meaning to life? Where do you begin?"

I watched a plate of steak appear before me. It was singed on the outside, raw in the center and sprinkled with coarse salt. Somebody had remembered to place a lettuce leaf and a tomato beside it.

The same waitress placed a plate of chicken rice and beans before the Doc. The Doc, who was still watching me, waiting for a reply.

"Where do you start? Try Helmand Province in Afghanistan.

I've lost friends who were a lot closer to me than Ash was. I'm sorry about him. But what outraged me was his daughter. Young, innocent..." I cut into the steak and watched it ooze blood into the oil. "The Buddhists have an explanation for why we die. You know what it is?"

"No."

"We die because we are alive."

She didn't react. I shook my head, stuffed a hunk of meat in my mouth and chewed. After a moment I said:

"There is no meaning in nature, Claire. There is no right or wrong about a bear killing and eating a salmon. A mountain lion catches a lamb and kills it and eats it. There is no reason or meaning. It's just the way it works. Meaning is something we humans overlay on things." I smiled. "If we were rabbits, we'd be eating because we were hungry. You would eat this lettuce leaf here, and this tomato, and I would be a horrible, mutant carnivorous wabbit, eating the steak, and then possibly you. But we would be eating to survive, because that's how it works." I shrugged. "But we are humans, not wabbits, so we are sitting here eating while we try to give things deep, complicated meanings." I shrugged again. "She died because she was alive, but her life gave richness and joy to Ash's life, and the other people who knew her. That is what I have to take away from this."

She studied my face for a long time, with her fork halfway to her mouth.

"Boy," she said at last. "You are pretty intense, aren't you."

"I'm told it's because I was born in November."

She laid down her fork and shook her head. "Wabbits?"

"What's up, Doc? Never heard of wabbits?"

She started to laugh and put her napkin to her mouth. *"Horrible, mutant carnivorous wabbits?"*

I watched her laugh for a moment, enjoying it. She wasn't beautiful but she was very pretty. She was feminine, but you could tell from her steady gaze and the way she spoke that she was strong. Right now her cheeks were flushed and she was wiping tears from her eyes.

"I'm sorry. Delayed reaction. It has been a stressful couple of days, and it will take me a while to get over that image." She put her index and middle finger in front of her mouth like teeth and her left hand cupped like a bunny's ear beside her head. "The horrible mutant carnivorous wabbit. Boy!"

"I can feel a graphic novel coming on."

"So, when are you planning to go to San Francisco?"

"Tomorrow, the day after."

"That soon?"

"Not much point waiting."

We ate in silence for a moment. Then she laid down her fork and took a deep breath.

"Harry, will you do me a favor? Actually, a couple of favors."

"Sure."

"You have a real interest in the martial arts, right?"

"Sure."

"I know enough to know that the martial arts are rooted in the Tao and in Buddhism. Will you explore the possibility of real meditation, as a supplement to what you are doing?"

It was surprisingly difficult to do, but after a moment I said, "Yes. I'll do that. It's probably a good idea. What else?"

"Stay in touch." She saw me frown and added, "While you're in San Francisco. Stay in touch." After a moment she smiled. "I was born and grew up there. It's my hometown. You can tell me where you've been and what you've done. I don't want to intrude on your process, but you could call me, once or twice, just so I know how you're doing."

I nodded. "OK, Doc—Claire—I'll do that."

Later, the Patio Grill closed its doors as we stepped out into the quiet, nocturnal street. Doc Erickson was laughing about mutant wabbits again, and after a couple of whiskeys I was beginning to see the funny side too. It turned out she lived less than two hundred yards from the restaurant, so I walked her home and promised I would get a cab instead of driving. At the door to her house we paused for an awkward moment, looking at each other.

"What's the rule these days for a first kiss? Third date?"

"Something like that, I guess. Doctors don't get to date much."

"Third date, then."

"Sure."

I bent and kissed her for a long time. It seemed to be a beautiful, peaceful place and I didn't want to leave. When I let her go, she put a hand gently on my chest.

I stroked her cheek. "I have a problem with rules."

NINE

I watched her close her door and walked back to my truck, parked outside the now dark, silent restaurant. I could smell the night air. It smelt cool and green. It touched my skin and I had the illusion suddenly that I had woken from sleep into a dream, and I was standing on an empty, nocturnal stage set: an empty street illuminated by dead lights.

I stood a moment looking, then climbed in behind the wheel and slammed the door. The echo was loud and solitary in the silence. I did a U-turn and headed back home.

When I had crawled, lurched and bumped up the long, dark track to my house, I did not go to bed. I opened up my computer and booked myself a room for the next day at the Grand Hyatt in San Francisco.

Next I booked a Ford Mustang convertible rental car to pick up at the hotel. I packed a bag with the essentials, took it downstairs, slung it in the back of the truck and locked up the house. I took a moment to say farewell to Ash, the man I had never met, and to Sonia, and to ask forgiveness for having arrived too late. Then I started the fourteen-hour drive through Utah and Nevada to northern California.

It was tedious, especially for the first two hundred and thirty miles along US-189, and the climb up into the Wasatch Mountains before dropping down into Salt Lake City to pick up the I-80, with still some ten hours to kill on the road.

I watched the sun rise crimson in my mirrors, listening to Credence as the sky ahead of me turned gray-blue. I crossed the border into Nevada at just after seven and stopped at a gas station outside Wendell to eat a couple of donuts and drink a couple of pints of black, sweet coffee. I slept for an hour in the truck and pressed on.

At Sacramento I pulled off at the Promenade Shopping Mall and bought myself half a dozen disposable cell phones, and at four PM that afternoon I finally crossed the Oakland Bay Bridge into San Francisco, at Rincon Hill. Exit 2C took me to Fremont Street, which in turn led me through grotesque, sterile canyons of glass and steel to the One Rincon Hill Parking Garage. I spiraled up through echoing, oily black shadows, with screaming tires, to the very top where it was almost empty. There I left my truck.

At four thirty I stepped out of the high-rise parking lot onto Harrison Street, hailed a cab and had it take me to the Hyatt, where I checked in, shaved, showered and fell into bed. I slept deeply for four hours, showered again, dressed more or less respectably and went down to the bar to have a beer before dinner. I took my beer to a corner behind a palm and called Jamie La Fontaine.

It rang four times before it was answered. There was silence for four long seconds. Then a slightly high, nasal voice said, "Hello?"

"Is that Jamie La Fontaine?"

When he answered I was surprised that his accent was English. He said, "Why don't you tell me who *you* are first?" A short aspirated laugh and then, "After all, you called me."

"Sure. I'm a friend of a friend."

Another laugh. "Well, I mean, that doesn't narrow it down much I'm afraid, does it? Shall we be more precise? Whose friend are you? And what's your name? Those are two good places to start, don't you think?"

"Why not? I'm a friend of Slick's. You remember Slick? He's Sean's son. He gave me your number. He told me if I was in San Francisco I should call you."

"What for?"

I paused a moment, thrown by the question and unsure how to answer. He spared me the trouble and said, "I mean it's not as if we're bosom pals or anything. Your friend is my friend kind of shit. When did he do this, give you my number?"

"A while back. Have I made a mistake? He said you'd be accommodating."

"Have you got a name?"

"I had about two minutes ago, but I seem to have forgotten it. I was expecting a friendlier reception. Why don't we say it's John Smith and start again from the top?"

"Why don't we. I am not accustomed to people calling me out of the blue. That nasty little redneck should have known better. When did you say you saw him?"

"Must be couple of months ago. What's the problem, Mr. La Fontaine? I just want to do a little business is all. I don't want to get in the middle of anything."

"What kind of business?"

"Well, now, I'd like to buy some of San Francisco's traditional horticultural produce. Do you think you can accommodate me?"

He was quiet a moment. Then, "Can I call you on this number."

"Yeah."

"How long are you in San Francisco?"

"Just a few days."

"All right. I'll get back to you tonight—" He hesitated. "Are you alone?"

"Yeah, I'm alone. Slick doesn't give me all this trouble. We meet in a bar, I buy him a drink, he gives me the shit and I give him the dough."

"Yes, I'm sure. That's all very folksy and lovely. But things are a little different in the city. I'll call you in an hour or so."

He hung up and I went and had dinner. I picked up a newspaper from reception and took my time over an avocado and prawn salad and a sirloin steak. I was halfway through some blue cheese, a generous glass of Bushmills and an espresso, when my phone rang.

"Mr. Smith?"

"Speaking."

"This is James. If you've had dinner, why don't you join me over a cognac at Room 389?"

"Where's that?"

"Oakland, Grand Avenue. It's very groovy, in the old style. Live music and a DJ. But it's a wholesome, family place. So don't go pulling any tough guy shit, no shades or flick knives. We are just going to have a chat so I can get to know you. It's my way of doing things, and it works."

"Suits me, pal. I'm not aspiring to be Lex Luthor. I just aim to have a little fun."

"Good, well I'll expect you in...?"

"Give me half an hour."

I signed the check, strolled out to reception and told the girl to have the Mustang brought round. Ten minutes later I was burning rubber back across the Oakland Bay Bridge with a strange burning in my gut. I came off onto West Grand Avenue, followed it over the rail tracks and through an industrial wasteland of broad streets and low prefabs, to the more gentle, middle-class environs of Glen Echo Creek. The park slid by on my right, and pretty soon I was pulling up outside a row of buildings that looked like they'd been preserved without change since the Summer of Love. The 389 was set back from the sidewalk behind a trough full of palms. The walls were adobe-oxblood and the door was heavy, polished wood.

Inside it was dark wood and dim lighting, there were a couple of cacti on the bar, and plenty of dark corners where you could talk without being disturbed. There were no posters of Che or Jimi Hendrix, which was disappointing. The music, however, was distinctly vinyl.

I leaned on the bar and asked a guy with an intellectual beard and horn-rimmed glasses for a double Bushmills straight up. He didn't say anything to me, but went efficiently about his task. Janis Joplin was singing the most tragic version of "Summertime" ever recorded, and her husband was doing his best to screw it up by playing his guitar like it was a lute. I looked around, scanning for someone who looked English and was called La Fontaine. I decided he hadn't arrived yet, took my drink and went to look for a table. I found a place in a corner under a painted wall panel that made me think of Carlos Castaneda, and sat.

I was on my fifth sip and getting antsy when a short, bald man in a shiny brown suit and a pink tie came in on quick little feet. He looked like Poirot's evil twin minus the waxed moustache. He went up to the bar and had a word with the intellectual beard who nodded and jerked his floppy head in my direction. The little bald guy with the polished head strutted toward me, dodging the few patrons there were, and smiled at me with shiny cheeks.

"Mr. Smith?" he said, with an English accent. "Don't get up and don't shake my hand. I'll just sit. Alan will bring me my drink. He knows." He sat at right angles to me and smiled, with his palms on his knees. "Lovely place. Hardly changed in sixty years. 'Course they all used to meet here, you know, and talk sedition," he chortled, "out of Vietnam, down with the capitalist state, turn on, tune in, drop out! Ha! Good times. Never knew who you were going to wake up next to!" He laughed, then shrugged. "You're too young."

I figured he was sixty and asked, "You're not?"

"Seventy-five in October. Yoga, meditation, plenty of red meat and sex." He laughed with a wide mouth. I smiled. He went on. "I'm deadly serious. And absolutely no stress." He pointed to the door. "See that door? You start stressing me and I will get up and walk straight out of that door and go and sit by the water, meditating."

"I don't aim to stress you. I just want to have a little fun."

"Well I'm all for that. But let's chat a bit first. I like to know who my friends are, see?"

"What do you want to chat about, Jamie?"

The guy with the intellectual beard and the heavy glasses came around and deposited a cloudy green drink in front of La Fontaine. It had a lot of crushed ice in it, a piece of lemon and some mint leaves on top. He sipped it carefully, leaning forward, with his baby finger sticking out.

He made an appreciative noise and said, "So, how do you know Slick, then?"

"He's from Pinedale. I live near Pinedale. Anything I can't get at the mall, he's my go-to man."

"You've met his father, of course."

"Briefly, but my dealings were with Slick."

"So how did you two meet?"

I sighed like I was getting bored. "I was eating a burger at the Burger Barn. Got to talking with George. That's the owner of the Barn. He told me he needed two joints a day, one in the morning and one before bed. I hadn't smoked a joint since I was in New York. I was never into coke or H or any of that shit. You know what I mean?"

"Absolutely. I couldn't agree more."

"But I enjoyed more natural stuff. I don't like a joint, but I'd have a pipe of pure weed and listen to Floyd. Right?"

"Heaven."

"Sometimes I'd mix in some salvia divinorum."

"Oh indeed."

"So I asked George where the hell a man could get some of that shit in Pinedale. It ain't exactly the Wild West out there anymore. He told me he bought his stuff from Sammy Connell."

He arched an eyebrow. "Sammy?"

"Samuel, Sammy, Slick. Before he became a teenager he was

Sammy. Then he started doing weird shit with his hair and became Slick."

"Oh," he said without smiling. "How amusing. So what are you in the market for, Mr. Smith?"

"What you got? Something a bit trippy. I got hectares of land out there. Something I can take, and go and lie under the stars and just go."

He laughed. "But you don't want to take acid because it's a chemical. You really are an old hippy, aren't you? Well," he shrugged, "there are always mushrooms. But if you really want to connect with what I call the *spiritual entities* of America, from Tierra del Fuego to Alaska, it has to be peyote." He took another pull from his weird drink and smacked his lips. "I mean to say, the place to take peyote is in Mexico, with a *brujo*. Then the Earth spirits really come to you. New Mexico also, but there is a *darkness* in New Mexico. Portals were opened in the desert down there, and in Nevada, by Jack Parsons and his friends. You know Alistair Crowley appointed Parsons as the head of his lodge in California, in 1942?"

"No kidding."

"Did you know that? The man who founded the Jet Propulsion Laboratory and the Aerojet Engineering Corporation, was a devotee of Crowley's. When his second wife, Sara Northrup, left him for L. Ron Hubbard—I tell you, *those* were the days!—Parsons went into the desert and conducted the Babalon Working."

"The what?"

"The Babalon Working, a series of rituals designed to invoke the Goddess Babalon. Of course, to do that, portals have to be opened in the space-time continuum, and lots of other nasty things slip through. Since then, that whole area of New Mexico, and all of Nevada, have become very dark places."

"Well, I don't plan to go down to New Mexico or Nevada."

"No, quite. I don't blame you. But Wyoming, by the Wind

River Mountains, my word, that would be a wonderful place to do peyote."

"So, how do I get hold of some peyote, and how do I use it?"

"You get hold of some peyote by buying it from me. And I shall explain to you how to use it. Now tell me something, is this just for you, or are you likely to do a little business of your own. It's an expanding market, you know?"

"Yeah?" I took a pull on my whiskey, like I was thinking about it. "I mean, what kind of numbers are we talking about?"

He rolled his eyes up to the ceiling and opened his hands, like he was invoking the Mother Mary, or maybe Babalon.

"My dear man, how high is the sky? How high is your ambition? I live modestly because that is my nature, but believe me, if I must take a car I take my vintage Bentley; if I must fly, I fly first class, on the rare occasions I dine out, I dine at Atelier Crenn, Gary Danko, Saison..." He paused to smile. "And believe me, my house is modest, but I don't *want* a palace. I have a couple of Picassos, I have a Monet and a few Manets, *lots* of wonderful first editions."

"From selling peyote? Forgive me, but I find that hard to believe."

He chuckled. "I can see I am going to have to educate you, my dear fellow. Peyote, marijuana, salvia...these are for hippies, nice people like you. They are the Napoleon brandies, the cask-aged single malts, for people like us who know what they want. Ironically, they are at the cheap end of the scale, and long may it be so. But for the rabble, for the noisy glitterati and the barely human apes who burn away their lives in dirty bedrooms, who, in the immortal words of the Eagles, drive themselves to madness with a silver spoon, there are other products which are less wholesome, and far, far more expensive."

"Oh man—"

"Perhaps I have overstepped the mark."

He sipped and watched me over the edge of his glass while I shook my head.

"No," I said and then made a show of thinking for a bit. "No, I was just expecting to buy a bud or two. I hadn't really thought about getting involved in..." I cleared my throat. "I mean, I thought Slick did all that."

"Slick is dead."

I was surprised he knew and didn't hide it. He picked up his glass and sipped, and as he set it down he said, "And if I am not very much mistaken, you killed him."

TEN

I frowned hard. "Hey now, slow down there pal."

He smiled at a passing couple. The woman gripped his hand a second and said, "Jamie..."

He kissed her hand and said, "Hello darling," before letting them move on. In the same tone, and without looking at me, he said, "Oh, come on now, Mr. John Smith! You can cut the howdy ma'am y'all cowboy act. You may have been a couple of years consorting with bison and farm girls, but I know you're a New Yorker, you said so yourself a moment ago, and you have the Bronx written all over your cow-hide face." Now he turned and fixed me with his eye. "I also know you're Harry Bauer." He paused. I said nothing. He went on, "So far I have developed some respect for you. Keep up the pretense and I shall lose it all and leave."

I nodded once, slowly. "So Slick is dead. Now what?"

"He was trailer trash, like his father and his mother. They consumed everything they bought and I hardly made a penny out of them. And they have the effrontery to get on the phone and start whining to me that you killed their son. If you hadn't done me the favor, I would've sent someone anyway."

"Sent someone?"

"Don't be naïve, Harry. Wyoming is remote and sparsely inhabited. But there is a good market there among the young, college kids, high school kids with rich parents, and there is always the Wind River Reservation. That should be a good market. An enterprising man could exploit that, and you also have Idaho, Utah—believe me, those young Mormons are *gagging* for it! Colorado, Montana. I mean, it's not like New York where you have eight or nine million people on your doorstep. But then in New York you also have the NYPD and the FBI breathing down your neck all the time. In Pinedale you have a sheriff and a couple of deputies, whom you can probably pay off anyway. A man of your experience and intelligence, it'd be a cinch."

"I came here for a chicken, and you're offering me an elephant farm."

He narrowed his eyes and licked his lips. "Why *did* you come here, Harry?"

"You said Sean called you?"

"He called me, sobbing on the telephone. It was nauseating. He was drunk and crying like a child. He said that you had killed his son, you had robbed them not only of their child, but of their income. He wanted me to send someone to kill you."

Inside I felt a terrible stillness and a coldness. He held my eye 'for a long moment. He knew who I was. He recognized what I was. He could smell it. After a moment I asked him:

"So what did you tell him?"

"I told him to kill you himself and I might consider not cutting off his supply. He telephoned again three hours later saying you had broken his leg, his arm and his jaw, and that I had a duty to send someone to kill you. I told him to go and screw himself and if he ever phoned me again I'd send someone to kill him."

"How did you know I was going to come?"

"I didn't. I thought it was even chances. I am a very intelligent man, Harry. I have an IQ of one hundred and forty-five. That makes me a genius. I know men like you. You want to get away, back to nature, chop wood and hunt. But what you're really doing is trying to escape from yourselves while at the same time trying to justify your animalism and your lust. Sooner or later something happens to stir it up again. I don't know what it was in your case, but Slick clearly crossed you, and you killed him. Now you've tasted blood again, you want more. You're too old to join the SEALs, so you seek to get involved in some dark business where, with a bit of luck, you get to kill somebody every now and then."

I leaned back in my chair. "You got all that from one phone call?"

"Oh, no. I had all that before you phoned. You're a type. So, Harry, with Slick dead I now have this large potential market that needs not only servicing, but opening up. We supply groovy stuff to the *cognoscenti*, we sell coke to the glitterati, and we sell heroin, meth and fentanyl to the scum. Do it right and you stand to make a seven figure yearly income. And if you have any problems, I have boys who can go out and back you up."

"Like they did with Sean?"

"Sean was a loser, he was wasting my time and my money. He was lucky to come out alive. You are a different kind of man. Do it right and I will back you to the hilt."

I drained my glass. "I need to give this some thought."

"Bullshit."

"What?"

"If you didn't come here for the purpose of making this deal, do you mind telling me what the hell you did come here for?"

It was a dangerous moment. I held his eye, then looked away, smiled and improvised on his assumptions.

"OK, you're right. The man's a genius. But I have been living as a cowboy in the Cowboy State. I drive a Dodge RAM and I drink cans of Rainier on my decking. I was kidding myself I wanted to come here, have a look, get some peyote and come to terms with what I had done." I shrugged and sighed. "You slammed the truth in my face. I need to think about it. Let me sleep on it tonight. I'll call you in the morning, after breakfast."

He nodded. "All right." He eyed me a moment as I stood. "You understand that your best advice is to accept the offer?"

"Yeah, I understand that."

He smiled broadly, everybody's favorite uncle. "Super, splendid. We'll have another little chat tomorrow, then."

"I can't wait."

I stepped out into the night, feeling the whiskey warm on my breath. I watched a couple of desultory cars roll by under the streetlamps, pushing misty amber cones in front of them along the yellowed blacktop. I climbed in behind the wheel and drove slowly back to my hotel.

I awoke suddenly, staring out at an orange sky. I was still dressed, lying on top of the bed. My cell said it was eight AM. I sat up, feeling physically hollow, and made my way to the bathroom where I washed my face and stripped off my clothes, telling myself he had known I was coming. La Fontaine had known I was coming. Even chances, he'd said. Because I'd killed Slick and broken Sean's leg. But that didn't make it even chances.

I climbed into the shower and turned on the cold water. It made me gasp and shook me awake. I let it drench me till it felt good, then gulped down mouthfuls of it before turning it to hot and soaping my head and body.

Killing Slick and breaking Sean's leg did not make it even chances I would want to step into Slick's shoes. That was bullshit. He was bullshitting me and using the seven-figure yearly income as a glamour to blind me.

I stepped out of the shower and dried myself off. Jamie La Fontaine had other reasons. He had other reasons for offering me Slick's business; other reasons for wanting to lure me into the family, and other reasons for wanting to know me. Sean had called him and told him what I'd done. La Fontaine had called his boss and they had decided to reel me in and see who I was and what happened if they poked me.

I was willing to bet if I had not shown up, they would have come to find me. Now, as I was here, they wanted to keep me close, where all good enemies should be.

I went down for a breakfast of wholegrain toast and a pint of espresso. After my third cup I called La Fontaine. He answered after the first ring.

"Good morning. I hope you slept well and have had a good think."

"Like a log, and I do all my best thinking when I am unconscious."

"I am very glad to hear it."

"So, if I accept your proposition, what happens next?"

"I thought you said you'd had a good think. If we are still at the 'if' stage, nothing happens. And I'll tell you something else, Bauer, keep me waiting much longer and you can go and screw yourself. The deal is off. One thing I do not need on my team is an indecisive cunt."

The word shocked me in spite of myself.

I let a beat go by and put a smile in my mouth. "Watch your mouth, La Fontaine."

"Yeah, why don't you watch it for me, cowboy. Now stop wasting my fucking time."

"OK, we are past the if stage. What happens next?"

"Oh, well that's super. Lovely to have you onboard. What happens next is that we agree on an order, what I like to think of as a starter pack. Maybe a kilo of coke, a kilo of H, and maybe four pounds of marijuana. You take that back to Wyoming and sell it, and if all goes well, we repeat the operation with double the product."

"How much is all that going to cost me?"

He laughed. "If you have to ask, you can't afford it! Isn't that what they say? My dear fellow, the coke you can have for twenty grand, the heroin you can have for thirty. The hash I'll let you have for ten thousand dollars. So we are talking about a startup of sixty thousand dollars."

"And where am I supposed to get that kind of money overnight?"

"Ah, but you see, my dear man, that is why I am not like all the rest. I am here to help you. You prosper, and I prosper. I will let you have the product on spec. You sell it at the prices I will list for you, and you will make a very handsome profit. Enough, I hope, that you will want to repeat the operation on a monthly basis, with an ever expanding market."

"So I sell it, pay you and order more."

"That's the idea."

"OK, so where and when?"

"Relax. There's no hurry. You said you were here for a week. Chill, enjoy this glorious city. I'll call you later and arrange a place where we can meet quietly, we'll go over some details and then we never meet again."

"Stop, you'll break my heart."

"I'll call you in a bit."

He hung up.

I signed the check and took myself for a walk through the city. I walked down Sutter Street till I came to Powell, and turned down the steep slope toward Union Square, and without knowing exactly why I called Doc Erickson. It rang five times before she picked it up.

"Harry, I wasn't sure you'd call."

I stopped, leaned against the wall of the Drake Hotel, and, wondering what the hell I was doing, I said, "I thought it would be nice to hear your voice. I hope that's OK."

"Of course." She said it with no particular emphasis. "Where are you?"

"Oh, um." I looked up and down. "On a hill."

"High on a hill?"

I laughed. "Yeah, Powell Street. I was just walking down to Union Square."

"How are you?" It was simple and direct, because she wanted to know. It made me long for normality, for school runs, visits to the doctor and the dentist, family Christmas and Thanksgiving. All part of a reality that was not for me. Not for men who make a living killing other human beings.

I shrugged, like she could hear my shrug. "You know, I've been better. I have to figure out how this works."

"Slowly. One step at a time. Like learning to walk."

I was going to ask her if she would help me, but the words got stuck in my throat, because she was good and kind and I was feeding her a lie. That was when she said, "I'll help you if you'll let me."

I nodded. "Yeah." I gave a stupid laugh. "I'll let you." I was about to add that there were things she didn't know, that I needed to come clean about, but she said, "I have a patient, Harry. I have to go. Will you call again?"

"Sure." I laughed the same stupid laugh. "Why don't you grab a plane and come and join me?"

"Oh! I wish..." and then, "We'll take a rain check. Maybe some other time?"

She hung up and I stood with my back against the wall, looking down at the silent cell.

I walked around for an hour or so, trying not to think about Sonia, sixteen, pale blue and waxy, lying beside her dad in the next freezer drawer; or about Slick, staring into my eyes as his horrified heart gripped at the knife. Trying to think of wholesome, kind, normal Claire.

I made my way back to the hotel and had them bring up the Mustang. Then I drove around for an hour until eventually I came to Lowe's Home Improvements on Bayshore Boulevard, in Bernal Heights. There I parked in the vast parking lot and walked into the vast warehouse, faintly scented with sawdust and wood preserver. There I strolled around for an hour and bought a roll of duct tape, a broad-headed screwdriver, a large pair of pliers and a box of Blue Hawk latex safety gloves. I paid cash and carried my goods out to the Mustang.

Then I drove across town under a bright, spring sun, and had lunch at Papa Mak's Burgers, near Ocean Beach. The growing question in my mind now was whether or not I waited for La Fontaine to contact me. I was beginning to feel impatient, but I knew that impatience was the warrior's greatest enemy.

The call came when I was halfway through my burger, sitting outside in the sun. The sun was warm, but the breeze was cold in the shade. There were two women behind me in coats, and one of them was advising the other that if Nigel no longer fulfilled her, she should leave him before the relationship became toxic.

I picked up the phone and spoke with my mouth full.

"Yeah."

"You know where I live?"

"Slick gave me your address."

"No doubt you were very persuasive when you asked him for it."

"He thought so."

"Come over this evening at seven. I'll have the stuff ready for you."

"Fine, listen, I wanted to talk to you about the laundry."

He sighed audibly. "We can talk about that when you get here, but believe me it gets harder every year. You know, it's this fucking New World Order and the World Government. *Everything* is controlled and they want their twenty percent of everything."

"So what, you're saying cash?"

"That is the safest thing, for sure."

I dropped my voice. "What about offshore accounts like Belize, the Bahamas, Switzerland?"

"Oh, my God! Don't touch Switzerland! Switzerland *belongs* to the European Union! Lord no, Belize is OK, but the problem is getting the cash there. They are not as corruptible as they once were, you know. You are far better off in Panama, where everybody is corruptible. You get your tame officials at the border, and as many government officials as you can bribe, and you're laugh-ing. Once you have *that* account you can open another, legitimate one in Belize. We'll discuss it when you're here."

"I'd appreciate that. But in principle you recommend cash…"

"Oh, far and away, dear boy. I mean, of course have your offshore accounts where the bastards can't get you, in case you need to make major purchases like houses or yachts, but keep plenty of cash available in case Big Brother decides he's going to move in and freeze your accounts." He laughed. "But we are getting a little ahead of ourselves, aren't we?"

"I guess." I glanced at my watch. It was twenty to three. "I'll see you in a while."

I hung up, finished my burger and stood. The two women behind me had their elbows on the table, leaning in close to each other, and an empty cappuccino cup each in front of them. I slipped my phone in my pocket and leaned toward the one who was going to dump her husband.

"You know what," I said, and they both looked up, surprised and affronted in equal measure. "Sometimes what you need to become fulfilled is to stick with the project through the difficult times as well as the easy ones, and make it work. Taking the easy option is not fulfilling. Being selfish and egocentric is not fulfill-ing. Working through the problems, having the humility to recog-nize when you're wrong, and the self-belief to know when you're right. That's fulfilling."

The one who was not leaving her husband looked me up and down a couple of times. "Excuse me, who invited you to this conversation?"

I smiled at her. "Nobody, and if they had I would have turned them down. It's a pretty stupid conversation." I looked back at the one who was preparing to leave her husband. "Good day, ma'am."

ELEVEN

I DIDN'T WAIT TILL SEVEN. I DROVE TO THE ONE Rincon Hill multi-storey Parking Garage, where I'd left my truck on the top floor. I parked the Mustang beside it, slung my purchases in the trunk and made my way across the bay to Oakland, where Van Buren met Lenox Avenue. I arrived just after four PM and left the truck at the corner of Lee Street, a hundred and fifty yards away from La Fontaine's house. I climbed the five steps to his front door, which stood under a mock Georgian pediment supported by two mock Georgian pillars. I rang on the bell and after a couple of minutes the door was opened by a black guy who was big enough to be two black guys. He had a voice like a geothermal disturbance, and a face like a tectonic plate.

"You was told seven."

I frowned at him. "How do you know that?"

He put his head on one side and gave me that, "You trying to be clever?" look. "Mr. La Fontaine jus' told me, is how. Now get lost till seven, stupid."

"Yeah, sure. Now you go and tell Mr. La Fontaine that I have urgent news from my friend Seth which cannot wait. And unless you and your boss want to see the inside of a state penitentiary in the very near future, you'd better advise him to let me in."

He narrowed his eyes at me. "You say *what?*"

"Don't try and understand it, genius, just tell La Fontaine."

"Stay there."

"No, I'm going to go away and come back at seven."

He frowned at me. I shook my head. He closed the door and went away. A minute later he was back, jerking his head at me to go in, the way they did back when the world was black and white.

He closed the door behind me and led me upstairs and along a corridor to an office that occupied the corner of the house. It had two windows, one either side of the corner, overlooking a large lawn with flowerbeds, skirted by a high wall and tall cypress trees. Visibility into the garden was minimal.

La Fontaine was standing behind a large, oak desk which was probably five hundred years old. He was shaking his head and wagging his finger in the negative.

"Don't do this. Don't do this ever, Harry. If you do this the whole deal is off. I never heard of you and I don't want to know you. People who do this get people killed, themselves included. I thought you were better than this..."

He stopped because I had stepped up to his desk. He was still frowning at me when I leaned forward, reached out and smacked him on the tip of his chin. His eyes rolled up, his legs wobbled and he dropped back into his chair.

As a rule of thumb, in a situation of high risk, if you do something completely unexpected, you probably have between three and four seconds in which to act before somebody else reacts. In a moment of high risk, three seconds can be a whole lifetime.

Before La Fontaine's ass had hit his chair I had sprung back in a long stride and smashed my heel into the side of the big guy's knee. Before he could scream, which I knew he was going to do, I twisted and rammed the angle between my left index and thumb hard into his windpipe. He had a neck like a redwood, so I did it twice.

He didn't know whether to reach for his broken knee or his paralyzed throat, so I made it easy for him. I kicked his feet from under him and guided him down to a crash landing on the floor on his right side. Once he was there wheezing with his eyes bulging, I told him to relax and breathe, the air would come. I told him that as I pulled the Fairbairn and Sykes from the sheath on my calf.

"Relax," I said again. "I am in no hurry to hurt anyone. I just need to know how many of you there are in the house right now." I leaned a little closer and placed the blade on his struggling windpipe. "Lie to me, and I will cut your windpipe. Then you'll drown in your own blood. It's one of the nastiest ways to die. Are we communicating?"

He nodded. I said, "OK, don't try to talk. Besides you and La Fontaine, how many people are in the house?"

He shook his head. I smiled. "So, if I lean out the door and shout, 'Hey, come on up, boss needs you,' nobody is going to come tripping up the stairs?"

He rasped painfully. "'S just me. Boys is comin' at six thirty, man."

"Oh, OK, that's cool."

I put his lights out with a right hook, then carefully drove the knife down behind his left collarbone, severing the aorta and the carotid artery before penetrating the heart. Death came in less than a second, but all the bleeding was internal and made no mess in the room or on the carpet. I cleaned the knife on his shirt and slipped it back in the sheath.

Then I pulled on the latex gloves and made my way over to where La Fontaine was sprawled in his chair. I dragged him down to the floor. He grunted and groaned like he was trying to wake up. I pulled off his shoes, then pulled out the laces. I used one to tie his ankles together. He was starting to come round, so I rolled him on his belly, pulled his hands behind his back and tied his wrists together with his other shoelace. Finally I rolled him on his back again, balled his socks, stuffed them in his mouth and pulled the masking tape from my pocket. I put a strip across the socks and went down the corridor to the bathroom to get a glass of water. I took it back to the study and threw it in his face.

He started making gasping, screaming noises like he couldn't breathe. I sat in his chair and spoke quietly.

"Relax. Stress is bad for you, remember?"

He tried to articulate sounds through his socks and the tape: one short syllable and two long ones, probably "I *can't breathe!*"

"Breathe more slowly, more lightly, through your nose. As long as I feel you're useful to me, Jamie, we're doing OK. The problems begin if you start to be a pain in the ass and I feel I'm getting diminishing returns. Blink once if you understand."

He blinked once and swallowed.

"Now, I have a series of questions for you, Jamie. Most of them are pretty simple, practical questions that you should have no trouble answering. One or two are more kind of abstract and subjective, and have no correct answer. They are just to satisfy my curiosity. Still with me?"

He blinked and swallowed again.

"Good, so let's begin with a very simple one." I pulled the pliers from my pocket and held them up for him to see. "You know what these are?"

He went sickly pale. His eyes stared wide and he started making noises.

"Blink once for yes, Jamie. Don't start giving me problems." He blinked. "Sure you do. I'm willing to bet you've had your boys use them more than once, right? Now, here is a slightly more abstract question. Do you believe that I am prepared to use them?"

He blinked. His breath was noisy.

"What I am asking you is, do you take me seriously? If you look a little to your left there, Jamie, you'll see your big friend. He didn't take me seriously."

Jamie stretched his neck around, saw his dead boy and looked back at me. He was more scared than upset.

"Now, in a moment I am going to take your gag off. I am

going to ask you some simple questions and I want quick, no-bullshit answers. Dither, hesitate, prevaricate or lie and I will take off your left thumb. And for every hesitation, prevarication and lie thereafter, I will remove a digit. Now, here's the big one: do I need to prove that I am serious?"

He shook his head a lot. I knelt beside him and took hold of a corner of the tape. I paused. "Give me the information I want and you get to live. If I catch you in a lie, I'll kill you."

He blinked and I ripped off the tape and pulled out his socks. He gasped noisily for a while sucking in air. When he'd settled down a bit I said, "Slick got his produce from you, so who supplies you?"

He answered quickly, almost gabbling the words. "I get my stuff from a man in San Diego."

"And where does he get his stuff?"

"He farms land and has labs in Tamaulipas, in Mexico."

I closed my eyes and smiled. I had the scent. "He's with the Gulf Cartel." I frowned. "So what the hell is he doing in San Diego?"

"Trying not to be noticed, I should imagine."

"Name, address and contact number."

He squeezed his eyes shut. He really wanted to tell me he could not give me that information, but the words came out in a rush. "His name is Otropoco. His number and his address are in my black diary, in the safe. Behind the Picasso."

I looked around and saw for the first time that he had a Picasso on the wall. I had no idea if it was authentic, but everybody in it had their eyes on the same side of their head, so I guess it might have been. I stood up and moved to the picture. It opened like a door and revealed a pretty standard safe.

"Combination?"

He told me and the box opened revealing a stack of cash, some documents and a small, black diary. I opened the diary, turned to O and found Otropoco, an email address, a telephone number and a street address.

"He gave you this?"

I must have sounded incredulous because he snapped, "No, of course not! I have people who carry out investigations for me."

I nodded. "You commission research on me? That's how you knew about New York?"

"Yes."

"You have other suppliers?"

"They're in the book. Blue ink is suppliers, black ink is buyers."

I leafed through it. He had five different suppliers. I stopped a moment and asked, "Red ink?"

He hesitated a fraction of a second. "People who have become a problem."

I put the book in my pocket and took out the files and documents. "These?"

He sighed heavily. I looked over my shoulder at him and he had his eyes closed and was sobbing. I snapped, "Answer me! Don't bullshit me, Jamie!"

"It's what I have on certain people, files, background, dirt..."

"How much cash is that there?"

"Half a million."

"Where's the rest?"

"No please! *Please!* They'll kill me!"

"I think you've stopped taking me seriously, Jamie. See? This is what happens when you're too nice."

I picked up the pliers and he started a shrill shrieking. "*All right! All right! No! No! No! I'll tell you! I'll tell you! In the attic! It's in the attic!*"

"You know what will happen if I come back and I haven't found it."

"Up the stairs. There's a door. Key's in my pocket. Open. Go in. It's, it's, it's under a false bottom in a chest full of old bedclothes and curtains, across the room under the skylight."

I rummaged in his jacket pocket and came out with a bunch of keys. He told me which one it was and I walked quickly down the corridor, and up a short flight of steps to a door. I unlocked it and found a large, empty room with a slanting ceiling, bare floorboards and a lot of old junk like sofas, armchairs, boxes of paperbacks, a wardrobe and, as he had said, an old trunk under a skylight. I crossed the room in a couple of strides, opened the trunk and pulled out the old sheets, curtains and pillowcases until I came to the wooden base. I felt around for a moment and found the edge of the double bottom, pulled and opened it up.

It was a cavity about six inches deep, five foot long and three and a half feet wide; and it was stuffed full of cash.

I didn't waste time. I searched the attic and his bedroom and eventually found a Samsonite suitcase on top of his wardrobe, and a sports bags full of books under some junk beside the trunk. I emptied them both out and stuffed them full of the cash. Then I carried the case and the bag back to the office.

He wasn't there. It flashed through my mind in a millisecond. I had made an elementary mistake. I should not have left him alone. I should have killed him then. But I needed him alive in case he'd lied.

There was a whisper of movement behind me. I pivoted away but the lamp caught my right shoulder an agonizing blow that put my back muscles into spasm. It was a second, but it was enough for him to rush toward the desk. A gun. I tried to go after him but the shards of pain in my back were crippling. He clawed at a drawer. I kicked the desk hard with my heel. It didn't do much. The desk probably weighed two hundred pounds.

I pulled the Sig Sauer from behind my back and yelled, *"Freeze!"* as he yanked the drawer free and hurled it at me. I didn't fire. I ducked. The last thing I needed was a firefight and for the neighbors to start calling the Oakland PD. The heavy, oak drawer struck me. Its heavy, wooden corner bit deep into my forehead and narrowly missed my left eye. There was a loud clatter. The sound was unmistakable. A semi-automatic hitting the desk where it had fallen from the drawer. He lunged, squealing, and I lunged too.

I saw in slow motion the silver Colt 1911, with its rosewood butt, dance on the ancient desk. It was only six feet away, but it seemed like miles. I saw his face, twisted with rage and fear, and his hand close like a clumsy claw on the weapon. Then I was colliding with the desk. My right hand lashed out and I struck his temple with the butt of the Sig. He let out a sob of panic as he went down, but he did not release the Colt.

Without thinking I vaulted the desk to approach him from behind. I pointed the Sig down at him and snarled, "Don't move!"

He was struggling into a squat, supporting himself between his desk and his bookcase. The weapon was still in his hand. He was groggy and unsteady and fell forward, out of my line of vision. I kicked the chair out of the way and moved around it, yelling, "*Stay down, Goddammit!*"

But he was on his feet again, running for the door. He wrenched it open, turned and let off one shot that went wide and smacked into the bookcase. Then he was out through the door.

I sprinted after him, slipping the Sig into my waistband. He was just three paces ahead of me staggering badly, with blood oozing down the side of his head. He was leaning on the wall with his left hand, trying to run on unsteady feet.

I lunged. He half turned to shoot but I grabbed his right wrist in my right hand, twisted hard and palmed his elbow, smacking him face first into the wall. I twisted again and pounded his elbow with my forearm. He dropped the gun. I slipped my arm around his neck, wedging his throat in the crook of my elbow, slipped my left arm behind his neck and gripped it in a choke hold, then tensed my arm muscles. His bare feet danced. He twitched and made ugly noises for a few seconds, then went to sleep. I laid him down on his back and slipped the Fairbairn and Sykes in behind his left collarbone, as I had with the big guy. He twitched a bit more, but not much, and after a few seconds that was it. I removed the knife, washed it thoroughly in the bathroom and made my way downstairs.

I stepped out the front door and had a quick look around to make sure nobody was passing, then moved down the steps with the suitcase and the sports bag in my hands. At the corner of Lee Street I slung the case and the bag in the trunk, climbed behind the wheel and pulled away. I drove north, found the I-580 and took my time, cruising steadily, allowing my heart to slow down and my breathing to ease.

I followed the interstate as far as Hayward, trying hard to focus on the blue sky, the smell of the ocean, the traffic. I took the San Mateo-Hayward bridge across the water, breathing deep and slow, staring at the boats, and the wheeling, laughing seagulls. From the bridge I drove slowly back to the multistory parking garage. There I left the case and the bag in the trunk of the Dodge, transferred myself to the Mustang, and drove back to the hotel.

I cleaned myself up, changed my clothes and paid the bill at the Hyatt. Then I took a cab to Salesforce Park, which was a short walk from the parking garage. I collected my truck and headed back across the bay as dusk was closing in. I didn't have a concrete plan yet, except that I was headed for San Diego, but I had a feeling I was going to make a detour first through Nevada. I was going to Las Vegas.

TWELVE

Las Vegas is the kind of place I'll probably go when I die, if I've been very, very bad. It's an eight or nine-hour drive from San Francisco, and I had no urgent desire to arrive. So, after about four and a half hours, once I'd passed Bakersfield, I stopped at the Redhouse BBQ in Tehachapi, got myself a couple of burgers and a six-pack of beers before pulling in at the Willow Springs Motel, just outside town. I climbed down from the Dodge and stood looking around. There was a pool at the side where a couple of families were sitting drinking beer and laughing.

I pushed into the reception and asked the woman behind the desk for a room at the back, by the parking lot, as far from the pool as possible. She had the kind of face you get after you realize you've failed to pursue one single dream in your life, and now it's pretty much over. She didn't speak, but she did what I asked.

I drove my truck around to the room. It was tucked in beside a high wall, a couple of pine trees and three dumpsters. It suited me fine. I carried my stuff into my room, set it on the bed and locked the door. It was ten thirty at night.

I put the beers in the fridge and the burgers on a small table. And when I'd done that, I emptied the bags on the bed. It was a cascade of money. It spilled off the bed and onto the floor where it lay in drifts. It was a lot of money and it made me laugh quietly to myself.

I cracked a beer, took a long pull and ate one of the burgers, sitting and looking at all that green lying on the bed and on the floor. When I'd finished the first burger I wiped my mouth, spread the faint, sticky smell of fried onion round my chin and cheeks, and set about counting the money. I had to pause halfway to get another beer and eat the second burger. By half past eleven I had counted it all. It was just over two and a half million bucks in assorted bills. For a moment I wondered how much pain, misery and self-destruction that money had bought. Then I dismissed the thought and packed it away, showered and brushed my teeth, and slept till six AM.

I woke up knowing exactly what I had to do. I made coffee and while I was drinking it and dressing I called the Brigadier.

"Harry, have you something to report?"

"Yes, sir. I need you to book me an Augustus Premium Suite at Caesar's Palace on Las Vegas Boulevard, for just shy of a thousand bucks a night."

He was quiet for a moment. "Las Vegas... Is that where Otropoco is?"

"No, he's in San Diego, sir."

He waited. I didn't say anything. Finally he said, "Care to explain?"

I made a couple of false starts. "I want to start a foundation." He didn't say anything. "The Ash and Sonia Cooper Foundation, to help kids get off the streets and keep them away from drugs."

"What happened, Harry?"

"We found Sonia. She'd been murdered by an eighteen-year-old kid who was pushing drugs in Pinedale. We found Ash, too. He hadn't been murdered, not as such. He'd found her body in the lake. He clung to her and couldn't let go. He drowned. I'm sorry. I know you were friends."

"Thank you."

"I've seen a lot of dead people, sir. But this…" I searched for words, but there weren't any. In the end I shrugged. "It has to stop happening. It's not enough to kill them. It's a sickness."

"Harry, are you all right?"

I smiled. "Is that irony, sir? I'm OK when I can kill and face death without feeling, but when I want the killing to stop I am not OK?"

"I suppose that is a bit ironic, yes, Harry. But I am going to ask you again. Are you all right? Do you need a break?"

"No, I'm going to finish the job." I told him about Slick and Jamie La Fontaine, and the money. "So I need an attorney in Vegas who specializes in laundering. I need this money cleaned, and then invested into a foundation in their name. All I've ever done in my life is kill. Now I'm going to do something to give kids their lives back, before I have to kill them."

———

By seven AM I was on my way, speeding west toward Barstow and the I-15. At nine AM I called Turo Luxury Car Rentals and told them I wanted a Corvette to pick up at the airport at noon. The girl on the phone told me that would be four hundred bucks a day. I told her that would be fine and I was on my way to pick it up.

When I hung up, I had a sudden sense of urgency. I hit the gas and covered the distance in a little less than four hours, and at eleven thirty that morning I pulled off the I-15 and into the Harry Reid International Airport.

I left my car at the long stay parking garage and carried my bags to the Turo office. A fluffy girl with lots of blonde hair, blue eyes and freckles made me sign some papers and show her my credit card. She told me what a wonderful car the Corvette was, what a wonderful town Vegas was, and how much she really did hope I had a wonderful time. Then she led me to the Corvette.

I managed to stuff my bags in the trunk, lowered the soft-top, rolled out of the lot, hit the gas and roared all the way up Paradise Road to Flamingo. There I turned left under the desert sun, among the tall palm trees, the faded, '60s architecture and the ostentatiously '50s neon and plastic adverts and billboards. I growled down Flamingo, going too fast and weaving in and out of the traffic, feeling my adrenalin surge, an antidote to the soul-searching of the last days.

I crossed Las Vegas Boulevard and two minutes later I pulled in at the Palace. I had never been there. I had always avoided Vegas. Now I sat in the Corvette and looked up in awe at the enormity of the grotesqueness of the building. It was truly a temple to ugliness.

I let the bellhop carry my case with my clothes, but kept a firm grip on my money bags. I booked in, told the concierge I did not know how long I would be staying and let the bellhop carry my case to the suite. There I gave him fifty bucks and told him to bring me a bottle of Bushmills.

When he'd gone, I slung the money bags under the bed and was about to step into the shower when my cell rang. It was the brigadier.

"Sir."

"I've made the appointment. He's a chap we use when we need to move invisible cash. The Firm Company use him too from time to time. He works mainly for the Sinaloa, but his status is protected. Name's Les Divine. Address is on South 7th Street. He's expecting your call."

I thanked him and made the call.

"Les Divine, criminal attorneys." It was a woman's voice, delivered in a singsong she must have repeated a thousand times, and she still wasn't bored of doing it. "How may I help you?"

"I want to talk to Les."

"Whom may I say is calling?"

"Tell him it's Harry Bauer. He's expecting my call."

"Uh-huh, I'll see if he's in."

A moment passed and a slightly nasal voice came on the line.

"Mr. Bauer?"

"I think you just got a call from a friend of mine."

"Indeed." He injected a smile into his voice. "Anything I can do to help out an old friend. What can I do for you?"

"I got lucky at the casino."

"Oh? That's pretty unusual."

"I mean, *really* lucky. And I have a feeling I am going to continue getting very lucky. So, I could use someone with your kind of expertise to help me administer that luck before it becomes a problem."

"Really?" What sort of ballpark figure are we talking about, Mr. Bauer?"

"Right now, about two and a half million dollars."

"That's very lucky. Very lucky indeed. I have never heard of anything like it."

"Can I come and see you?"

"I think you'd better. Hang on—" The line went dead a moment. Then he came back. "Have you had lunch?"

"No."

"Good. Come over to my office, we'll have lunch. Where is the, um..."

"Under my bed."

"You'd better bring it. I'll give you a receipt. We'll discuss what to do with it while we eat."

It was three and a half miles up Las Vegas Boulevard, right on East Clark and left on 7th. It was a mock Georgian building in redbrick and white stucco, with lots of arches and tall windows. I left my car in the parking garage and rode the elevator to the reception. It was spacious, carpeted in dark blue with lots of blond pine. The receptionist studied me with narrowed eyes when I told her who I was and why I was there. She arched an eyebrow and spoke into the phone.

"Mr. Bauer is here to see you, Mr. Divine."

She smiled at me with a complete absence of feeling and pointed to a walnut door at the end of a corridor on my right.

"He'll see you right away. It's the door at the end."

I figured she didn't deserve a reply and made my way toward the door. I knocked and pushed in. It gave on to a small, windowless office, where there was another door, a desk with a computer and a telephone on it, and a very attractive woman behind it. She had long black hair and black eyes set off by a white lace blouse and a string of pearls around her throat.

She stood and spoke with a mellow, Mexican accent. "You are Mr. Bauer?"

I said I was, she knocked on the door and opened in, leaning in to say, "Mr. Bauer is here, Mr. Divine."

The way she said "Divine" was nice.

She opened the door for me all the way and I went inside. This office was bigger, but still of a modest size. It smelt of furniture wax and was clearly a place of work, not a sign of status. Three arched windows overlooked 7th Street. Mahogany bookcases lined the walls. There was a heavy, mahogany desk with a green leather blotter, and a large, black leather chair behind it. The chair on my side was also black leather, but less impressive.

Beside the desk, looking like he'd just stood up, was a tall, thin, angular man in a charcoal gray suit. He had dimples and lots of dark hair which made him look boyish in spite of his fifty-plus years.

"Mr. Bauer," he gestured to the smaller chair, "please come in, sit." As I sat he said, "I notice you haven't brought anything with you. I hope you haven't left it under the bed, or there will be some very happy cleaners partying in Las Vegas tonight."

"It's where I can lay hands on it. I am not sure yet I'm happy to exchange it for a receipt. If I sued on the strength of the receipt, I think the cops and the IRS might start asking questions about where the money came from in the first place."

He smiled a tolerant smile. "Of course that's true, Mr. Bauer. But on the other hand, if word got out that I had stolen two and a half million bucks from one of my clients, I would lose all my other clients overnight—and believe me, some of them are worth a lot more than two million dollars—and if just one of them got the idea I had done the same to him, my life would not be worth a gnat's shit." He paused and his smile deepened. "Have you ever seen a gnat's shit?"

"I can't say I have."

"Nobody has. That's how small they are."

I smiled and nodded. "OK, so everything I tell you here, now, is privileged, right?"

"Here, right now, over lunch, at four in the morning discussing women over a bottle of Scotch. Keeping secrets is something I do very, very well. My livelihood, and my life, depend on it."

It made sense and my gut feeling told me that, professionally at least, I could trust him. Bottom line was, if the brigadier had recommended him, I wasn't going to get a better guarantee. I nodded.

"Believe me, Mr. Bauer, it does not pay for a criminal attorney to screw his clients. Best bring it up and let me put it in the safe."

So I went back down to the parking garage, grabbed my bag and my case from the trunk and brought them back up to the office. There I dumped them on Les's desk. When he opened them, he smiled like he wanted to laugh. He pressed a buzzer on his desk.

"Maria, can you come in and help me count this, please?"

I scowled. "Can you trust her?"

"Oh yes." He nodded. "Implicitly. Believe me, it's not the first time she's seen a million dollars."

The door opened and she came in. She pulled up a hardback chair and, without a trace of surprise, the two of them sat down to count, like it was something they did every day. When they were done she said crisply, "Two million five hundred and thirty-two thousand dollars."

She smiled at me and I didn't miss the appraising flick of her eyes. Les dismissed her and told her to prepare a receipt, and got busy locking the money in a large wall safe behind his desk. When he was done he clasped his hands and leaned toward me.

"OK, Mr. Bauer, I have not eaten yet, and as I understand it, neither have you. Let's adjourn to the Antojitos de Sinaloa, where we can discuss your case in more depth."

"Sinaloa?"

He smiled. "It's a Mexican restaurant that belongs to a client of mine. The meat is exceptional, as is everything else. We'll see what direction our discussion takes, but he might prove useful to you in the future."

The Antojitos de Sinaloa was not the kind of restaurant where you'd find the Brigadier. It didn't have white linen napkins or a wine waiter. It was on East Charleston Boulevard, painted adobe orange and set back from the road beside a second-rate boutique and a payday loan shark.

Inside, the walls were painted that same adobe orange, and were decorated with paintings that looked like they'd been lifted from the covers of Carlos Castaneda paperbacks. It was a wide open space with rough wooden floors, lots of simple wooden tables and chairs, a bar fronting a kitchen and lots of cute girls dressed like mariachis racing to and fro with trays laden with food and drink. The music was what you'd expect.

The head waitress recognized Les as we walked in, gave him a peck on the cheek and guided us to a table near the bar. We ordered a couple of beers and, as she left us, she muttered to him, "I will tell Nestor you are here."

"Yeah, do that. I'd like to introduce him to our friend."

We sat, a waitress threw a gingham tablecloth on the table and set it with gingham napkins, which I noticed nobody else had, and Les leaned back and spread his hands.

"So tell me."

I thought for a moment, inhaling the almost intoxicating smell of chargrilled meat. I said, "I have two and a half million bucks I want to deposit in a bank in Panama. I will be adding to that money on a fairly regular basis—"

He grunted. "OK, step by step: You say you'll be adding fairly regularly. What amounts are we talking about, and how often? And also, why do you want to send it to Panama?"

I hunched my shoulders. "I don't know, a hundred grand, two hundred grand, five hundred grand. Six figures, anyway. How often? Two, three times a year, maybe more often than that. Why Panama? Because then I want to open another account in Belize. The dirty money goes to Panama, gets cleaned and then transferred to Belize as clean money. Will that work?"

He shook his head. "Not like that, no. In the first place, unless you launder it here first, you'll have to take the money over by hand, as cash, which has considerable risks attached. Then, once you've deposited it, it will have to be passed through some kind of shell corporation."

"What's that?"

He splayed his fingers on the tabletop and pushed out his lower lip. "A shell corporation is basically a company that only exists on paper. A fictitious identity, or a ghost. It has no office, no employees, no assets, but it might have one or more bank accounts."

"If it has no office, where does it have its company address?"

"Oh, that's not a problem. You can register it at the address of a company which provides a service setting up shell companies—such as mine." He smiled. "Then I would act as the company's agent for receipt of official or legal correspondence. Obviously we would charge a nominal fee for that.

"People generally use shell companies for, *inter alia*, tax evasion, tax avoidance and money laundering. Or to preserve their anonymity from spouses, creditors, government authorities and a long list of et ceteras. But what interests us here is that a shell company can be used to transfer assets, or money, from one company to another. So if we set up a second shell company in Belize, it can receive funds from your Panama account for 'services rendered,' which do not have to be specified. So the money you have in your Belize account will be perfectly legitimate money, and outside the jurisdiction of any American court. They won't even know you have it."

"So what about the money going into the account in Panama?"

"That is not of itself a problem. The account is numbered and Panama has the most lax banking laws in the world. And believe me, it is in *nobody's* interest that that should change anytime soon. There would be *a lot* of very unhappy people in DC if Panama suddenly got a conscience. That is not a problem. No, once the money is in your Panamanian account, it's safe. Your problem is getting it there without being caught and arrested."

"So what risk there is, is getting the cash to Panama."

"That is correct."

"Any suggestions?"

He nodded. "Yes. I'll see to setting up the account. Then we'll book you a flight. Once we have the details of the flight I'll pull some strings in Panama and nobody will bother you going in or coming out. But this is something I can do once. It cannot become a regular thing." He leaned forward. "This will be a favor to me, personally, from friends in the Sinaloa Cartel. That is something I cannot abuse. You understand?"

THIRTEEN

He ordered Argentine steaks and a bottle of *Casillero de Diable*. It was good and I realized I was hungry. Halfway through the steak I drained my glass and while he refilled it I sat back and told him:

"I killed a drug dealer in San Francisco, and stole his money."

He paused for just a moment, then refilled his own glass and set the bottle down on the table.

"I imagine you took care of the forensics."

"Yes."

"Two and a half million bucks is a lot of money, even for a dealer. I am guessing he was a reasonably big dealer."

"He wanted to employ me to expand his operation into the Midwest."

"So you killed him?"

"He was responsible for a friend of mine's death."

"He got her hooked?"

"No. His dealer killed her while he was high on peyote."

He narrowed his eyes. "Doesn't that make the dealer who was high on peyote responsible?"

"I killed him first. I made him tell me who his supplier was." I pulled off half my glass. It warmed me inside and I could feel my body relaxing. "They were planning, between the two of them, to get the kids hooked at high school. They wanted to take heroin and cocaine to the towns and villages around the Wind River Mountains, to the reservation. Their purpose was to destroy lives and suck the kids dry of their money and their parents' money."

"What was the name of the guy in San Francisco?"

"James La Fontaine."

He took a deep breath, crossed his arms and leaned back in his chair.

"This is pretty heavy, Harry. I need to reassess the level of risk you pose."

"You knew La Fontaine?"

"No..."

"Do you know a guy in San Diego called Otropoco?"

I was watching his face carefully. He didn't flinch, he just sighed again and said, "No."

"Then the risk to you is zero."

"How's that?"

"Because I am not going to go after Sinaloa. The guy I am going after is from the Gulf Cartel."

"You had better tell me what it is you're planning to do, Harry."

I leaned forward and cut into my steak again.

"It's not so much a plan as..." I shrugged, stuffed rare red meat into my mouth and chewed. "It's just something I have to do."

"What is, exactly?"

I held his eye, aware I was saying things I had not even articulated to myself until then. "I have a contract to kill one man. He is not Sinaloa. Like I told you, he's from the Gulf Cartel. But since they killed my friend and his daughter, I have taken a decision."

"What decision?"

"I am going to kill everyone who is responsible for my friend and his daughter's deaths."

He closed his eyes and raised both hands.

"Wait, wait, slow down, Harry. No, you can't do that."

"Who, or what, precisely, is going to stop me?"

His eyebrows went high on his forehead. "Well, law enforcement, for one."

I smiled and took another pull on my wine. "Yeah? Like they stopped Slick, and his dad, and La Fontaine?"

He made a complicated face that said things weren't supposed to be like this. "That's organized crime. It's different, Harry. You know it is."

"I do? In what way, exactly, is it different? OK, I know you have your share of white collar criminals whose bag is stealing from people who have their money insured anyway, and that's fine. But I know you also have a percentage of customers who make their money preying on victims. They sell death. They sell heroin and all its byproducts to people who are too weak or vulnerable, or plain stupid, to say no. And we both know, as those dealers know, that from that first rush, ninety-nine point nine percent of people will be addicted. And day by day they will die inside. They will lose their souls, their wills, their very selves will die, and their sole purpose in life will be to get another rush. Those people kill to make money, and it is your job to protect them. So explain to me how their situation is different to mine."

"You're playing with semantics, Harry."

"Then you should be right at home. Lawyer's paradise, right? I will tell you the one and only valid difference between what your other clients do and what I do. They have the backing of organized crime: the Mafia, the Russian Mob," I jerked my head at the sign over the bar behind his head, "Sinaloa. I have nobody backing me up. But that means that there is nobody, except you, who can sell me out. I am not even a shadow. Right now I don't even exist."

I stuffed the last piece of steak in my mouth, drained my wine and leaned my elbows on the table as I swallowed.

"Here's how it works. I am making a list of the people I hold responsible for my friend and his daughter's deaths. Each one of those people will die, and I will take their money. And most of that money will go to you. And that is something else we need to talk about further down the line. That money will be used to set up the Ash and Sonia Cooper Foundation, to help get kids off the street and away from drugs.

"Eventually I will decide the 'but-for' chain of causality has ended, and I will stop. Or I will be killed by one of my targets. Until then I keep going, and you keep getting paid. My targets are Gulf Cartel. Right now I have no beef with Sinaloa, except what I've just eaten. The beauty of it for you is that you can claim total ignorance. There is no comeback on you."

He looked unhappy. He nodded because he had little choice, but he looked me in the eye and said, "It's not healthy, Harry. You may laugh at this, but a lawyer has a duty to his clients, not just to look out for their interests, but for their well-being. Sure, I have clients who are gang members, killers, hit men..." He hunched his shoulders. "I don't know how to say this. It's who they are. That's all they have known from the day they were born. Life has little value for them, so taking it is not traumatic. They're like animals. In some bizarre way it's healthy! But you, this is not you. I can see that, I can hear it in the things you say, the things that are important to you. You are in a dark place, Harry, and the more you pursue this path, the darker it's going to get."

"I appreciate your advice." I meant it. "But this is what I am going to do. If you want out, that's fine. But don't try and change my mind."

He shook his head. "No, I'll be your attorney. But please, think about what I've said. Maybe you've done enough already. Maybe stop before it gets out of control."

I frowned. "Why would you care?"

"You know what, Harry?" He nodded for a bit. "You're right. Why *would* I care? But let me tell you something. There are many categories of people in this world, and some of the worst are those who categorize others according to their own small prejudices. 'He's an attorney, he must be a sub-human species of scum;' 'She's a whore, she must be frigid and doesn't know how to love;'

'He's a thief and a killer, he has no soul and no compassion;' 'She's a good Christian, so she must be a good person.' Well, let me tell you something, Harry, you're a killer and a thief, and if you think your motives set you apart somehow from all other killers and thieves, I am here to set you straight. You are just like all the rest, because all the rest are human beings, like you, and like you they all believe they are justified in what they do. We are all human, Harry, and the worst of us are the judges and the victims."

He didn't wait for an answer. He turned in his chair and signaled to the head waitress. "Tell Nestor I want to introduce him to a friend."

Nestor must have been waiting because he appeared almost immediately and came over to the table with a big smile on his face. Everything about him was big except his height. He had a big belly, big arms and big legs, and a big moustache that was turning gray, but he was only five foot five if he was an inch. He came over with his arms open and Les stood to greet him. They embraced and pounded each other on the back, then exchanged words in Spanish that sounded obscene but made them laugh. Finally Les turned and gestured to me.

"I want you to meet my friend..."

I went to stand but Nestor started waving his arms and telling me not to. Instead he grabbed a chair and sat between us, holding out his hand to me.

"Nestor Gonzalez. Any freng of Mr. Divine is a freng of mine. Welcong to my home. You eat good? Everything good?"

I took his hand and we shook. "Perfect. Everything was superb."

Les spoke. "Listen, Nestor, my friend here is going to make a trip to Panama."

Nestor's eyes went wide and he turned to me laughing. "Yeah? Panama? Sensational! They really know how to party in Panama, amigo!"

"Yeah, Harry is going to enjoy some Panamanian night life.

But, listen, he would like his visit to be discreet. You understand? It could be embarrassing if he was stopped at customs going in or coming out."

He turned to me, still smiling, and held up his hands like I was pointing a gun at him. "You not carrying a bomb! I can't do nothin' about the metal detectors! Don' carry no iron, OK? But I can guarantee nobody gonna look in your luggage. That my promise. *Promesa!*"

Les gestured me with his head to say nothing. He spoke for me, "We are very grateful, Nestor. I owe you, pal. And you tell Fabian I miss him and I am still hoping we can meet soon for a party."

"Hey, you got it. Anything you need, you come to Uncle Nestor!"

He laughed like he'd said something hilarious and gripped Les's hand in a complicated handshake.

After a moment he'd gone, laughing and slapping shoulders as he went. Les watched him go, then turned to regard me with a raised eyebrow.

"An evil bastard. A hit man for Fabian Ochoa, responsible for trafficking many tons of cocaine into Arizona and California over ten years, from the millennium till 2010. Father of five wonderful, well-educated children who have no idea what their father used to do, a devoted husband and a man who has probably spent more on helping the destitute and marginalized underclass in Vegas than just about anyone I have ever met."

"After having helped to put them there by creating their addictions and feeding on them."

"OK. So now he is going to help get you in and out of Panama unmolested. That is a favor. I am in his debt, you are in mine."

"Understood. I appreciate what you're doing to help."

We had some tequila on the house and he called Maria, his secretary. "Book Mr. Bauer on a flight to Panama, will you. Business class. He'll need a hotel room, make it a suite, and a rental car…" He looked at me. "Any preference?"

"So long as it's not a Mercedes, a BMW or an Audi I don't mind. A Mustang, Jaguar…"

"Get him a Mustang or a Jaguar, nothing German. Something with class. And arrange a meeting for him with Oscar, at the Panama International Investment Bank. Tell Oscar I'll call him in half an hour."

He hung up. He'd drunk a lot but he could hold his liquor. "So, Harry, I need to get to work arranging your trip. I hope you are happy with the arrangements so far. Please give some thought to what we have discussed. If you will accompany me to my office, I will have my secretary drive you home."

"I have my car."

He grunted and smiled at the same time. "I *really* don't want the cops taking you in for driving over the limit. Once they know I am your attorney they will be all over you like eczema. Where have you been? What have you been doing? Whom have you seen?"

"OK, I get the idea."

"Maria will take you home in your car, and she'll get a cab back."

It seemed odd, but it also made sense. So I agreed.

Dusk was moving toward evening by the time I handed Maria my keys and we climbed into the Corvette. We growled out of the garage onto 7th Street, with the headlamps making amber holes in the grainy, gray air.

"I like the balance since they put the engine in the middle," she said unexpectedly. "The performance has improved big time. But I'm not crazy about the transmission."

She glanced at me like she wanted me to agree. I dragged my mind back from Panama and San Diego and tried to frown like I was interested. She had the fingertips of her left hand on the bottom of the wheel, and held her right hand out like she was holding Yorick's scull.

"OK, manual transmission is gonna be hard when you've got eight gears. But do you really *need* eight gears on a Corvette? It's a muscle car, right? It's a driver's car. It's not a speed machine. This baby will do zero to sixty in less than three seconds. That's great. But let me do it in half a second more, and give me the manual transmission. I'm just saying." She glanced at me again and said, "What?"

I smiled. "Is this what happens to you when he lets you out?"

She shrugged. "You gotta have your office personality to meet and greet the clients. You have to be polite, enunciate and speak in a pretty voice. It's OK. I don't mind. But when I leave the office, that's me time. Besides," she grinned, "you look to me like a regular guy, I figured I could be myself."

"I'm flattered. Tell me something."

We were cruising down the Boulevard now. The big V8 was rumbling comfortably, and nocturnal Vegas was easing by in alluring lights.

"What's that?"

"Has Les sent you to spy on me?"

She laughed, but it was a brief, disappointed laugh. "Man." She shook her head. "In the first place, if Les wanted to know about you—no, let me rephrase that. Les definitely wants to know about you. He wants to know what color shorts you wear. He wants to know what time you get up and what color your toothbrush is. And he will find out. He is finding out right now. Because you are a high-value client and he needs to anticipate every risk to you, and to him. He has the means and he will do it. But that is not *my* job."

"OK."

"Second, do you realize how insulting your question was?"

"I apologize."

"I mean, let me ask you something. How would you feel if somebody asked a question like that about a woman in your family?"

"I'd be mad."

"Of course you would. So why should I be any different?"

"You shouldn't."

She gave me another quick glance. "Are you humoring me?"

"No. I agree with you. Believe it or not, I am in uncharted water."

"How's that?"

I thought about it and decided I had drunk too much tequila.

"I'd love to tell you, but I can't. If I ever do, I'd better not have half a bottle of tequila inside me."

We drove in silence for a while. I could see Caesar's Palace approaching on the right. Suddenly she said, "Hey, mister."

"What?"

"Les's instructions to me were to take you back to the hotel and make sure you had everything you needed." I arched an eyebrow at her, wondering where she was going. "Which means I am still on the job, and bound by the same confidentiality as Les. So, you want to talk to me, spill your guts, bare your soul, feel free."

I was well on the "had too much" side of "just about enough" and I knew my judgment was impaired. I also knew what she was suggesting was a bad idea on many levels and the correct answer to her suggestion was, "Thanks but no thanks." So I drew breath and said firmly, "You want to get some dinner?"

FOURTEEN

She took me to an Italian restaurant called the Trattoria, in the Ahern hotel, which was located in a big red building so ugly only an architect could love it. There were a lot of bicycles hanging from the ceiling, which must have meant something to whoever put them there. But the food was good and we had a bottle of Barolo which, according to the Brigadier, was about the only Italian wine worth drinking.

We had a plate of scampi first, which we shared while drinking martinis, and ordered a couple of the chef's father's lasagna. Apparently, the chef's father was good at lasagna.

While we were still eating the scampi she gave me a look that was startling in its directness and asked, "So what's the story, Harry?"

It was the first time she'd used my name, and just like that she was inside my defenses. I took a deep breath and leaned back in my chair, speaking my thoughts aloud.

"Les knows the whole story. He'll probably tell you sooner or later, so I may as well tell you myself." I picked up my glass and considered the ice cubes. "I used to be in the military, in special operations. Most of our work was in war zones, but we also did a lot of work in South America. It's hard to talk about. There are experiences that become a part of you, and you can never un-live them.”

I paused, trying to find a way to communicate what was impossible to understand unless you had lived it.

“There was a child, a little girl of four or five. They massacred the village, raped all the women and the girls. The children were forced to watch. The parents were forced to watch. We were up in the hills. There were only four of us. There were a couple of hundred of them, with heavy machine guns, grenades…” I trailed off. It sounded even to me like an excuse. “That little girl, her eyes, her fear… It’s not imprinted on my mind. It’s more than that. It’s a part of me. There are no words…”

I trailed off. She didn’t say anything, and eventually I spoke to fill the silence.

“When I saw Sonia, she was only sixteen, lying dead next to her father, both of them pointlessly, needlessly dead because some son of a bitch wanted to push drugs to them. It took me back to Helmand Province and that little girl, it took me back to so many other villages and little girls in Colombia, Mexico…” I spread my hands. “I’m drunk. You don’t want to hear all this.”

For a moment she looked away. We ate in silence for a bit, though I had lost my appetite. Then she pulled off half her glass of wine and frowned at me.

“Tell me to mind my own business if I am intruding.”

“It’s OK. It’s almost a relief to talk about it.”

“When did this happen, to your friend and Sonia?”

“About a week ago.”

“So how do you get from there to depositing two and a half million dollars in a bank in Panama, in a week?”

I sat back and regarded her face. It was a very beautiful face.

“I guess because at heart I am the meanest son of a bitch in the valley.” She laughed uncertainly and I smiled. “I killed the kid who killed Sonia. But first I made him tell me who his supplier was. It turned out he was a guy in San Francisco who got his supplies from the Gulf Cartel. So I went to San Francisco and killed him too. I took all the money he had in his house, which amounted to two and a half million bucks."

She sat staring at me, blinking. "You're out of your mind. I mean, why? I mean, do you realize how dangerous...?" She shook her head. "I mean, I get killing the kid in hot blood." She frowned. "I kind of get killing his supplier, because of everything that happened in New York. But the money? I don't get that."

I shook my head. "I'm sick of these bastards killing vulnerable, innocent people. I am sick of them preying on daughters, on small girls who can't fight back. On women, old people. Always it's the weak and the vulnerable. So I am going to use their money to establish a foundation to help put an end to it."

We sat staring at each other for a long time. With anybody else it would have been uncomfortable, but with her it felt natural. Finally I said:

"If you want to go, if you feel..."

But she was already shaking her head. "No, no, don't think that. I can't imagine what you have been through. I am not judging you, far from it. I'm just kind of stunned. It's—" She seemed to search for the word and finally settled on, "*intense*. It's very intense. I have never known anyone as intense as you."

"I guess I've become kind of habituated. I wish I could let it go, but I wouldn't know how." I smiled and gave a small snort. "Boy, I sure know how to show a girl a good time, huh?"

"Hey!" She returned the smile. "That's not what this is about. C'mon. These guys are going too close. Let me take you somewhere where we are going to drink tequila. And then I am going to take you home and tuck you up safe in bed."

We went to a dive off East Tropicana called the Born Loser's Café where there were a lot of people jostling each other. They had live country music, giant cocktails served in jugs shaped like cowboy boots, beer in plastic cups and shots in shot glasses. Maria found us a table in a corner and we did shots of tequila. We shouted a lot into each other's ears, with our heads close together to try and be heard, but I'm pretty sure we didn't hear most of what we said. For some reason, even though we couldn't hear each other, we laughed a lot; and then, at some time after two in the morning, she drove me back to my hotel. She took me up to my room, pushed me on the bed, and the last thing I remembered was her taking off my boots.

WHEN I AWOKE in the morning, with a bad headache and a nauseous pit in my stomach, my clothes were still on and Maria was not there. I drew my own conclusions. After I had spent fifteen minutes in the bathroom taking the first steps toward curing my hangover, I emerged having showered and shaved, and with clean teeth. That was when I saw the note scrawled on hotel notepaper on my bedside table. It said: *You were a perfect gentleman—just my luck! M.*

I closed my eyes and sat on the edge of the bed, telling myself I did not need this kind of complication right now. She was cute—she was more than cute. And she was deep. But I could not even think about that now.

I dressed, negotiating occasional recurring waves of nausea, and remembered that the best cure for a hangover was a high-protein breakfast. So I called room service and had them bring me a double serving of eggs, bacon, sausages, two aspirin and lots of black coffee.

At eleven thirty my phone rang. I answered without looking at the screen, assuming it was Maria.

"Hey."

The voice on the other end did not sound very amused.

"Hi. I thought I might have heard from you by now. How are you? I don't want to worry you, but Sheriff Levi dropped in this morning to see if I'd had any news. Otherwise I wouldn't have bothered you."

I closed my eyes. "Doc, Claire—"

"It's an improvement on Doc Erickson, I suppose."

"I'm sorry. I've had my head kind of…" I trailed off, not sure what to say.

"I know. I just wish you'd talk to me. I don't want to pressure you, Harry, but I do worry."

"I know. I appreciate it. I'm OK. I'll be back in a few days and then…" I trailed off again. "What did Seth want?"

"He said the DA is giving him a hard time about you and he's tired of covering your ass. You need to come back pretty soon, Harry, or they're going to issue an arrest warrant for you."

"Why didn't Seth call me?"

She was quiet for a long moment. "He did. He called you several times yesterday evening and last night. He said you wouldn't answer the phone."

I had a look at my call register and saw there were six missed calls, all from Seth. With the noise and the music in the restaurant and the bar I hadn't heard it.

"Damn, I didn't hear it."

"Will you call him?"

"Yeah, I'll call him now."

"And, Harry?"

"Yes, Claire?"

"I'm not pressuring you. I'm asking as your doctor. Have you some idea of when you're coming back?"

"Couple of days, maybe four at most."

"OK." She hesitated a second. "It would be nice to see you again. That's me, Claire, not your doctor."

"Yeah," I fumbled. "Me too, I mean, I would, it would, I'd like that too."

She sighed. "Take care of yourself, Harry. Stay in touch, please."

She hung up and I had just enough time to sigh before the phone rang again. This time I checked the screen. It was Seth. I thought about not answering it, but pressed the green button instead.

"Hello, Seth."

"Tell me something, Harry. Do I need to put out a federal BOLO on you and your truck? Tell me something else. Do I need to apply for an arrest warrant?"

"Why would you need to do either of those things, Seth? I'm at Caesar's Palace in Vegas. You have my telephone. All you have to do is call me."

"I did call you, like a dozen times. You just ignored me. The DA thinks you've gone AWOL."

"I was in a noisy bar getting drunk. The DA's a prick."

"What the hell are you doing in Vegas? Doc Erickson said you were in Frisco."

"I was in San Francisco. They don't like you to call it Frisco, Seth, or San Fran. It offends their sensibilities. It was too quiet and civilized there. I needed some noise and bright lights to blot out the noise in my head."

He sighed. "Yeah, I know, Harry. It's tough. I wish I could do something."

I shrugged. "Life sucks, then you die."

"So what do I tell the DA?"

"Besides that he's a prick? When you get through telling him to stick his prosecution up his ass, tell him I'm letting off steam in Vegas at Caesar's Palace and I will be back in a couple of days or four at the most. Right now I have a hangover, Seth. My first in a decade."

"Yeah?" He chuckled. "I ain't had one of them in a while."

"Yup. I went out with a gorgeous young woman. She came back with me, threw me on the bed and took my boots off. Next thing I remember is waking up fully dressed with a dead rat in my mouth."

He laughed a lot. "OK, Harry, do what you need to do. Get it out of your system, but remember this ain't just Sonia and Ash anymore. The DA likes you a lot for Slick's murder. We need to get this business fixed."

"OK, couple of days, Seth. I'm getting there."

I hung up and poured myself the last dregs from the coffee

pot. As I was drinking it my phone rang again. It was a Vegas landline.

"Yes—"

"How's your head?"

"Not as clear as it should be."

"Did I screw up?"

"Not at all. It was probably exactly what I needed. How are you?"

"Not as bad as you. You had a head start on me, remember?"

"Yeah, thanks for the note."

"Yeah... I was drunk. And anyway, what note?"

"Right."

"On another subject, I have a ticket here for you and a number of documents. You fly this afternoon at five thirty. If you plan to do some clothes shopping I'd say that was a good idea, but leave yourself time for a chat with Les before you go. Want me to drive you to the airport?"

"Um..."

"Go buy yourself a suitcase and a couple of suits, shirts, chinos, a sports jacket, socks, shoes—you know, the kind of clothes normal men wear. No jeans, no Wrangler shirts, no cowboy boots."

"OK."

"Then grab a burger, come here, have a chat with Les and I'll drive you to the airport."

"Got it."

I hung up and sat wondering why. They could not possibly provide this kind of service to all their clients, and I was willing to bet a good deal of their clients were worth a damn sight more than a couple of million. Les had said as much the day before. So why were they falling over themselves to accommodate me? Or, more precisely, why was *she* falling over herself to accommodate me?

I went to the bathroom and looked in the mirror. Maybe it was my rugged, outdoor, manly good looks. I couldn't think of any other reason. So I packed my other pair of jeans and my other shirt and went down to settle my bill. They had forgotten to charge me the surcharge for breathing, but aside from that they had charged me for pretty much everything else.

According to Maria's instructions I went to Macy's on Spring Mountain Road and bought myself a suitcase and the kind of clothes normal men wear, including a couple of suits. After that I grabbed a burger and arrived at Les Divine's office at two PM.

FIFTEEN

I was sitting in a large, leather armchair gazing through the porthole at the runway as it slipped past and suddenly dropped away beneath me. I was in a Gulfstream G 500, rising effortlessly above the Nevada desert. We leveled off at thirty thousand feet and the stewardess, who might have been a beautifully constructed android, came and asked me if there was anything I needed. It seemed to me that if I was flying in a Gulfstream G 500 from Vegas to Panama City, the very least I should do was have a dry martini. I told her so and she laughed like I was the funniest guy in the world, which was oddly gratifying. I wondered what else she could do if I pressed the right buttons. Then she went away to get my drink.

A couple of hours earlier Les had held up a sheet of paper in front of me and said, "This is your reservation at the Hilton on Balboa and Aquilino de la Guardia. You're booked in from eleven PM tonight." He put that down on his desk and lifted up a glossy envelope with several more sheets of paper in it. "This is your reservation on a flight out of Harry Reid this evening. You fly business class to Tocumen, Panama City International Airport, arriving at eleven thirty tonight. Here is also a reservation for a fancy car rental. It's a Mercedes or something. I know you don't like them, but that doesn't matter." He put the whole lot in a manila folder and placed the folder to one side on his desk. "Because you will use none of these."

I arched my eyebrows. "Say again?"

"I am a very careful man, Harry. I have not survived this long in this trade, in this city, by being careless and hoping for the best."

"I'm not following you, Les. I need to get that money into a bank in Panama."

"Oh, you're going to Panama, Harry, and you're going this afternoon. We both need you to get that money into a bank. But you killed a San Francisco dealer who was selling product on a medium to large scale for the Gulf Cartel. Not only that, but he was expanding his operation. They will not be happy and they will want to make you pay. More, they will want to make an example of you."

"They have no idea who I am."

"You hope, but you don't know. They employ expert investigators. Did La Fontaine know that Slick was dead? Did he know that you'd killed him? Can you be one hundred percent certain that he had not passed this information on to the man in San Diego?"

"Otropoco..."

"That guy."

"No."

"Where did you leave your car while you were killing La Fontaine?"

"In another street."

"So you had to carry that case and that bag from his house to your car. Can you be one hundred percent certain nobody saw you?"

"I guess not."

"So we are going to be careful. It won't be cheap, but you can afford it."

He pulled out a drawer in his desk and removed a manila

envelope. From that he extracted one sheet of paper and showed it to me. "This is your reservation at the Westin, a fancy hotel in old Panama, on Rotonda Avenue. We got you a suite. You'll be staying just one night, two at the very most. The reservation was made in person, manually, by a colleague over there. There is no electronic record of it. The reservation was made using the firm's credit card, so it is not traceable to you. Don't worry, I'll bill you for it."

He pulled out another glossy envelope and extracted another sheet of paper. "This is a reservation for a private jet, also booked by the company. We get special rates. You fly from the North Vegas Airport to Albrook Gelabert International Airport, at the west end of the city. Again, this reservation was not made online, and again it was made using the company credit card." He fixed me with his eyes, "And again, you *will* be billed. Finally—"

He pulled out another glossy folder and extracted another sheet of paper.

"We booked you a Jaguar. It will be waiting for you at Albrook Gelabert Airport. So, *if* anybody is looking for you, with a little bit of luck they'll be looking for a Mercedes at Tocumen and the Hilton, while you will be discreetly arriving at the other end of the city in a Jaguar and residing four miles across Panama Bay."

He collected up all the papers, put them back in the envelope and tossed them over to me. I picked them up and asked, "What about the bank?"

He smiled and pointed at the manila envelope. "Your appointment has been made with Oscar Morales, at the Panama International Investment Bank. The details are in there. But here's the nice bit. The bank is one hundred and twenty-five yards—a short walk—from your hotel. You need hardly step out of the hotel."

"Nice."

He held up both hands like he was framing a picture. "Touch down at Albrook Gelabert Airport, collect your car, drive to the

Westin, check in and stay in your room. Somebody from the bank will contact you and make arrangements for the cash to be collected and for the necessary documents to be signed and handed over. When that has all been taken care of, you call me and I will have the jet waiting for you at the same airport. All good?"

It had all been good. After that Maria had driven me to the airport. She had been quiet and undemonstrative: She was Les's secretary and I was a client. The night before hadn't happened.

She had seen me safely to the check-in at the VIP lounge, wished me a safe trip and disappeared. Now I was hurtling at five hundred and fifty miles an hour, thirty thousand feet over Arizona, toward Panama. I closed my eyes and dozed, and when I opened them again it was dark outside and the pretty android was shaking my arm. "Sir? Mr. Bauer? We are coming in to land."

As promised my bags were not checked at customs, and I was waved through passport control without a second look. At the car rental desk I signed for the Jag and was taken to collect it from the parking lot by a young guy with a bow tie, who showed me there was no damage to the car, told me the gas tank was full and asked me to sign a paper to that effect before he gave me the key. And so I was in Panama, ready to open a two and a half million dollar bank account.

I fired up the big V8 and rolled out of the airport onto the Omar Torrijos Avenue. It was night and there wasn't a lot to see besides long streams of headlamps. I followed Torrijos through a spaghetti junction with crumbling blacktop and no road signs, and followed the Avenida Central searching for Avenida Balboa among jostling, speeding traffic that seemed hell-bent on tailgating anything in the fast lane. I spent five minutes shielding my eyes from the headlamps glaring at me from my rearview mirror, and was just considering stopping the car dead, getting out and dragging the SOB out of his window and beating him to death, when I realized that the Avenida Balboa was actually also the Pan-American Highway. What's in a name?

I took the exit and left the manic rush behind me. The exit led me to another broad, busy three-lane freeway, which was also called the Pan-American Highway. This one had no markings and no central reservation. It was a stimulating drive.

But, after ten minutes of intense certainty that I was about to die, mangled among tortured steel and burning gasoline, I found myself suddenly eased onto a broad, four-lane highway, like a peaceful stream after mountain rapids. It was flanked by sweeping lawns dotted with palm trees and jacarandas, and illuminated by streetlamps that looked like H. G. Wells' idea of Martians: tall and spindly with big, glowing eyes. The landscape was a sci-fi vision of dystopia, dotted with widely spaced, ultra-modern skyscrapers in brilliant white, steel and glass, reaching high into a sky rendered black by light pollution. This road was called the Cinta Costera, which translates roughly as the "Coastal Strip." It was also called the Pan-American Highway, and the Avenida Balboa. Like I said, what's in a name? It paid to ignore everything except your SatNav.

The SatNav led me past the sweeping gardens and lawns that fronted the glowing glass and bronze edifice of the Panama Hilton and Casino, and from there onto the South Corridor, the extended bridge that ran for one and a half miles across the Panama Bay.

At the other end, after almost two minutes of flying across the black, nocturnal ocean, I peeled off onto Rotonda Avenue and, thirty seconds later, found myself at an intersection with the Panama International Investment Bank on my right, and the Westin Hotel directly ahead of me. I'd arrived, and Les and Maria had been as good as their word.

I pulled in and before the engine had died the doorman was opening the door for me and saluting, a bellhop was standing by the trunk with a brass and mahogany trolley, and the kid from valet parking was standing by to get my key. I distributed sixty bucks and made my way through the big, brass-and-glass doors to the reception desk to check in.

I told them to send me up a sirloin steak, a bottle of *Casillero del Diablo* and another of Bushmills, and had the boy take up my bags. When he'd gone and I was alone I called Les. He answered on the first ring.

"Harry, I'm glad to hear from you. How was the trip?"

"Fine. I am installed in my suite, waiting for dinner. No hitches, no problems. Tell me something."

"What?"

"My Jag has a push-button starter and no handbrake. How do you do a handbrake turn in a car with no handbrake?"

"I don't know. I have never done a handbrake turn."

"Boy, you haven't lived. I bet you've never ridden a bronco either or hunted with a bow, have you?"

"Not recently. Please don't do anything crazy. I can't look after you over there."

"Is that what Maria was doing last night? Instructed to look after me?"

"I mean it, Harry. No getting drunk, no going out on the town. You stay in your room and wait for the call from the bank."

"Don't worry about it."

"OK, I'll hope to see you tomorrow or the day after."

"You got it."

I stood on the terrace looking out at the lights reflecting off the palm trees and the vast sweep of the Pacific. There was a knock at the door and a small knot of anxiety twisted my gut as I opened up, but it was only room service with my food and my drinks. I told him to put it out on the terrace and gave him another ten bucks. He opened and poured my wine and left.

As I ate, the moon inched over the roof of my terrace and laid a shimmering, uncertain path across the ocean. I looked up at her a moment. She smiled at me. It was an inscrutable smile, hard to read. So I ate my steak, drank a glass of wine and had a nightcap of Bushmills. Then I went to bed and tried to sleep.

· · ·

I was awoken at nine AM by the jangle of my cell phone. I grabbed it and sat up.

"Yeah."

"Good morning, Mr. Bauer?"

"Yes, who is this?"

"I hope I did not wake you after your long flight yesterday. This is Oscar Morales, from the Panama International Investment Bank. Is this a convenient time to speak?"

"Sure."

"At a time that is convenient for you—I would recommend the earlier the better—we will send four security guards with an armored van to collect the items. We recommend that you stay in your room until then. I will accompany the team and I will identify myself with my ID card and my bank credentials. The team will wait while we finalize the formalities of your account, and then they will take the items—you will accompany us, please— and you will watch us place the items in the bank vault. Is this acceptable to you?"

"Very much so."

He told me he'd be there in an hour. I told him that was fine and called down for coffee and croissants.

I had just stepped out of the shower and was toweling my hair when there was a knock at the door. I checked my watch. It was only half-past nine. I pulled on my pants and opened the door. I'd got as far as, "You said you'd be..." and stopped. There were four guys, but they were not security guards, and ten got you twenty the gorilla looking up at me was not Oscar Morales. He tilted his head on one side and smiled. He had an accent.

"What?" he said. "I'd be what?"

"I'm waiting for my breakfast. You're not it."

"You are Mr. Harry Bauer?"

"Says who?"

"Says the hotel register. May we come in?"

"Not really."

"We have some very important business to discuss with you, Mr. Bauer."

"Important for you. It is not very important for me. Also, I don't like your face, and I don't like the fact that you brought three bone-breakers with you. So take a hike, pal."

"You are making a big mistake."

"No, Clyde, *you* are making a big mistake. You want to try and get heavy with me in this hotel, go ahead and try. Let me tell you what's going to happen. First I will break both your legs and put your big brown eyes in your jacket pocket for you, where you won't lose them on account of being blind. Then I'll break that guy's shoulder, I will rupture that guy's testicles and then I'll rupture that guy's liver. By that time my breakfast will have arrived and the waiter will call the cops to take your twitching bodies away and dispose of you in the Canal." I smiled. "Have I been ambiguous? Do I need to illustrate?"

His eyes had glazed. I knew the look. He was ready to kill. There was a moment of extreme stillness. Then the elevator pinged down the corridor and a trolley rattled as it emerged.

"You boys have yourselves a nice day."

He turned and looked at the kid approaching with the breakfast trolley. Then looked slowly back at me. He was calculating the odds and the risk. Finally, as the kid squeezed past and pushed the trolley out to the terrace, he nodded.

"You gonna have a nice day too, Mr. Bauer. We gonna make sure of that. My boss wants me to give you a message. He say he sending regards from Jamie, and from Mr. Otropoco. Special regards. You know?"

He stabbed at my chest with his index finger. There are a couple of things you practice above all others in Jeet Kune Do, and one of them is explosive speed. Everything happens in a fraction of a second. His finger hadn't touched my chest when I had it gripped between my left index and my middle finger, and my fist squeezed closed and twisted back toward his elbow. His eyes bulged and he went up on tiptoe. He was staring hard at his finger, like he could stop it snapping with the sheer force of his will.

I jabbed hard at his windpipe with the inner edge of my right hand, let go his finger and shoved him back at his friends. Then I closed the door and went to look for my wallet, to give the breakfast boy another ten bucks.

By the time the guys from the bank arrived I was dressed and sipping coffee. The security guards stood around the suite looking bored while he and I had coffee and he made me sign several documents which made me officially the owner of a numbered, Panamanian account with just over two and a half million bucks in it.

Eventually he handed me over a credit card and a debit card, neither of which had a name on it. Each had an envelope containing a randomly generated PIN number. We discussed different account options and interest rates and settled on an annual rate of five percent, which was going to give me a yearly income of one hundred and twenty-five grand. I told him that was better than a kick in the head and he blinked and smiled without feeling. Then he asked me to accompany them to see that the money was safely placed in the vault.

SIXTEEN

By noon we were done and I strolled back to the hotel, scanning the street and the cars for the four gorillas. I didn't see them, though there were a couple of dark Audis with smoked windows that I noted for later reference. Nobody jumped out at me, and nobody tried to shoot me.

Up in my suite I packed my single remaining bag, then went down to reception to settle my bill and had the boy bring round my Jag. I pulled out of the hotel and headed south and west toward the bay. It wasn't long before I noticed one of those dark Audis on my tail, not making much of an effort to conceal his presence. I was pretty sure his intention wasn't simply to follow me. I figured his intention was more likely to take me on the bridge, where I would have no way of evading him. I knew the Jag could outrun the Audi any day of the week, but on the bridge my speed would be limited not by my car, but by whatever vehicles I had in front of me. So I swung the wheel sharply and took a sudden, unexpected left onto Avenida Centenario and accelerated fast toward the shantytown of Los Yoses.

I drove too fast, doing sixty down shabby streets of dilapidated houses and apartment blocks that had once promised homes to families, but had long since gone to seed. Now they were covered with graffiti and their gaping windows, like wounds, reflected no light, because they had no glass.

I doubled back on myself and described figures of eight, weaved among marketplaces and narrow streets among ramshackle houses made of boards and corrugated steel. Kids playing soccer scattered and women came out to scream after me, shaking their fists. All the while the Audi stayed with me, glued to my tail.

Finally I fishtailed into 103rd Street and floored the pedal to the end where it turned sharply into Calle Gilma Santimateo Brown. I just had time to do a double take at the name before I accelerated again to the next intersection. All around me there were people on the street staring at me, barely dressed in ragged T-shirts and short pants, standing in the doorways of their lean-to shacks, staring at the crazy chase.

And then I was at a dead end.

If I'd had a handbrake I would have done a handbrake turn. But, as the brigadier was always pointing out to me, the whole ethos of modern corporate thinking was to rob the individual of control and free choice. So I slammed on the brakes and spun the wheel and fishtailed until I was facing the oncoming Audi. Then I hit the gas, hurtling toward a head-on collision. He chickened first because he cared and I didn't, and as he swerved to my left, I spun the wheel left too, braced and rammed into the driver's door at sixty miles an hour. There was a horrible, violent jarring, a screaming of tortured tires and scraping, screeching metal.

The airbag deployed. The world took a second to stop spinning. I pulled the Fairbairn and Sykes from the sheath on my calf, pierced the airbag, released my seat belt and climbed out of the car. I was unsteady on my feet. A large crowd had gathered to watch. I ignored them and scoured the Audi. The driver's door was wrecked and the window was shattered. Through it I could see the driver. His eyes were open and, in real life, as in the movies, that's a fair sign that the guy is dead. Lateral whiplash will do that for you.

I put the knife away and noticed the nearside rear door was opening. I vaulted the crumpled hood of the Jag, pulling the Sig from my waistband, stepped around the door and saw a guy in a suit with a Glock in his hand. His pupils were wide and he looked dazed. I put a single shot through his temple. A plume of blood and brains sprayed over the smoked window and he sagged down between the door and the car.

I peered in and saw the back of the head of the guy whose finger I had nearly broken. He was moving and he was groaning. I put a round through the back of his skull and he stopped groaning and moving.

The far door was opening. I put away the Sig and took three long strides around the trunk. The third guy staggered out reaching inside his jacket. I trapped his right wrist with my left hand and smashed his nose with the heel of my right. It probably wasn't what he needed right then. He whimpered, I grabbed his wrist with both hands, twisted it in on itself and dragged him out of the car. As he staggered forward I smashed my right elbow into his eye and made him scream. He reached for his eye and I lashed my instep into his balls, and as he bent his legs, gripping his ruptured organ, I stamped on the outside of his right knee. I felt it snap and he screamed again and collapsed sobbing on the road.

I knelt beside him.

"You speak English?" He just sobbed. I repeated, "*You speak English?*"

He nodded and shook his head, saying, "*Si, si, si...*"

"I will let you live," I racked my brains for some vestige of Spanish, "*Yo te dejo vivir...*but you give a message to Otropoco. *Tu dices a Otropoco*, I am coming for him, and I am going to kill him. *Yo voy a por el, y yo lo mataré.*"

I stood and the crowd watched me walk back to the Jag. The front left wing was caved in and the airbag was ripped, but it got me as far as my hotel, where they were only too happy to find me a cab to take me to the airport.

In the cab I called Les. He answered on the first ring.

"Everything OK?"

I told him, "Just fine. Everything sorted. I'm on my way to the airport. I had a small accident with the Jag. Some guy in an Audi collided with me and took out the front left wing."

"Some guy?"

"Yeah. It was his fault. He was driving too fast on the wrong side of the road. I figured we didn't want any complications, so I paid him off and he was all good."

"So you're in a cab?"

"Yup."

"Everything went OK at the bank?"

"No problem. They were courteous and very helpful."

He laughed. "Good, get used to it. That's the way it goes when you're a millionaire. I'll have the plane ready for you when you get to the airport. Just go to the AMCO Air Taxi desk and give them your name. Everything will be taken care of."

"I could get used to this."

I hung up and wondered about what I would do next. Otropoco—or at least the Gulf Cartel—had found out where I was a little too fast. How? Had it been, as Les had suggested, simply a case of using first-class investigators? Or had they received their information from somewhere else? It was hard to tell. Les had gone to some lengths to ensure my anonymity, so that I could open the account as planned. That might have been simply a convenient way to have me taken care of outside the jurisdiction of the United States, and without getting his own hands dirty. What to me might seem an elaborate arrangement, to him might be routine procedure—from which he might just come out two and a half million bucks richer. Even so, it had seemed unnecessarily elaborate if all he wanted was to have me taken out.

I thought it over and ran through the procedures we had followed on setting up the account. In the end I decided that my account was about as safe as any account could be. If Les Divine had arranged the hit, or helped the Gulf Cartel to arrange it, it would have made sense to have them get the money before it was banked. That hadn't happened. In fact they had barely made the effort.

I thought back to how he had sounded when I'd called him. He hadn't sounded particularly surprised to hear from me, or upset. Was that because he was a good actor, or was it simply because he wasn't particularly surprised or upset?

The simple answer was that I didn't know. All I had were gut feelings.

At the airport I made my way through the shabby main hall of faded marble floors and smoke-stained walls, redolent of the early 1970s, and found the AMCO Air Taxi desk. The girl behind it gave me her permanent smile and I showed her my passport. Just for the hell of it I added, "Bauer, Harry Bauer."

"Oh, yes, Mr. Bauer. Your plane is ready. Would you like to come with me?"

"Yeah," I said, returning her meaningless smile, "I'd love to, but there's a problem. Something's come up and I need to change the flight plan. I need to go to San Diego instead of Las Vegas."

She tipped her head on one side. "That is not a problem, Mr. Bauer. I'll just inform the pilot and he'll make the necessary adjustments. You have five hours before you reach the USA."

She made a brief call and I followed her across the concourse, down a short passage that smelt of stale tobacco, through a perfunctory passport check and into a lounge where there were armchairs and sofas that had once been luxurious, back when peace and love were going to save the world.

There was a bar with a guy in a burgundy waistcoat and a bow tie, and a door out onto the tarmac. My bag was taken out by a man with a moustache and a short-sleeved white shirt. He slung it on a small truck and drove it a hundred yards to the same Gulfstream that had brought me here.

I then followed the smiling woman across the tarmac to the jet. She showed me her smile one last time and said, "My name is

Carolina, if you are in Panama again don't hesitate to call. I'll be glad to help with anything you need."

"I'll remember that, Carolina."

The captain welcomed me on board and a flight attendant who'd got her smile from the same parlor as Carolina, showed me to a highly polished mahogany table with a luxurious leather armchair. The captain leaned out the cockpit door and asked me, "We're going to Long Beach, Mr. Bauer, is that OK for you?"

"That's perfect. Thanks."

I settled myself and set about booking a studio suite at the Hyatt Centric, and a Mustang convertible at the airport. I had the flight attendant bring me a martini, dry, and called Les Divine's office again. When Maria answered I said:

"Hello, Maria. It's Harry."

"Oh, hello Mr. Bauer, I'll just put you through—"

"No. Actually, Maria, it was you I wanted to talk to."

"Oh—"

It was hard to make out whether she sounded pleased or worried. Maybe she sounded neither.

"I've settled everything. I'll soon be going back to Wyoming."

"I'm very pleased." Now she sounded like she meant it.

"But there are still things left unresolved."

"Oh? Like what?"

I put a smile in my voice that was on the rueful side of humorous. "Like, was that Maria I went out with the other night, and, if it was, what have you done with her? Because I'd like to go out with her again."

There was a moment of silence that almost went on too long, but when she spoke there was a reluctant smile in her voice.

"I think she might like to go out with you too."

"I wasn't sure."

"I told you, there is one Maria at work and another after work."

"That might take some getting used to."

"It's always good to have a project, cowboy."

"That's more like it. Listen—"

"I'm listening."

"I'm not going to Vegas."

A moment of stillness, then, "Oh?"

"I'm going to Long Beach."

"What's in Long Beach that I need to know about?"

"Nothing much. I've done what I had to do. You know what an addiction is?"

"Not from personal experience, no. You're not going to a rehab, are you?"

I gave a small laugh. "No. An addiction is when you can't free yourself from a deep pain, but there is something—beer, whiskey, dope—something that anesthetizes you for a while. It numbs the pain."

"What are you telling me?"

"I found something that numbs the pain, but I don't want it to become an addiction. So I am through with that. I want to spend a few days at Long Beach, learn to enjoy being a rich man, and then go home to Wyoming, where I will decide what I am going to do with my future."

"That sounds wise."

"Yeah, it is wise. Maria, what I would like you to do is forget that I am your boss's client, take a long weekend and join me here. No strings, no pressure. I had a good time with you the other night. I like you, I like your style, and you helped me. We go swimming, we dine, we dance, and at the end, you go back to work and I go back to Wyoming and we decide, do we want to do it again? Or was it something that just belonged to the moment?"

"My goodness, Mr. Bauer! If you're not careful you're going to become some kind of wise philosopher!"

"Is that a no?"

"Not at all. I think it could be an amazing weekend. I'll have to clear it with the boss, but as far as I am concerned it's a definite yes."

"I'll be arriving at the hotel in about six hours. The Hyatt on

Bay Street, Long Beach. I have the studio suite. I'll be expecting you."

I hung up and sat staring a long time at my phone. After a time the stewardess brought me some lunch, and after that I slept.

When I eventually opened my eyes the sky was dark. Navy blue and streaks of smoky, fire red were fading from the western horizon, and far below us the Earth was like a black Christmas tree.

We touched down at seven PM and I was ushered painlessly through customs, to collect my waiting Mustang. My hotel was not far from the airport, I had chosen it that way, and the SatNav took me there on a gentle, California cruise, with the soft top down, under a translucent moon and towering palms. I rolled down Lakewood Boulevard and along the Pacific Coast Highway to Pacific Avenue, through the incessant stream of headlamps, among family homes with cactus gardens, and high-rise apartment blocks, fringed with almond trees and cherry trees; and millions and millions of people. They were all walking the prescribed path from birth to death in bewildered obedience, guided by their omnipresent screens, living out their moments by accident, never quite knowing why, until it was too late and it was all over.

And then, I told myself as I watched them flow past, painted amber by the streetlamps and the shop fronts, as they are lowered into the ground, all their yesterdays having done nothing but light a dusty path to death, those they leave behind will say, with empty, borrowed wisdom, "He had a good life."

A good life, lived by accident, leading inevitably to death.

I pulled in finally at the hotel and checked in at reception. I had the bellhop take my bag up to my room and made my way to the bar. It was empty and I climbed on a stool and ordered an Irish, straight up, from a six-foot-three Australian barman in a burgundy waistcoat with a clip-on bow tie.

He gave me a Bushmills and set a bowl of peanuts in front of me, then set about polishing the bar.

"What's that thing," I asked him, "about tomorrow and tomorrow and tomorrow?"

He smiled. "I dunno, mate. What is it, a quote?"

"Only piece of Shakespeare I ever tried to memorize." I thought for a moment, then recited quietly, "Tomorrow, and tomorrow, and tomorrow, creeps in this petty pace from day to day, to the last syllable of recorded time; and all our yesterdays have lighted fools the way to dusty death. Out, out, brief candle! Life's but a walking shadow, a poor player, that struts and frets his hour upon the stage, and then is heard no more. It is a tale told by an idiot, full of sound and fury, signifying nothing."

"That's pretty heavy."

It wasn't the barman's voice. I turned. She was there, with her black hair and her black eyes, dressed in a violet gown, split from ankle to hip. It was the kind of image that would make a bishop kick a hole in a stained-glass window.

I said, "You came like that from Vegas and the pilot didn't crash?"

She smiled. "So you *do* know how to make a girl feel special. No, silly," she added as she climbed on the stool beside me. "I went up to our suite and I changed for the evening."

SEVENTEEN

Over dinner at the hotel I asked her, "Is this a Cinderella kind of thing?"

"A Cinderella kind of thing?"

"Now you are this version of you. But on Monday are you going to turn into a pumpkin and start calling me Mr. Bauer again?"

She methodically removed a prawn from its shell with her fingers before answering. Then she smiled and said, "I don't think so." She popped the prawn in her mouth and frowned as she chewed. "But you're a worrying man, Harry. You don't exactly inspire a feeling of security and stability."

"Is that important?"

She was still frowning as she peeled another prawn. "Yeah, I think it is. You shouldn't make me feel like I'm some kind of safe, boring, stay-at-home..."

"That's not what I meant."

"Well, what did you mean? We all want some degree of predictability, don't we? That's why you asked if I was going to be Cinderella."

I hesitated a moment before answering.

"I'm going to have to go down to San Diego at some point."

She sighed and sagged back in her chair, wiping her fingers on her napkin.

"You asked me to spend the weekend with you, and now that I'm here you spring this on me?"

"I didn't say I was going this weekend."

"Oh." After a moment she nodded. "So this is about you inspiring a nice, cozy sense of security?"

I sipped my wine, watching her. "I was thinking of going Monday. When I return that will be it."

"If you return." She shook her head and closed her eyes. "Harry, what do you hope to achieve?"

"Stop. After San Diego, if you still want to know me, I'll find a shrink, I'll get help, whatever it is I have to do. But first I have to go to San Diego."

She closed her eyes again. "That is code for something *so* ugly."

I nodded. "I'm sorry."

"Is there nothing I can do, Harry, to change your mind?"

"No."

She stared unhappily at her remaining prawns.

"What will you do? How does that work? You'll book a hotel? How long will you be there?"

"I don't know. I guess I'll book a room at a hotel. I'll stay there two or three days..." I trailed off. "Why?"

"I don't know, morbid curiosity I suppose. I want to think of you doing something normal, healthy, positive. I want to think of you rebuilding your life." I waited, watching her face. She said, "Where will you stay?"

"A hotel."

"I know, you said that, but which one?" I frowned, then laughed. "Don't laugh at me, Harry."

I spread my hands. "I don't know. The Hilton, I guess. The Bayside Hilton. Why do you want to know?"

"I wish you wouldn't go. I'm going to pray for you."

"Really?"

"I know you probably don't believe in that kind of thing. But my mother was a Catholic, and my grandmother before her. And I am a Catholic too. I know that Jesus is going to look after you if I ask him to. I am going to pray to Jesus and the Mother Mary, to help you walk away from this thing you want to do." She gave a small shrug with her exquisite shoulders. "If I am going to pray for you, I need to be able to see you in my mind, where you are. I need to visualize you."

"I'm touched, thanks."

"Sarcasm?"

"No, I mean it."

The waiter came and took away our plates and our glasses, and replaced them with two plates of roast lamb and two glasses of red wine from the Napa Valley. I asked her, "Does this mean you'll go back to Vegas?"

"No, Harry." She picked up her knife and fork and stared at her plate for a moment while I cut into my lamb. While I chewed she put her knife and fork down again.

"What I am trying to tell you... Look, I think you have an idea of me, because I work for a criminal attorney, because I live in Vegas, maybe because I am Mexican, you think I am some kind of crazy, bad-ass, ruthless operator. You couldn't be more wrong."

"You said that, not me."

"Whatever, Harry. But just because I am a Mexican chic from Vegas doesn't give you the moral high ground."

"Can we stop this, please? I never said it did."

"So, what I am trying to tell you—do you know how long it takes two people who have never met to decide they want to have sex?"

I smiled, then laughed. "I have no idea. Is this relevant?"

"Yes, very. It takes them seven seconds."

"Seven seconds! That long?"

"Now, maybe for New Yorkers that isn't a big deal, but for a good, Catholic girl it is. Because contrary to what you might think, most Mexicans do *not* belong to a drugs cartel, and to sleep with a man is a big deal and a commitment."

She had tears in her eyes and suddenly I didn't feel like laughing.

"I think you are a good man, I like you—a lot—but I think you are badly lost and I would like to help you find your way back. I don't know how you feel about me. I don't think *you* know how you feel. Because your mind is full of darkness. But if you will let me, I am going to stay until Monday, and on Monday, and Tuesday and Wednesday, every day until you return, I am going to pray for you to find your way back to the path."

"Wow..."

She smiled an odd, shy smile. "Did I just fill you with panic? I am not normally that direct, but you put my back against the wall."

Dressed the way she was, looking the way she did, Maria with her back against the wall was an image I was going to have to struggle to put out of my mind. I nodded and sighed.

"OK, so let's declare moratorium until Monday. From now till then, we'll swim, dine, explore. And on Monday we'll see what we do. Deal?"

"Deal."

The rest of the evening was good. She was funny and sexy and made me almost forget the nightmare I had come to accept as my life over the last few years. We laughed a lot.

At ten thirty she excused herself and went to the ladies. While she was gone I pulled my phone from my jacket and called Les.

"Harry, how are things?"

"Good, listen, I'm sorry to call you at home and I'll keep it brief so you can enjoy your family."

"Don't worry."

"Maria will be returning Monday,"

"That's fine. I was quite surprised you two had hit it off so fast. She's a good girl."

"That's nice to know. Now I need you to know this. After

she's gone I'll be going to Escondido before heading back to Vegas and then home."

"What's in Escondido?"

"An appointment. I have a meeting with someone who is going to help me finish this thing."

"I wish I could persuade you to drop it."

"I know, and I appreciate that, Les. But this will be the end of it. I don't want it to continue. I'll be staying at the Motel 6, on Quince Street. I'll be there till Tuesday morning, then I'll head back to Vegas."

"OK, thanks for keeping me in the loop, and be careful, Harry."

I hung up and shortly after that Maria came back. As she sat she stretched and yawned elaborately before grinning.

"I don't know about you, cowboy, but I am just about ready for bed."

So we went up to bed.

FOR THE NEXT forty-eight hours I managed to make myself believe that I was the luckiest man on Earth. It was a fantasy, and I knew it was a fantasy, but I buried that knowledge under laughter, music, restaurants, beaches—where she shone with a burnished bronze beauty that was hard to believe. Through those hours, which we filled almost obsessively with activities to blind ourselves to their finite nature, I pretended she was mine, and that I really could start to rebuild my life. And in the wild, loving hours of the night, I actually came to believe it.

On Monday it ended quietly in the morning, with no words, no drama. We rose early, before the sun, and I drove her in silence to Long Beach Airport, through the dark, sleeping streets. Occasionally a set of headlamps would sigh past on the far side of the road, and vanish into the dark behind us.

When we finally pulled up in the parking lot it was almost empty. Amber light glowed in the terminal building and touched the sidewalk, but there were no people visible. I climbed out and pulled her bag from the trunk.

She stood in front of me and placed her hands softly on my chest.

"I guess you're not coming with me."

"No."

"Don't come into the airport. Leave me here. Otherwise you'll start talking about hills of beans and how we'll regret it, not today, not tomorrow..." I tried to smile and failed. "I'll call you when I get to Vegas. Will it be you, or the other Maria?"

"If you call, it will be me."

We kissed. It was a long kiss, but it felt too short. The last moments before the end are always too short.

She watched me get back in the car, and as I pulled out of the parking lot I watched her in my rearview mirror, immobile, holding her bag, receding into the dark. A violent twist of bitterness clenched my gut and I almost turned around. But it was as though ice had settled inside me and frozen my limbs. So I moved on instead, on until I joined the I-405. That carried me into the gray of dawn as far as Lake Forrest, where I stopped and, in the sterile light of a drugstore, I bought things that I knew I was going to need before the day was out. After that I took the I-5 to Escondido, and all the way there, the past receded relentlessly behind me.

I arrived at the motel at eight AM and pushed through the glass doors into reception. There was a large man in his forties watching me through heavy spectacles with thick glass that made his eyes look very small and black.

"Good morning, I need a room until tomorrow. As far away from people as possible." His brows contracted over his nose, like he felt it was somehow his business that I wanted privacy. I smiled. "I'm writing a novel."

His face told me he knew all about novelists and he didn't like what he knew. He checked me in, handed me a key, took my money, and managed to do it all without saying a word. His words were not for the likes of novelists and people like me.

The room was three thirty-five, in back, on the third floor and overlooked the blue, disabled parking spaces. Two orange trees flanked the entrance to the stairwell, taking up the available space, so I had to leave my Mustang on the far side, beside the trash. That meant that though the room was secluded, the car was not. It was highly visible. And that was OK. That suited me.

I climbed to the third floor, pulled on a pair of latex gloves I had bought at the drugstore, let myself into the room and lay on the bed, drifting in and out of sleep, waiting.

I waited four hours.

At noon there was a knock on the door. I swung off the bed and opened it. There were three guys there, in leather jackets and jeans. The one doing the knocking was in his early thirties. He had Ray-Ban aviators perched on his head, blue eyes so pale they were almost white, and a black T-shirt under his brown leather.

Behind him was a guy who must have been six foot three, with hair cut real short and a scar on his cheek. His eyes were dark brown and his leather jacket was black. Next to him was his shorter clone. His shorter clone hadn't shaved that day and had black sandpaper all over his face. Something told me the two guys at the back were Mexican.

The brown jacket said, "Harry Bauer?"

I looked him over for a second. "You want to give me a reason why I should tell you who I am?"

"Yeah," he said, and moved his head like a turtle, "'coz I'm a cop."

"No, you're not."

"Sure I am, and I got a badge to prove it." He flipped open a leather wallet with a badge in it. "Special Agent Lofthouse."

I jerked my head at his two friends. "Who are they, Attic and Cellar? Since when do the Feds hunt in threes?"

"Since we got word that Harry Bauer was a dangerous son of a bitch. Go ahead, show him your badges."

They showed me nice shiny badges in nice leather wallets. The tall one in the brown jacket said, "Mendez," and his shorter pal said, "Silva." I thought I caught an accent with both of them. I said to Lofthouse, "They don't talk much, do they."

"What, you wanna have a conversation? That suits me. So are you Bauer or not?"

"Yeah, why?"

"We're investigating the death of a kid in Wyoming. Sheriff says you went AWOL after the kid died."

"That's bullshit."

"Maybe so. Why don't you let us in so we can talk about it."

I sighed. "What the hell? Fine."

I went inside and sat on the bed. Lofthouse followed and Mendez and Silva closed the door and stood either side of it. Lofthouse pulled the chair from the desk and sat on it, but before he could say anything I asked him, "How'd you know I was here?"

He only hesitated for a fraction of a second, but it was long enough to catch. "We're the FBI. It's our job."

"Yeah, but there was only one person on this planet who knew I was coming here today. See, I planted the information to see if he was the leak."

Mendez and Silva glanced at each other. But Lofthouse frowned like that didn't make much sense to him. Then he shrugged. "Looks like your hunch was right then."

"So what do you want?"

"I'm authorized to offer you immunity from prosecution if—"

"You can cut the law enforcement bullshit. I know you're not Feds. I just told you so. You work for Otropoco, right?" Again the brief hesitation. I pushed. "So what does Otropoco want?"

"He wants his money back."

"It was La Fontaine's money."

"It was Mr. Otropoco's money, because La Fontaine was going to spend it on merchandise from Mr. Otropoco. See? So that makes it Mr. Otropoco's money."

"Yeah, well, it didn't work out that way. So now the money is mine."

"Mr. Otropoco wants it back."

"OK, so how does he plan to get a hold of it?"

He leaned forward. His pale eyes said he was getting impatient. "That's what I'm here for, Bauer. If you're smart, you'll give it to me."

I smiled. "Do you know what a detonation cap is, Lofthouse?" For the third time in a few minutes he frowned. I went on, "Right now you're sitting on one. It's located under that cushion you're sitting on. If you release the pressure exerted by your ass on the cap it will explode with just enough force to set fire to your pants and tear your balls off."

"You're bluffing."

I watched a single bead of sweat stand out on his forehead. Mendez and Silva edged away from him.

"Am I?" I asked him. "You said there were three of you because I was a dangerous son of a bitch. I told you I planted the information because I wanted to see where the leak was. You think I'd do that and not be prepared?"

He shook his head. "You're bullshitting me. Detonation caps don't work that way. That's mines, antipersonnel mines. It's when you lift your foot off..."

"And what kind of detonation cap do you think it is, genius?"

"Shit!"

"But your real problem isn't the detonation cap, Lofthouse. It's the ounce of C4 it's wedged into. That will make a real mess of you."

Mendez and Silva had both pulled their weapons, but looked like they weren't sure what to do with them. I held up my hands and said, "I am going to reach for my cell phone." I pinched the lapel of my jacket and reached in for my cell. I held it up and showed it to them. "I know a lot about bombs," I said. "If you've done your homework you know I was the SAS. I did all the courses and I learnt a lot about explosives." I flipped the screen to the telephone keypad and set it on the bedside table beside me. "If I press one of these numbers it will deactivate the cap. If I press any of the others it will be the testicular spectacular."

He was working hard to control his breathing, but wasn't doing a great job. His brow was now beaded with sweat. "This is *not* a good idea, Bauer. You don't realize who you are up against!"

"I think," I said, "we should all just calm down. I think you two boys should put your weapons away and we should all have a little chat. That is, after all, why you came here, wasn't it? To chat?"

"You're making a big mistake."

"You said that." I put my phone on record. "Now I want to hear you say it. Who sent you?"

EIGHTEEN

"Mr. Otropoco sent us."

"Who told you where I was?"

"Mr. Otropoco got a call."

"Who from?"

"He didn't tell us. He just said to come here and get the account number from you."

"Give me your gun."

I held out my hand and for the first time he saw I was wearing latex gloves. He shook his head. "Don't, please. I'm telling you the truth."

"I'm not going to shoot you. You're sitting on a damned bomb. Why would I shoot you?"

As I said it I pulled the P226 from under my arm. "Give me your gun."

As he pulled it carefully from its holster I said to Mendez and Silva, "Open the door."

"What are you doing? What are you gonna do?"

"Shut up. I need to know who told you where to find me. I need you to say the name."

Mendez opened the door. I said, "Step outside, both of you."

Lofthouse said, "I told you he didn't say who..."

"Yeah? You two—" They were both outside now. I said, "Back up, another step, another." I shot them both in the chest. Then I dropped the gun, stepped inside, grabbed Lofthouse by his collar and dragged him screaming to his feet. I took a hold of his belt with my right hand, lifted him off his feet and hurled him over the rail. He landed with a sickening thud in one of the disabled lots. I guessed that was OK. He looked pretty disabled. I went inside, closed the door and phoned reception.

"Yes?"

"I specifically asked for a quiet room, and all I keep hearing is people screaming and firecrackers going off. What the hell is going on?"

HALF AN HOUR later the place was crawling with cops. A small detective with gray hair and intelligent eyes sat on the edge of the chair Lofthouse had recently vacated and watched me in silence. It would have been unnerving if I had given a damn. He had a blue and white checked shirt with short sleeves. His hands looked like he played the piano, or the guitar. I figured he was sensitive, probably a good guy. But I have a prejudice about short-sleeved shirts. I don't think young boys wear them beyond the age of nine.

He had looked at my driver's license and then sat considering me, gently tapping his fingertips with it.

"Wyoming," he said at last.

"Pinedale, I was visiting. I'm from New York." I said, and nodded like I was agreeing with him.

"What are you doing in Escondido, Mr. Bauer?"

"A friend of mine and his daughter were murdered recently."

"I'm sorry."

I nodded again. "Thanks. They lived in Pinedale. We knew each other from when he lived in New York. His wife was killed a few years back and he moved to Pinedale to have a safe environment for his daughter." I spread my hands in a "what can you do?"

He frowned. "Man, that's harsh."

"Yeah. He called me because he was worried about his daughter, when I got there they were both already dead. It was pretty upsetting. So I went to San Francisco, Vegas..." I trailed off. "I've been moving around, trying to think and put things into context." I smiled and gave my head a twitch. "The doc who advised me to get away for a few days, she's a really special person. We hit it off pretty good, and I've been struggling with that too."

He sighed. "I know what you're saying, are you clinging to her for support? If you were not in an emotional crisis because of your friend and his daughter, would you feel the same way?" He nodded, like I'd said it and he was agreeing. I gestured at him with my hand. "That's exactly it."

"So what brought you to Escondido? I mean, it's my town and I like it, but..." He shrugged.

"I'd spent the weekend with a young lady—"

"Oh? Not the doc?"

"No," a short laugh, "I was actually trying to—seeing if I could—forget the doc. This was just a kind of friends with benefits thing, in Long Beach. I'd taken her to the airport, early flight back home. When she'd gone I just started driving. I'd been up most of the night, and when I saw the motel I thought, 'I'm going to get a couple of hours' sleep.'"

"Wasn't your lucky day."

"I guess not. I'd asked for a quiet room. Next thing I heard shouting and screaming..."

"Did you catch what they said?"

I looked up at the wall, then shook my head. "Oh, not really. It was kind of, 'No, no, what the hell?' that kind of stuff. I was dozing, in my own little drama, you know? Then I heard like firecrackers and a scream."

"Sure." He handed me my license. "You're free to go, Mr.

Bauer. We'll be in touch if we need you to testify. I hope things work out."

I drove back to Long Beach, packed my bags and checked out.

It's less than a two-hour drive from Long Beach to San Diego along the I-5, but I took my time and managed to do it in two hours and a quarter. I had a lot to think about.

It would be no great surprise to me that Les had sold me out, but it bugged me that I'd not been able to make Lofthouse say it. There were other things that troubled me too. Things that didn't square up, like, if Les was going to sell me out to the Gulf Cartel, or to Otropoco, why the hell did he arrange a successful deposit at the bank? It was true that those four boys had found me at the hotel. But if he had shopped me, why not arrange a hotel that was five or ten miles from the bank, where they would have had a better chance of nailing me? Why go through the whole charade of booking a flight and a hotel as a red herring? It didn't make a lot of sense.

He was a cartel lawyer, so in principle at least it made sense that he would shop me, but not that he would do it so badly. So maybe he was being cautious, playing a deep game and hedging his bets. That might make more sense. He was a cautious man and, maybe, if I was successful and managed to take out Otropoco and hurt the cartel in a significant way, maybe he wanted to be able to show me a clean pair of hands and say he had in fact looked out for me. If that was the case, he was going to have to explain to me how Lofthouse and his two pals had known where to find me. And I would be asking him, but not yet.

But one thing troubled me more than anything else. And whichever way I turned it, I couldn't make sense of it. The Gulf Cartel had been around a long time, and since its rupture with the Z Cartel it had grown weaker. They were still powerful, but nothing like what they had been. Whereas Sinaloa was very much in the ascendancy.

Les's clients were Sinaloa, he had made that clear, and the Gulf and Sinaloa were sworn enemies. So what the hell would he be doing helping the Gulf Cartel? That would be a very dangerous game indeed.

I had no answer to those questions, so, as I approached the town, I filed them under a big question mark for later consideration.

La Fontaine had given me an address for Otropoco. Not surprisingly, it was in the Torrey Pines area of San Diego, among some of the most expensive real estate in the US. I came off the I-5 at exit twenty-nine onto Genesee Avenue and followed it onto North Torrey Pines Road. After a couple of twists and turns I found myself on La Jolla Farms Road, cruising among mansions as large as small hotels, with swimming pools and tennis courts and sprawling lawns and gardens.

As the road wound its way along the cliff, I thought about how those people—that political class—who, some three hundred and fifty years ago, had imposed the grid system on our cities and towns because it was more logical and generally better, all lived in areas where there was no grid system, where roads meandered, gardens sprawled and each house had its own style and character. What is good for the goose, is not necessarily good for the golden eagle, it seems.

I slowed as I came to a great mass of tall, spindly palm trees, oaks and towering pines. There were also ferns and yucca, and they all seemed to explode like crashing, green breakers around a high stone wall with a large iron gate. It was set back from the road in a broad driveway. Over the gate there was a scroll, fashioned from wrought iron, that bore the motto, *Melius Quam Alius Paulo.*

I didn't go to the kind of school where they taught you Greek and Latin. I had no idea what it meant. Glimpsed through the iron rungs as I drove past, I saw a long gravel drive descending through the shade of abundant trees toward a palatial house.

La Jolla Road didn't really lead anywhere. It described a big loop, changed its name to Blackgold on the lower part of the loop, and found its way back to where it started. On the way it passed the Saigon Trailhead, which looked like it led down to the bottom of the cliff. I noted the fact and filed it away under possibly useful. Then the road ushered me, along with all other undesirables, out of the loop and back to the grid system, with the rest of the plebian mass.

About a mile down North Torrey Pines Road I pulled into the Hilton and checked in to a room with a balcony and a view overlooking the pool and the ocean.

Once in my room, I spent a while gazing out at the Pacific, with the sun shattering its photons on the surface. About a quarter of a mile out at sea, roughly opposite Otropoco's mansion, I saw a white schooner riding at anchor. It was very white and gleamed against the darkness of the sea, like it meant something. It made me wonder how hard it would be to get a small sailboat and take a short trip up and down the coast. I didn't think it would be too hard.

And as I thought about that, it occurred to me also that Yuma, just across the border with Arizona, was maybe three hours away, or less, along the I-8. I knew a man there who had a shop out in the desert, not far from the Mexican border. I smiled to myself. When I said "man," I used the term in the most flexible sense of the word.

I went into the en suite, stripped off and stood under the shower for twenty minutes, switching from scalding hot to cold, letting the ideas consolidate in my mind. Then I dried off, dressed and went downstairs to the reception desk. There was a guy with a thing on his lip that really wanted to be a moustache but lacked the courage to assert itself. He looked at me with eyes that hoped I would be nice.

"I'd like to rent a small pleasure boat. Something with a sail and a motor. Not too big. Something manageable. I am competent, but I am no expert," I laughed like it was funny that I wasn't an expert. "Something I can just potter up and down the coast in and maybe do some fishing. Can you arrange that for me?"

"As a matter of fact," he smiled, "we have an arrangement

with Ocean Blue Rentals. We have anything from forty-foot sailing and motor yachts to six-foot rowing dinghies. Would you like to see the catalogue?"

I told him I would and took it away with me to the bar where I had a beer and burger while I pored over the options. I'd learned to sail and got my skipper's license when I was in the army. All I needed was a thirty-foot sailing boat with an outboard.

Eventually, when I had finished my burger I went back to the man with the frightened moustache and told him to arrange a thirty-foot sailing yacht for me with an outboard motor, and that I would want it for a few days, maybe a week. He looked worried when I said I hadn't brought my license, but was reassured by a hundred bucks and the promise that I really was an experienced sailor, and would not go beyond the immediate coastline. As an afterthought I told him to arrange some skin-diving equipment too.

"A frogman suit?"

"No, just the air bottles, flippers, mask, a weighted belt. That'll be fine."

He said he would have it for me by the following afternoon. I thanked him and went to fetch my Mustang.

I drove fast, with an increasing sense of urgency and aggression in my gut. A plan was assembling itself in my mind as though of its own volition. I could see the different parts as physical things: a jigsaw of living scenes acting themselves out in my mind.

By the time I'd crossed the border into Arizona, the afternoon was turning to copper in the west and the palms and the mesquite trees were casting long shadows across the burnished dust. I came into Yuma on the Kumeyaay Highway, crossed the Colorado River at Gateway Park and followed the I-8 for ten miles as far as exit nine, out in the desert. After that I followed a series of black-tops and dirt tracks scratched into the empty sand in some kind of a grid, until I came eventually to a large, hangar-like prefab with blue walls and a red roof. It had a sign over the door that read,

"The 2nd" and was set in a couple of acres of desert surrounded by a broken-down fence.

There was a broad, gravel parking lot out front, shaded by a handful of acacia trees. I parked between two of them, climbed out of the Mustang and pushed through the big plate-glass doors into the store. There was a blue wall fifteen feet ahead of me, littered with bills and posters advertising survival courses, shooting events and political rallies in defense of the second amendment. There were also three doors. One said MEN, the other said, WOMEN and the third said, PRIVATE. It had a picture of a Colt .45 beside it that somehow managed to suggest that this was one private room you really didn't want to go into.

The entrance hall formed a dogleg, and over on the right, where it turned left and disappeared, there was a long counter. The only person there was the guy behind it. He had his elbows placed either side of a glossy magazine that, from where I was standing, looked like the Gun Club's version of *Playboy*. It probably had a centerfold with a picture of a stripped Smith & Wesson 500.

I knew the guy. I'd known him for many years. Nobody knew his name. They just called him Viper, or Vipe for short. They said he'd picked the name up in the army, but nobody knew how.

He looked up as I approached. He had a face like fossilized granite that had sprouted a goatee, and blue eyes hard enough to cut glass. Those eyes became hooded with humor as I approached.

"I'll be a son of a gun," he said, and reached across the counter. I clasped his hand and we shook. "What is it, five, six years?"

"Five."

"What happened to you? I heard the Brits invited you to go home."

"Yeah. We captured Mohammed Ben-Amini, the Butcher of Al-Landy."

"Yeah? So they should give you a medal, not kick you out."

"But the CIA showed up, wanted to bring him back here, give

him a pension and a nice house in Cali. Me and the guys thought it made more sense to execute him right there in the cave where we found him. We had words and the CIA recommended I be sent home."[1]

"Son of a bitch. So he got away."

I shook my head and smiled. "I happened to bump into him later."

He grinned. "So what you doin' these days? Anything legal?"

"Nothing I could tell you about without shooting you afterwards."

He laughed. "Son of a bitch."

I leaned on the counter with my elbows. "Listen, Vipe, I need to talk to you in private. It's important."

His eyes acquired a glaze and he nodded. "Yeah, sure, no problem."

He came round the counter and took his time flipping the "open" sign on the door to "closed," then led me down the dogleg to a fourth door which he opened onto a warehouse that could have won the war in Ukraine and kept Taiwan going for at least six months. There were steel shelves twelve foot high stacked with wooden crates holding everything from handguns and assault rifles to bazookas, by way of sniper rifles and crossbows in-between.

I stood looking around for a minute while he closed the door behind me. Up against the wall behind me there was a row of filing cabinets, a desk and a couple of chairs that formed a makeshift office. I turned to him and frowned. "You shift this much merchandise?"

He shrugged. "Some of it's not for sale. A lot of it is export. I have a lot of special clients."

"Who do you export it to?"

"I only have three rules in business, Harry. I don't sell to Islamic fundamentalists, I don't sell to Communists and I don't

---

1. See *The Dead of Night*

pay taxes unless I have a .44 shoved down my throat." He pulled out a chair and sat looking up at me. "Lately I am offering special rates to some nice guys in Ukraine. But enough about me. What happened? If you're here you're looking for a weapon. You in some kind of trouble?"

"You remember Ash? He was with the Feds, did a lot of work with the DEA."

"Sure. His wife was killed. Took his kid to Wyoming. Must be..." He rolled his eyes to calculate but I cut him short. "She's dead." He went very still. I went on. "She was murdered. He died too."

"Who did it? You want me to take care of it?"

I pulled out the chair and sat, with my forearms on the table and my hands clasped, and told him the story. When I was finished I said, quietly, "Who did it? All of them, Vipe. They all did it."

"What the fuck's that supposed to mean? Don't you go fuckin' crazy on me, Harry."

I shook my head. "I'm not going crazy. I killed the kid who killed her, I told you." I took a deep breath, trying to find words that could express feelings that had no words. "But when I looked down at his body, dead, empty, I could not..." I stared at him, knowing nobody could ever understand what I was trying to say. "I could not say that I had avenged her or Ash. I couldn't say justice had been done, that the debt was squared. I wasn't satisfied, Vipe, because he wasn't the only one responsible for her death. He was just the hand at the end of a guilty arm that reached all the way back to a poisonous corporation that kills millions of people every year; not just kids, but anyone who is weak enough, vulnerable enough to get sucked into their blackness."

He stretched out his legs and studied his boots while he sighed quietly.

"Oh, man... You know I agree with you, Harry, but what are you telling me?"

"I killed his supplier, too. He worked for the Gulf Cartel."

"Jesus, you're on a fucking crusade again. You're always on a fucking crusade, Harry, trying to save the world."

"He wanted me to sell for him in Wyoming. He wanted me to push heroin to kids at school, Vipe."

"I am not questioning the righteousness of what you did, Harry. Hell, I'd exterminate the whole fucking breed, like cockroaches. You know me! If more people killed drug dealers, there would be fewer drug dealers out there. I am not questioning that, but I *am* questioning how smart it was. The whole fucking federal government, the FBI and the DEA, with the backing of the SEALs and Delta force, can't get a handle on this thing. You're gonna come along with an M16 and put an end to the Mexican cartels?"

I ignored the rant and said, "The cops can't connect either killing to me."

"Yipee. The cops can't, sure! But what about the Gulf Cartel? They don't need proof beyond a reasonable doubt. 'Maybe it was Harry Bauer,' is enough for them."

I nodded. "They can, and they know I am in San Diego. I made sure of that."

"You made sure of that. Sweet. And you are in San Diego, because...?"

"I am going to kill Otropoco."

"Who the hell is Otropoco?"

"He's the Gulf's man this side of the border. He has farms and labs in Tamaulipas, on the Gulf, he brings his produce to San Diego and then distributes it through his networks. I am going to kill him, take the proceeds of his crimes, and give the evidence of what he was doing, and all his contacts and supply lines, to the Bureau. Then I am going to disappear from view."

"You're on a rampage." I didn't answer so he went on. "It's a thing. You know that. It happens to soldiers who are under intolerable stress. They go berserk and they start killing everyone they think is the enemy."

We stared at each other a moment. I still had nothing to say. I knew he was probably right. It was probably why I had joined Cobra in the first place.

"Ask yourself something, Harry. Was Sonia hooked on drugs?"

"I doubt it."

"Was she killed by an overdose?"

I sighed. "No."

"Now, honestly, Harry, ruthlessly honest, was the drugs trade, the Gulf Cartel, *directly* connected *in any way* to Sonia's death?"

I didn't hesitate. "Not directly, no."

"So what are you doing? What kind of revenge is this?"

I gave my head a single shake. "Vipe, I am going to kill Otropoco because it's my job. You know enough not to ask, so don't. But you're right. I am on a crusade. That kid, Slick, he didn't kill Sonia because the peyote drove him crazy. Peyote doesn't work that way. That kid killed her and destroyed Ash because he'd spent the last two years snorting enough coke. We both know the kind of daemons that are born from cocaine abuse: paranoia, narcissism, towering ego. Everybody's after you, but you don't give a damn because you're the biggest, the baddest, the most powerful indestructible—you are God."

He scowled and stopped me. "You're saying he killed her because he snorted coke? A lot of people snort coke, Harry. They don't go around—"

"No, Vipe. He killed her because he spent two years snorting coke, playing at being the kind of badass dude he saw every night on TV, and then he took peyote in the forest with Ash's daughter! That peyote opened the gates for those daemons, and *that* is why he killed her. If Otropoco and La Fontaine and all the rest of those bastards had not created the conditions, those kids would have had a couple of beers, communed with nature for a couple of hours and gone home. As it was, Slick brought with him the sickness he had been given by La Fontaine, who had been given it by Otropoco, and Ash's sixteen year-old daughter paid the price."

"Are you going to kill the CEOs of the TV networks too? If you're going to kill everyone who created the conditions, where do you stop?"

"I don't know. Like you said, I am on a rampage. I am killing all those I see as the enemy. I hope, when Otropoco is dead, I'll stop."

"You hope. Swell. The most likely thing is they'll stop you first. And if they don't, they will sure as hell come after you later."

"I'll take care of that."

"That simple, huh?"

"Yes."

NINETEEN

He took a long time to reply. He seemed to be making a careful study of his boots before saying anything. Eventually he asked them, "Why are you telling me all this?"

"Because I am going to ask you a favor. And if you decide to help me, I want you to know what you're doing—what you're getting yourself into."

Finally he looked up at me. "What do you want?"

"I want twenty pounds of C4."

He laughed long and loud, with his head thrown back. When he was done pounding his thing he wiped his eyes and said, "*Seriously?*"

"Yeah, seriously."

"You're one of a kind, Harry, you really are. What do you plan to do? Blow his house off the cliff?"

"It's best you don't know what I'm planning, Vipe. I also need a crossbow. Seventy or eighty pounds will do, but the heads have to be broad, hunting heads and I want them razor sharp. I'll need at least twelve."

He nodded. He wasn't laughing anymore. "You are serious."

"Yes, I'm serious. I want a Kevlar vest, night vision goggles, I want an M16A3—"

"With or without a grenade launcher?" His tone was only slightly ironic.

"I don't need a grenade launcher, but I do need a suppressor for my Sig Sauer P226, and I'll need another for the M16."

He shook his head. "Harry, noise suppressors are big and cumbersome and add significant weight and length to the barrel. They change the rifle's balance, make it less maneuverable. Plus, you know yourself they don't silence the shot, unless the ammunition is subsonic. You really don't want—"

"And I'll need some subsonic cartridges. I'll need a couple of magazines with subsonics and a couple with regular ammo. I've written a list for you. Are you prepared to help me?"

He heaved a big sigh and leaned forward, reaching out his hand. "You know damn well I will. Show me your goddamn list."

I pulled it from my breast pocket and handed it to him.

"Vipe, I need these weapons, and the ammo, to be untraceable. I know you used to do that. I need you to do that for me on this job."

He raised an eyebrow at my list. "Job? What are you doing, Harry? You trying to legitimize this? What you're doing is murder. Don't kid yourself. Ask me and I'll tell you it's moral and you're doing God's work. But moral or not, it's murder, plain and simple."

"OK."

He nodded again. "Yeah, I can make them untraceable. But you gotta use latex gloves. And remember, the gloves are gonna have your prints on the inside. So you burn them after you use them."

"I know that. How soon can you have this?"

He glanced over the list again and shrugged. "I got it all in stock. As long as it takes me to put it together. You got a plan?"

"I'm putting that together."

"You need help?"

I thought about it, then shook my head. "No, thanks. I'll let you know if I change my mind."

He got to his feet and I stood too. I said, "There's one other thing, Vipe." He paused, watching me. "Can you buy me a truck, cash? I'll give you the money. Something anonymous that's not going to die on me halfway through the…"

"Yeah. I can do that."

"And leave it somewhere I can steal it."

"You going to paint it and change the plates?" I nodded. "I'll do that for you. Come back tomorrow. I'll have everything ready."

I ARRIVED BACK in San Diego after dark and had some lamb chops and a couple of beers in the restaurant. After that I slept the sleep of the damned for eight hours until the sun leaned in through the window and started poking at my eyes, forcing me to fall out of bed and stagger to the shower, as though I had not slept at all.

After breakfast I collected my boat reservation at the front desk. "The boat is moored at the Ventura Yacht Club, in town," the concierge told me, "a mere ten-minute drive or so. Once you have collected it, you can anchor it off Black Beach's Lookout, just a mile across the golf course." He simpered apologetically. "We are not really a beach hotel."

I assured him that would be fine and took the Mustang down to San Diego, to the Mission Bay Park. With the soft top down, as I killed the engine, the air was full of the clang and clatter of shrouds and the splosh and creak of boats moored at the quay. Overhead a seagull laughed on the wind.

I climbed out of the car and a brisk, cool breeze whipped in off the bay, across small, glistening waves under a flawless blue sky. It was a Southern California sky. I crossed the broad parking lot, squinting in the sun despite my heavy, black shades, and found the offices of the Ventura Yacht Club. It was a low building of highly polished dark wood, with large plate-glass doors furnished with big brass handles. I pushed through and found myself in a small reception facing a dark, wooden counter behind which a pretty blonde with blue eyes tilted her head to one side and offered me a pretty, California smile.

"Good morning," she said, like she was pleasantly surprised to see me. "How may I help you this morning?"

I put the booking form in front of her on the desk. "I want to pick up my boat."

She looked through the papers and cocked her head on the other side. Her teeth, her face and her hair were all made out of pure sunshine.

"Sure, it's right here by the pier."

I followed her out along the planking among rows of yachts of various sizes, all creaking and bobbing in the gentle swell. We soon came to a thirty-foot sloop with a small cabin and an open cockpit in back. We stepped aboard and she showed me around, asked me how long I wanted it for and gave me her card in case I needed anything. I thanked her and watched her leave, wondering if she gave her card to all the boys.

I got the outboard going and let it take me out of the harbor, where I turned north. There I hoisted the spinnaker and the mainsail and the yacht surged, slapping across the small waves.

The breeze was mild, coming out of the northwest. So I kept the mainsail close hauled and tacked gently up toward La Jolla and Torrey Pines. After about ten or fifteen minutes I rounded the La Jolla peninsula and came in close, to within a quarter of a mile of the beach. From there I followed the coast, slapping over the waves and hurling small showers of spray high into the wind, that somehow always found their way back into my face. I moved on, coming at last to the Scripps Pie, where the cliffs began to climb toward Torrey Pines. And there, half a mile or a little more from the Torrey Pines City Beach, I saw again the white yacht I had seen earlier.

It was an exquisite schooner, long and sleek, with three masts plus a fourth thrusting out from the prow. It looked real still and peaceful, riding the small waves. I couldn't see a name and I wouldn't have any binoculars till the evening.

I dropped the sails and moved along the cliffs real slow, using only the small outboard, examining the face of the cliffs. As far as I could see there were only two ways up, unless you wanted to go climbing. There was a broad, easy path that rose from the Torrey Pines City Beach and climbed to what was pretty much the entrance to the Torrey Pines residential area. Or there was a narrower, more difficult track that started from the base of the cliff beneath Otropoco's house, and climbed to La Jolla Farms Road, less than three hundred yards from Otropoco's front gate.

The second was tempting, but on reflection neither was much use to me. The only other option was a deep, narrow ravine that dropped almost vertically from between Otropoco's house and his nearest neighbor on the left: a space-age affair that looked like a captured spacecraft converted to a house. The gully was steep and heavily overgrown with bushes and stunted trees, and even though it was overlooked by two houses, I figured it would be narrow enough and dark enough at night to afford cover.

Just past the so-called razor house I turned the boat around and started back south, scanning the cliffs for a second time, and slowly my plan started to take real shape and consolidate in my mind.

After an hour or so I raised the sails again and, with the wind slightly more in my favor, I sailed back to the Ventura Yacht Club, where I swapped the yacht for the Mustang and burned rubber out toward Arizona, for my second visit to Vipe.

The drive from San Diego to Yuma is flat, dry and straight. There is a lot of desert and at that time of day, when the sun was high in the dome, the glare and the heat were intense. I drove fast, too fast, reckless as to whether I would get stopped, but I kept one eye on the rearview and another on the sky; and I guess that day I was lucky.

I made Yuma in just under two and a half hours, and ten minutes after that I had crossed the Colorado and was raising billowing plumes of dust on my way to Vipe's warehouse.

When I got there he had a couple of clients he was talking to at the counter. He saw me push through the door and jerked his head at the back.

"Make yourself some coffee. I'll be right with you."

I went through the door into the warehouse, found the desk and the chairs pretty much where we had left them the day before, and found also a coffee filter on top of one of the filing cabinets. The coffee was still hot so I spilled some into a mug and took a stroll.

There were seven broad aisles that ran the length of the hangar, and each aisle was composed of steel shelves about twelve feet high and six feet deep. At the far end, in the first aisle on the left, I found a wooden case on the floor. It was about five or six feet long and some three feet wide. It was lined with heavy plastic and contained an M16 A3 assault rifle with a laser sight and night scope attached. There was also a suppressor, and two boxes of subsonic rounds. I didn't know if I was going to have the opportunity to use them, but if the opportunity arose, I wanted to have the option.

More silent, and arguably more deadly, was the crossbow. I picked it up and examined it. It was also equipped with a laser sight and a night scope. Its range was limited, but at eighty pounds draw weight, with razor-sharp broadheads, it was the perfect balance between power and accuracy. One of those barbs would slice clean through a man, severing tissue, veins and arteries. Hemorrhaging would be massive and death would come in seconds. And it would do all that in almost total silence.

There were also five packs of C4 plastic explosive, each one holding five half-kilo tablets, slightly over a pound. He had thought to add a number of detonators, some mechanical but the majority remote, the sort you can sync with your cell phone.

Then there were the magazines I had asked for, for the assault rifle and for the Sig. All the other stuff I had included on the list was there too, plus a box of .22 cal rounds and a small .22 revolver I had not asked for.

"I'm surprised you didn't put it on your list." I put down the weapon and turned to look at Vipe. He was leaning on the shelf, looking down at me. "It's the assassin's weapon of choice," he went on. "It leaves no casing behind, because it stays in the chamber, and the slug hasn't the energy to exit, so it stays inside the skull or the chest cavity, bouncing around causing a lot more damage. The report is also a lot quieter than a nine mil."

"Never occurred to me. It's not a common weapon."

"All I ask is you bring it back. I've lost a lot of pals over the years." He shrugged. "One thing is losing touch. You expect that, right? Guys tend not to stay in contact. There are too many memories you don't want to share. But losing a pal, that's different."

I nodded. "I hear you."

I stood and he stepped up close, put a hand on each shoulder. "Be sure you want to do this, dude. It's one of those things, you know? There's a before and there's an after. There is no going back."

"I passed that point already, Vipe. I can't live, day to day, going through the daily routine, knowing *they* are out there, alive, they are swimming in their pools, sailing their yachts, snorting their damned coke, laughing..."

"OK," he sighed and patted my shoulder, "so the truck is parked out front. It's painted off white and it's covered in dirt. It's got Cali plates and the keys are behind the sunshield."

"I appreciate it. How much do I owe you for this?"

"Come back alive and we'll talk about it. Now, you want to explain to me how you're going to get the Mustang and the truck back to San Diego at the same time?"

"No problem. I take the Mustang now and come back on the Greyhound."

"Forget it. I'll take the truck. I'll leave it at the parking garage on 6th Avenue, opposite the Moonshine. Tomorrow I'll report it stolen. Obviously with its previous color and plates. You take the Mustang. Give me a twenty-minute head start. Make sure you put gas in the tank as you come into San Diego and get yourself seen on the gas station CCTV. It'll give you an alibi for stealing the truck, if you need one. I'll get one of the boys to come and get me."

"Thanks."

He shook his head. "I don't know why we don't just send the Air Force over and napalm the fuckin' fields, man. What, this isn't a threat to national security?"

I slapped him on the shoulder. "I'll see you in a couple of days." I smiled. "Keep watching the news."

TWENTY

I went into Yuma and had a burger and a coffee at Arby's, where I could keep an eye on the road. Eventually I saw the dirty, off-white truck roll past, headed west. I gave him twenty minutes like he'd said, and went out to the Mustang.

I didn't go to 6th Avenue. I drove slowly, staring at the vast, flat desert. My mind was a blank, unfertile area, like the thousands of square miles of dead sand that surrounded me, and my thoughts were like the gnarled, dehydrated shrubs. I saw the Pacific in my mind: a cool, crystal-green contrast to the dust and the withered bushes. I saw the cliffs, and the paths that wound, almost vertical up from the beach. I saw Otropoco's rich, green gardens which surrounded his mansion, abundant in a luxuriant variety of trees.

But I did not see his face. I had no idea what he looked like. I became vaguely aware that I had assumed that sooner or later it would become apparent who he was. I would eventually need to know. Alternatively, I could simply kill all the men in his house. I was aware that that option should trouble me, but it didn't. It did, however, become clear to me that I needed to know who my target was, and what he looked like, before I went in.

I had my cell on the charger and glanced at it.

"Hey, Siri, call Maria."

It rang a couple of times and her voice came on the line.

"Good afternoon, Mr. Bauer."

"Cut it out, I'm not in the mood. I need information about Otropoco."

She sounded cool. "What makes you think I have information about Otropoco?"

"Nothing. I need you or Les to make inquiries. I need to know what he looks like. I need photographs—something."

"Isn't this something you need to discuss with Les?"

I thought about it. The last time I had given Les information I had almost been killed. But maybe that wasn't such a bad thing. I said, "Yeah, OK, put me through to him."

Fifteen seconds later he came on the line. "Harry, where are you?"

"Listen, I need some information on Otropoco."

"That is both difficult and highly risky."

"Put a private dick on it. I need to know what he looks like, or at least where he hangs out so I can go and take a look."

"It will be expensive."

"I don't care."

He sighed audibly. "All right. How soon do you need this?"

"The day before yesterday will do."

Another sigh. "OK, I'll be in touch."

I returned to my hotel and went to my room where I lay staring at the ceiling, putting all the pieces of my plan together, searching for the flaws, asking myself, if I wanted to sabotage this plan, how would I do it? Where were the weaknesses?

The sun began to decline outside and a sudden, bitter desire to be back in New York drinking a cold beer twisted my gut. I sat up, looking out at the blueness of the ocean. It looked infinite under the sky. I told myself, "A shower, beer and a whiskey chaser, dinner."

My cell rang.

"Yeah—"

"Harry, it's Maria."

"You got something for me?"

"I'm fine thanks, how are you?"

"I've been better. Have you got something?"

"Yes and no. There are no known photos of Mr. Otropoco. He has managed to keep a very low profile and he goes everywhere with half a dozen bodyguards who are all bigger than he is. Nobody, and I mean nobody, is willing to go and take snapshots of him. Harry, he is a very, very dangerous man."

"So if he's in a group, he's the small guy?"

"I guess so, yes."

"That's useful."

"It is? This is more useful. He likes to go out on the town. He has a couple of clubs and a casino where he whitewashes his cash."

"Names?"

"Those are not my instructions."

I stared out at the bright ocean for a moment. "What?"

"My instructions are to fly to San Diego and accompany you to the casino. If you go alone you're going to stand out like a fluorescent dildo at a nuns' convention."

"That is a big risk to you."

"Not if you don't do anything stupid it's not. And if I know Les, that's half the reason he asked me to go with you."

"He's not my mother—neither are you. He's my attorney. I don't need looking after."

"He's your attorney, and the way he sees it he has a duty to look out for your well-being. I see it that way too, and in case you haven't noticed it, Romeo, you and I seem to have some kind of a relationship going. I don't sleep with all my boss's clients, just in case you were wondering."

"I'm sorry."

"Don't be. Just wise up a bit. I'll be there tonight."

Wise up.

I stood under a cold shower for five minutes, trying to find some solid ground in my head. There wasn't any. So I dried myself off, dressed and went down to the bar. I was having trouble understanding Les. I knew enough about the cartels to know the dos and don'ts, and I knew there were certain things you just didn't do. And one of them was that you did not represent more than one cartel. It was not just a conflict of interests, it was betrayal of the highest order and punishable by torture and eventual death. *Eventual* being the operative word.

I had been running that point over in my mind for several days now, and I could not make sense of the game he seemed to be playing. He didn't strike me as a big risk taker. Les was nothing if not careful, and yet it was made very clear to me from the start, from lunch on day one, that I was in Sinaloa territory, and whatever shit I wanted to lay on the other cartels was fine, but if I wanted Les's help, I had to respect Sinaloa.

And yet from where I was standing, at times he looked very much like a man, quietly, discreetly, sitting in the Gulf Cartel's corner too. And yet it was only sometimes. At others, like when I was in Panama... My thoughts trailed off. The barman was looking at me with a patient smile.

"Bushmills," I told him, "straight up. And give me some peanuts," I told him with unnecessary brusqueness.

Maria arrived an hour later, when I was on my second Bushmills. I had also read every section of the *Torrey Pines Recorder*. She looked the way she always looked: absurdly desirable, carelessly exquisite, too good to be true, and yet too real to be fake.

She stood a moment, found me and came and put her purse on my table and sat.

"I changed the reservation to include your wife," she told me. "You have to confirm it."

"We're married now?"

"That's what happens when you're careless, see?"

"Did you come in the private jet?" Somehow I made it sound like an accusation. Her eyebrows shot up. "Are you kidding? That kind of stuff is reserved for The Boys. I get to fly coach."

"Does that make me one of the boys?"

The waiter was coming over, but she called to him, "Gimme a dry martini. Shake it. Don't stir it." To me she grinned and said, "Uh-uh. You are definitely *not* one of the boys. Les is worried about you, and not just because you might wash up on a beach one of these days minus your hands and your head."

"Why else?"

"Because he has very powerful, very dangerous friends. And if you decide to go after them, you could put him in the middle of a very ugly situation."

"I wouldn't do that. I have no beef with Les. He's looked after me till now."

"I hope you keep seeing it that way, Mr. Bauer. You seem to be a little crazy at the moment."

"His friends are Sinaloa. I am not interested in Sinaloa."

She narrowed her eyes at me. "How do you know that?"

I laughed. "He warned me. He took me to lunch at a restaurant called something-or-other of Sinaloa. He introduced me to the owner and asked them to look after me or something. He was making it clear to me his friends were Sinaloa and he didn't want me going after them."

She shrugged. "OK."

I paused a moment, studying her face. "So what I am wondering is, why do boys from the Gulf Cartel keep showing up trying to talk to me?"

She frowned. "Who showed up?"

"Four guys in Panama who shouldn't have known where I was—"

"I heard about that. But that leak could have sprung anywhere along the line, Harry. They have real pros working on that kind of thing. And they have very persuasive ways of extracting information."

"And then three boys who came to talk to me in Escondido."

"What were you doing in Escondido, for God's sake?"

"Testing a theory. They knocked on the door pretending to be federal agents."

"Did you talk to them?"

I shook my head. "They developed respiratory problems and had to leave suddenly."

She spoke quietly. "You killed them?"

"But these boys were with the Gulf. So how the hell did they know I was there?"

"If you are looking at Les or his office, you are way off base."

"That information leaked somewhere between me and Les."

Her face went real hard and her eyes were bright. She pointed at her chest. "You're looking at *me?*"

"Any reason I shouldn't be?"

She nodded. "Yeah, the owner of the Antojitos de Sinaloa, where you went for lunch with Les...?"

"What about him?"

"That's my father. To me, the only good member of the Gulf Cartel is a dead one. You want to wipe out the whole damned cartel, that's fine by me."

I sagged back in my chair. "Son of a gun. I should have seen that."

"There is no leak from the office, Harry. The answer could be lot simpler than that."

"Simple like what?"

"Like they have tracked you down since San Francisco and they are following you. These guys are all paranoid, Harry. They spend a small fortune on security, surveillance, spying, bribing authorities..." She shrugged. "You name it."

"So that's the real reason you're here to help."

She studied my face a moment. "I'd like to see Otropoco dead, yes. But I am not the android you seem to be, Bauer! What has happened between us actually means something to me. Even if it doesn't to you." I drew breath but she cut me short. "Please! Don't apologize again. Just try to remember where you left your humanity and go back and recover it."

I didn't answer straight away. When I did all I could say was, "I'd like to do that, but I can't. Not yet."

We had a light supper in the restaurant and then took the Mustang and drove down to San Diego. Maria drove.

As she pulled onto the Pacific Highway, she said, "We'll go to the casino first. It's called the Wild Life Casino, because it's beside the National Wildlife Refuge. Imaginative, right? We'll hope to spot him there. If we do, don't look at him. They will notice if you look at him. OK? Just stay cool and look at me."

"You should run courses for special ops. They never taught us stuff like that."

"I'm serious, Harry. If they think you have recognized him they will take you out to the parking lot and cut your throat. And mine!"

"Got it. And then?"

"If we're not lucky, then we'll go on to his clubs. He has two upmarket strip clubs on Midway Drive, Gentlemen Prefer Nudes, called Nudes for short, and Otro Poquito."

"Another little bit?"

"Yup, apparently he sells coke to very select clients there. They never get caught because the people who would prosecute him are all there wiping their noses in the can."

"I love this guy." I said it without much feeling and she glanced at me.

"Don't go doing anything stupid, Harry. You could get us both killed."

"I am not going to do anything to put your life at risk. We're just a couple out on the town. I am just here to observe."

"Good. Keep it that way."

The casino was located on Lagoon Drive, right beside the Collins Aerospace Laboratories. When we dropped the car in the parking lot there were still a couple of windows illuminated, casting amber light on the leaves of the trees that surrounded the place. Maria linked her arm in mine and we crossed the lot to a flight of seven broad, marble steps that led up to a long, burgundy awning which, in turn, led to large plate-glass doors that stood open onto an ample foyer with a burgundy carpet, a cloakroom and several burgundy sofas which would have looked over the top in Rococo France.

Directly ahead of us was a set of walnut doors with big brass handles. They stood open. Beside them there was a guy in an evening suit with satin lapels and a bow tie who looked like he'd spent his youth breaking walls with his face.

We drifted past him and went inside. There was a lot of noise and a lot of tables where people were busy wasting their money playing cards and craps. I went over to the cashier, bought a thousand bucks of chips and gave half of them to Maria.

"What's this guy's game?" I asked her.

"I have no idea. You want to get a drink?"

There was a bar up some steps against the far wall, and waitresses in sparkling bikinis carrying trays around the room. I climbed the steps and told the barman to give me a dry martini and a Bushmills, straight up. Maria leaned against the bar beside me and scanned the room. I looked around with her, though all I could see was a seething mass of greed.

"There is a sickness in this place," I said, speaking more to myself than to her. She looked at me curiously. I said, "Did you know that the rutting of the white-tailed deer is controlled by the phases of the moon?"

She arched an eyebrow. "No kidding."

I nodded. "It's a fantastic thing to watch. The rut peaks seven days after the second full moon during October and November. That's why they call it the rutting moon."

"Who, the white-tailed deer?"

I ignored her facetiousness and went on. "Elk, on the other hand, start rutting during the September equinox, on the twenty-first of September." I looked out at the seething mass again and felt a momentary ache in my belly for the green grass, the snow peaks and the ice-clean brooks. "It's neat," I told her, smiling, "because it means the does give birth in spring, when the new green shoots allow the mother to produce abundant milk for their fawns."

"Is this where you tell me you were adopted as a young boy by the Shoshone Indians, and they taught you the ways of the mountain?"

I shrugged. "Then you complain that I never open up and I am never serious. Let's go look at the tables."

We moved among the tables, sipping our drinks and watching the games. After a while Maria took my arm and squeezed it, leaning in close. "I think I want to play craps," she said, "over at that table."

She guided me toward the game she wanted. Beyond it I saw a blackjack table. It was what she had wanted me to see. There were twelve people seated and maybe twice that number standing watching. Among them, on the far side from me, were four gorillas in evening suits with wires stuck in their ears. They were all gathered around one man who was seated, obscured from view.

I felt a hot, molten pellet of rage and triumph in my gut. I had found him. Now I would stalk him and kill him.

TWENTY-ONE

It couldn't have lasted more than a second, and probably lasted less than that. I saw his eyes and knew he was looking at me and taking in the features of my face—and the fact that I was looking at him. Time did not so much slow as cease to exist. I was suspended, like disembodied consciousness outside of space and time, looking at his single, visible eye beyond a dark-jacketed shoulder. His eye was large and very dark, almost black, his lashes were exceptionally long, to the point of looking feminine, and above the black arch of his eyebrow, his head was bald.

He blinked once, like the shutter closing on a camera, and I looked away, laughing and smiling to Maria, like I hadn't noticed him.

Maria was saying, "Oh my god, I lost. I can't believe I lost."

"How much?"

"Two hundred bucks!"

We played again a couple of times, lost all her money and I took her arm and told her, "I think I've had enough. Let's go get a drink somewhere."

We moved out to the foyer, where Maria went to collect her coat from the dressing room and I stood with my hands in my pockets, staring at the burgundy floor and thinking. I became gradually aware of a dark wall closing around me and looked up. There were four guys in evening suits surrounding me, watching my face. One of them had a pencil moustache and thick black hair. It was the only thing that set him apart from the other three, who all had crew cuts and no facial hair. I didn't say anything, because there was a fifth guy standing right in front of me. He was short, maybe five foot five, slim, bald and extremely well dressed. He was holding an unlit Havana cigar and was studying my face from large, dark eyes with excessively long eyelashes. He said:

"Do I know you?"

I smiled pleasantly. "I have no idea. I'm afraid only you can know that. But I can tell you that I don't know you, or your...," I gestured at the guys standing around me, "...friends."

"My name is Mr. Otropoco."

"I am Harry Bauer, how do you do?"

"I do good. You looked at me in there." He jerked his head toward the gaming room. "I got the feeling you knew me."

"I did?" I shook my head. "It was quite unconscious, I'm afraid. Perhaps we have run across each other in the past, connected in some way, and now it has slipped from our conscious minds."

There was no trace of expression on his face. "You're from San Diego?"

"No, I'm just visiting."

"Where are you from?"

I was going to tell him New York. Instead I paused for a tenth of a second and smiled. "I'm from Pinedale, in Wyoming." I pointed at where Maria was standing holding her coat, looking worried. "My wife has her coat. Will you excuse me? Perhaps we'll meet again, and this time remember where we met before. On that occasion you must let me buy you a drink."

He turned and stared at Maria. I brushed past him and we made our way out of the casino and into the night.

As we climbed into the Mustang I could see the five of them standing at the top of the steps, watching us.

"Holy shit!" It was Maria, I glanced at her. She looked sickly pale. "What the hell was that?"

"He saw me when you were playing craps. For some reason he had a hunch who I was and came and asked me if we had ever met. He's been expecting me, waiting for me."

She shook her head as we pulled out onto Lagoon Drive. "You should back off. This has got out of control. He will have you killed."

"It's too late. You take a cab to the airport in the morning. If I take you it will be too risky."

"I'm not leaving you alone, Harry! You have to come with me and call this crazy vendetta off."

I found my way to the John Montgomery Freeway and headed south toward Torrey Pines and the hotel. We drove in silence. I glanced at her a couple of times and saw the pallid glow of the streetlights wash rhythmically over her face. She had her arms crossed and was staring out at the headlamps streaming north, beyond the barrier. She was beautiful. And I knew suddenly that she was beautiful inside and out.

I said, "I'm sorry."

"You should stop apologizing." She didn't look at me. "It's your life, your death. Your choices. I have no right to ask you to do anything."

I couldn't answer. I didn't know how to. After a moment she exploded and there was bitterness and hurt in her voice. "Just because we slept together! Just because I was *stupid* enough to think we'd become close! It doesn't give me the right..."

She hugged her arms tighter and put her hand over her mouth. After a while I said, "The right?" Now she turned to look at me, uncertain what I meant.

"There is no such thing," I said. "It doesn't signify. Nobody had the right to kill Sonia Cooper or her father. Nobody gave me the right to kill her killer. When a mountain lion kills a white-tail, or a bear snatches a salmon from the river, nobody gave them the right. The universe is cruel, Maria, and dispassionate. There are no rights. You need something, or you want something, you take it, and you take the consequences with it."

"You really believe that?"

"Believe?" I shrugged. "Do you believe in gravity? Do you believe in the heat of the sun? Kings and priests invented gods, and the rights they grant to protect their property. They don't exist in nature."

"Jesus! You are some piece of work." She raised the hand that had been covering her mouth. "Don't tell me. It's just the way it is."

I didn't answer because I was focusing on the headlamps that I'd noticed shortly after we left the casino, and which were still behind us. She must have noticed my expression because she asked, "What is it?"

"I think they decided to come with us."

"Shit!" She pointed ahead. "Come off like you were going to the airport."

"Why?"

"He has a couple of clubs up there. He won't cause trouble at his own clubs. I'll call the cops and we'll wait for them there."

"Don't call the cops. I'll talk to them. I think he's just curious."

"Otropoco's curiosity is not something you want to stir up, Harry."

"OK, like you said, he won't cause trouble at his own club." I took the exit for the airport and kept going. "Stay in the car and keep your cell in your hand if you want. But for now just stay cool."

They stayed with us and after a couple of minutes I pulled off the Pacific Highway, onto Barnett Avenue and then Midway Drive. Everything on the road was low, flat and broad. It was like a high-tech industrial area, with broad lawns and huge parking lots. After a block, I pulled in at the *Poquito a Poco* club. The name was written in neon script and there were luminous pictures of cowgirls with lassos.

"This is it, right?"

"How did you guess?"

I found a vacant space near the steps that led up to a set of bright red saloon doors. I parked and raised the hood.

"Don't get out. Don't call the cops unless things get rough."

She sighed and shook her head, but she didn't say anything. They were pulling in as I climbed out of the Mustang. It was a large, black Audi Q8 and came to a halt ten feet from the back of the Mustang, effectively blocking my exit. The doors opened and four of the five guys I'd seen at the casino climbed out. The guy with the hair was there. He got out of the driver's door. Otropoco climbed out of the back, and two of his crew cut gorillas climbed out too. They all stood looking at us while Otropoco approached on small legs.

I watched him, thinking I could kill him right there. The thought excited me and I had to focus on relaxing. He spoke suddenly, and his voice had an odd ring in the broad empty space, with the traffic in the background.

"You left so sudden. I thought we were having a conversation."

"My mistake. I thought we had finished." I leaned my ass on the trunk of the car, crossed my arms and smiled. "You see, my wife was waiting for me."

"Your wife." It wasn't quite a question, but it wasn't a statement either. "What are you doing in San Diego, Mr. Bauer?"

I raised my eyebrows, like I was amused by the question. "I'm writing a story."

Still no expression, no gesture, no inflection. "You're a writer."

"I'm a writer."

"What's the story you're writing?"

"What all stories are about: struggles, sex, life, death..."

He wagged a finger in the negative. "No. Stories begin with life, and they end with death, but in between all stories are about power. Sex is not about creating life, Mr. Bauer, and it is not about love. Sex is about power, control, domination. That is why when one man kills another he gets a hard-on. Power."

"I'll bear that in mind. Maybe I should include you in the story, Mr. Otropoco, a wise man in the night."

He pulled his un-smoked cigar from his pocket, took a couple of steps closer and stood looking up at my chest before he raised his eyes to meet mine. I could feel the presence of death like a physical thing on my skin and wanted very badly to take hold of his neck and break it.

"Do you know, Mr. Bauer, what the most valuable commodity in the world is?"

I gave my head a single shake. "Oil? Perhaps heroin? I don't know."

"Violence. Violence is the most valuable commodity on Earth. Because violence backs every law and every rule that can be enforced. Think of this." He adjusted his feet as though to present the idea. "A country that cannot enforce its laws with violence—" He paused to shape the word and enunciate it. "—*decomposes* into anarchy. Look at Mexico. Who makes the law in Mexico? The cartels, because they have access to more violence than the government."

He took another step closer and wagged the two fingers that were holding the cigar in the air. The air had turned chill. A car hissed by.

"But, it is not just how much violence you can access and use. It is how much violence you are *willing* to use. Is it going to be enough to shoot the guy? Are you gonna cut off his arms and legs before you kill him? You gonna set fire to the village or you gonna set fire to the people too? How far are you willing to go in your violence? You gotta measure the violence in quantity, volume *and* degree. Because power comes with the *willingness* to use violence."

"I can't argue with that, Mr. Otropoco. It's as self-evident as gravity. But I get the feeling you are trying to tell me something, and I wonder if you have mistaken me for somebody else."

"Do you want to kill me, Mr. Bauer?"

His eyes were like two cameras scanning my eyes at a thousand frames a second. I raised my eyebrows high on my forehead and tried to look like a middle-class guy who is feeling out of his depth.

"I have to tell you, Mr. Otropoco, I am beginning to feel a little threatened. I am not sure what this is all about…"

"You didn't answer."

"I have absolutely no desire to kill you, Mr. Otropoco. In fact, what I would like, is to go home."

"Wyoming?"

I gave a small laugh. "No. I am from Wyoming, but I live in Vegas. But what I *meant* was my hotel."

"I scared you."

"Yes, a little."

"You're a writer."

"Yes."

"Now you got something to write about."

"That's definitely true."

"You like boats?"

"Yes. I, in fact…" I gestured toward the ocean but he cut me short.

"I got a yacht. She's beautiful. A white schooner. I call her the *Holy Spirit. Espíritu Santo.* I got her moored off the beach back of my house."

"That's wonderful." I made like I was trying to normalize the conversation and asked, "You live by the beach?"

He smiled to the extent that there was suddenly an ugly humor in his eyes, though his face did not change.

"You don't know where I live?"

"No, Mr. Otropoco. I don't know where you live."

"You should come over. We'll have lunch on the yacht. You can tell me about your book."

I made a face like I was astonished. "That's extremely kind of you…"

"I'll send a car. Where are you staying?" I paused, smiling, like I was worried but didn't want to show it. He said, "What?"

"I am staying at the Hilton, Torrey Pines, but I really do not want to kill you, Mr. Otropoco."

He didn't answer for a second. Then he said, with that same lack of expression, "I know. If I thought you did I would have killed you already. Good night, Mr. Bauer. Go home now. No more drinks tonight."

I nodded. "Yes, thank you."

He walked back to his dark Audi on his short, exquisitely tailored legs, and climbed in. Four doors slammed like four gunshots and the car took off into the small, quiet hours. I felt the tension ease in my shoulders and got back behind the wheel of the Mustang. Maria was staring straight ahead at the orange-washed wall in front of us. She was breathing hard and biting down on her lower lip.

I fired up the big engine and pulled slowly out of the lot. I found my way back to the freeway and cruised slowly back toward Torrey Pines and the hotel. We didn't talk again until we were in the bedroom and I opened the terrace to look out at the enormous ocean. There was no moon and the sea looked dark, like a limitless, bottomless pit.

I felt her arms encircle me and squeeze, and her head rest gently on my back.

"Do you know how close we were to death back there?"

"Yes."

"Please never do that to me again."

"I won't." I turned and took her face in my hands. "I won't, but tomorrow you go back to Vegas, and you stay there till this is over."

"I don't want to leave you alone, Harry."

"I can't do this if I am worrying about keeping you safe." I faltered a moment. "And I am worried about you."

"Leave it, Harry. Drop it. Let's go away, find a different way of dealing with the loss of your friend. We'll find a therapist, the best, we'll move back East, to New England. Anything, but please, Harry, leave it."

I shook my head. There was a burning, thrashing in my gut that made my voice come out, twisted. "I am going to kill that son of a bitch, for Sonia, for Ash, for a little girl I allowed to die in Al-Landy, and for all the souls he and bastards like him have stolen and all the hearts he has broken. I am going to kill him with my hands."

She clutched me and clamped her mouth hungrily to mine. Her body pressed hard against me. Hot hunger welled up in my belly and I tore off her dress, picked her up in my arms and carried her to the bed.

TWENTY-TWO

At seven AM I woke her and called room service for breakfast. We showered together, dressed and ate breakfast watching the violet dawn seep into the air. Then I took her down to reception, put her in a cab and told her I would see her in a few days. Her eyes told me she didn't believe that was true. She smiled, touched my hand, and then she was gone.

I walked back inside with my hands deep in my pockets, wondering whether Otropoco was going to kill me over lunch. A preemptive strike out at sea, catching me unarmed while my entire arsenal was sitting in a truck in San Diego. It would be ironic.

I took the Mustang and drove down to 6th Avenue, where Vipe had left the truck in the parking garage. It was yet another warm, sunny day in California, and I had the hood down to let the breeze clear my head as I cruised through the broad avenues and the low buildings under the huge, pale dome of the sky. It was obvious from our encounter the night before that Otropoco suspected who I was. It followed logically then that if I went to lunch with him, there was every chance he would cut my throat and feed me to the fish, simply to be on the safe side.

On the other hand, I also believed what he'd said, that if he had wanted to kill me, he would have done it last night. My gut feeling was that he was curious and wanted to know what I was about. Allowing for the fact that his curiosity could change to boredom in a matter of seconds, still from my perspective, a visit to the yacht and a longer conversation with the man could be invaluable.

I spun the wheel and pulled into the sudden darkness of the parking garage, where I was pursued by the insane screams of the tires as I spiraled up to the top floor. I found the truck at the far end, parked next to it, locked up the Mustang and got behind the wheel of the truck. There I sat for a good five minutes, drumming my fingers on the wheel and reviewing for the hundredth time the events of the night before.

Finally I fired up the truck, spiraled down through the screaming shadows again and reemerged into the bright, sunlit morning. I sought out the I-5, crossed the river and turned into Grand Avenue, among the superabundance of trees and tall palms which fringe that long, straight road; and the low, elegant buildings that nestle in their shade. And, just before I hit the beach, I turned onto Mission Boulevard which carried me to the Ventura Yacht Club. There I backed the truck into the parking space beside my rental yacht and, with some difficulty, I transferred the contents of the wooden crate into the bowels of the yacht, without those contents being seen.

After that I returned the truck to the parking garage, wiped off all my prints and returned to the yacht club in the Mustang. Nobody had seemed to take much notice, but even if they had, what they would have seen would have been unremarkable.

I checked my watch. It was ten minutes after eleven. I spent another fifteen minutes concealing the weapons and the C4 in the cabin in the prow, and then set off out of the harbor and into the open seas.

I spent about forty-five minutes playing around, remembering how a sailing yacht behaves and responds to the wind, getting the feel of the breeze and the movement and resistance of the ocean. Then, when I was feeling more confident, I made my way north, smacking and skipping over the small waves along the coast toward La Jolla, and Otropoco's yacht.

I approached it at about twenty past noon. I dropped my spinnaker and the mainsail and used the outboard to come within fifty or sixty feet of the towering, gleaming white schooner. A man appeared on the deck, leaning on the gunwale, smoking a cigarette and watching me. He didn't respond when I waved, so I called out to him, *"Is Mr. Otropoco aboard? Are we still on for lunch?"*

He took another drag without answering, then flicked his cigarette into the water and turned away. I waited a couple of minutes, wondering whether I was being ignored. Then Otropoco's bald head peered over the side.

"Mr. Bauer."

"Good afternoon! Are we still on for lunch? I thought I'd take the opportunity to put in some sailing."

"I said I would send a car."

I ignored him and grinned. *"Beautiful day, isn't it?"*

He spoke to someone out of my sight for a moment, then turned to me again as a sailor lowered a retractable set of stairs.

"Drop anchor. Use your dinghy to come alongside."

I did as he said, tied my dinghy to the steps and climbed up to the deck. There was a sailor there, and the gorilla with the facial hair. They stood behind Otropoco who was wearing very white pants, a blue blazer with brass buttons and a burgundy silk cravat. I ignored the boys and spoke to Otropoco.

"I hope I am not too early." Before he could answer I went on. "I asked the concierge at the hotel if he knew which was your yacht, because I was thinking of putting in some practice sailing. He said he didn't know, but as far as he was aware there was only one large, white schooner anchored here. So I figured it must be yours."

He watched me say all this with very still eyes. When I had finished he said, "You want a drink."

"Sure, why not? Dry martini would go down a treat." I looked around. "This is a magnificent boat."

He indicated the long, one-storey cabin toward the stern. The walls were highly polished mahogany, and through the windows I could see a luxurious saloon and a dining area with a long, mahogany table set with silver candelabra.

"We'll go inside."

I followed him through the doors into the saloon. I was struck by the strong smell of furniture polish and tobacco. There was a suite of leather chesterfields, a couple of sofas and a fully stocked bar with a barman in a white tux. Otropoco snapped, *"Martini seco para el señor Bauer. Champán para mi."*

He pointed to one of the large, leather armchairs beside a walnut table with a big, fat lamp on it and said, "Sit there."

I sat and he sat on a sofa at a right angle to me, perched on the edge, with his elbows on his knees. He didn't waste time. He came right to the point.

"I told you last night if I did not trust you, I would kill you."

I smiled. "You did. That made quite an impression on me. That's why I made a point of telling the concierge, the guy at the marina and several other people where I was going. That's also why I came in my small rental yacht."

"If you were afraid, why did you come?"

I gave my head a little sideways twitch. "I'm a writer. This is what Graham Greene called literary convertible stuff. I would be crazy not to come."

He looked at the guy with the hair. *"Es o no es, Joaquín? Es un pendejo imbécil, o es el hijo de puta que mato a La Fontaine?"*

I had enough Spanish to make out he was asking the hair, whose name was apparently Joaquin, if I was just an asshole or was I the son of a bitch who'd killed La Fontaine? The hair shook his head, then shrugged.

"No lo se, jefe. Mátelo de todos modos. Que hay que perder?"

He didn't know. He should kill me anyway. After all, what did he have to lose? I interrupted.

"Is it just us? Nobody is joining us?"

He turned to face me and for the first time there was an expression on his face. He was struggling to mask it, but it was something like incredulity. He slid back on the sofa and made a temple of his fingers, which he rested against his lower lip.

"What is the title of your book, Mr. Bauer?"

Without thinking, and without hesitation, I said, *"El Verdugo."*

"The executioner."

"Yeah."

"What has made you choose this title?"

"That's life," I said. "Life is the executioner. Nothing lasts, everything dies. We are all in search of permanence. We diet, we exercise, we install intruder alarms, we train in self-defense, we study at school and at college so we can get a job or a career so we can have money to be safe—to buy a house or an apartment, buy food and clothes—all for what? To preserve ourselves. We want to preserve ourselves unharmed and alive. But it is a pointless exercise because life itself is our executioner. We die, not because we are shot or stabbed, or strangled. We die, Mr. Otropoco, because we are alive."

"Philosophy."

"Fact."

I sat back and sipped my drink. He said, "What is the argument?" I frowned. He looked at Joaquin the Hair. *"Cual es el argumento?"*

The hair said, "The plot."

"What is the plot?"

I almost told him it was about an assassin avenging the death of a friend he had never met, and that friend's daughter. Instead I said, "It's about a man who sets out to find himself."

"Find himself. He didn't have a mirror?" No smile, just the bald question. I shook my head. "You don't find yourself with a mirror, Mr. Otropoco. With a mirror you find only your reflection. The true you is the one looking."

He gave a small frown and narrowed his eyes. "So what happens to this man?"

"He loses everything he most cares about. The people he loves, his wife and his daughter, his home, his health, even his sanity begins to go, but then he finds two things that save him."

"What things?"

"Love—he falls in love with his doctor, who is trying to save him—"

A fraction of an arch to his eyebrow. "And what else?"

"Death."

A fraction of a frown. "Death? He finds death?"

I didn't know what I was saying, but it sounded good and I was impressing even myself.

"Everything is mortal, Mr. Otropoco, except the pure essence. That pure force that drives us, that makes us breathe, that rouses us from the bed in the morning, that makes us take up our weapons again and keep fighting, that nameless, shapeless thing that drives us on to action. That is not mortal. And so, when death claims everything and drags everything we value and love down into the abyss, what is left, what survives, that is the one thing of true value."

Like I said, I'd made it up as I went along, cobbled together from things I'd read and bits and pieces I had heard along the way. But he seemed to find something in it. He was staring down at his blue, canvas deck shoes, placed neatly side by side on the end of his short legs, and eventually said: "Again, philosophy. You do not look to me like a philosopher. What is the story? What happens to the people, Mr. Bauer?"

"Well, his wife is killed, murdered. She is an innocent bystander in a shoot-out between gangs. His daughter is also killed..."

"And what does he do?"

My mind was racing. I was vaguely aware that his forcing this narrative from me was a dangerous game, because the temptation to tell Ash's story or my own was almost irresistible. I got some sense then of just how dangerous, and how intelligent, this strange man was. I took a deep breath.

"Well, he seeks the advice of his doctor, a beautiful, young yet wise woman. He asks her what meaning these deaths have. What is the meaning of his loss? But she is unable to help him. She herself has lost the man she loved, and is struggling with the pain. And for a time they are brought together by their pain, but eventually they are unable to satisfy each other's..."

"I am sorry," he said suddenly. "I have made you waste your time."

"I beg your pardon?"

"We can have no lunch today."

I laughed. "My story was that bad? Maybe I was too pompous?"

"You must leave. I have made a mistake, Mr. Bauer. I thought you were somebody else. I can see now that I was wrong. So, you will please leave."

"Oh, well. I am sorry." I took one last sip and set the glass on the walnut table. As I stood he stood too. "I was really looking forward to talking to you and getting some material for my novel. But I guess if you're busy..."

"This way."

He wasn't wasting time. He indicated the heavy mahogany door and I followed Joaquin the Hair out onto the deck. I hesitated a moment and Otropoco said, "Please, take your boat and leave now."

I nodded. "Sure, I'm um..."

But even as I said it he was walking away toward the stern of the yacht. I climbed down the steps and got uncertainly into the dinghy, then rowed the fifty or sixty yards to my small sailing yacht. As I clambered aboard I heard a kind of electronic humming behind me. I turned to look and saw a small crane lowering a motor launch into the sea. When it was in the water I saw that Otropoco was at the wheel and the Hair was beside him.

They gunned the engine and in a moment they were gone, leaving a broadening field of small waves in their wake.

I spent the afternoon sailing leisurely up and down the coast, turning over Otropoco's reaction to my story. It was weird, for sure, but then the man wasn't exactly normal. To say he was hard to read was an understatement. Had he decided I was no risk to him? Had he, as he said, decided I was wasting his time? It would be nice to think so, and his sudden lack of interest had come when I had started to focus on the romance between the man and his doctor. But I didn't think Otropoco was that stupid. In fact, I was convinced Mr. Otropoco had a mind like a scalpel.

In fact, the more I thought about it the more convinced I was that I had escaped with my life by a hair's breadth. He had invited me there intending to kill me and drop me overboard, just in case I was the guy. If he hadn't done that, it was only because I'd told him I had advised the concierge and several other people where I was going in my yacht. But if that had saved my life, it had also confirmed for him that I was no ordinary tourist. I had taken out insurance, and only a pro does that. A normal person just doesn't show up at all.

So why the questions about the book? To confirm I was who he thought I was. And when he'd done that to his satisfaction, he dumped me and left the yacht. For what purpose? To make arrangements for my discrete execution. That was the only thing that made sense, and it meant I had to act soon. Very soon. Sooner than him.

THE SUN WAS SITTING on the horizon, turning red and bleeding into the water. I had returned to within half a mile of the *Espíritu Santo* and dropped anchor. I sat for a while, listening to the small waves slap and splosh, lazy against the hull, watching the dusk quicken, and a couple of lights wink on onboard the schooner.

I went below then and made a few arrangements. I pulled on a pair of swimming trunks, a mask and a pair of air bottles, and when it had grown dark outside I took hold of a waterproof bag I had prepared, slipped up onto the deck, eased myself quietly into the water and allowed the leaded belt to pull me slowly down into the wet darkness. When I was a few feet below the surface I began to kick gently with the flippers, slowly closing the distance between my yacht and Otropoco's. It was hard to judge direction down in the murk, and a couple of times I had to surface very slowly and very quietly to make sure I was on track. But eventually I found myself just a hundred feet away, and when I went down again, after a few kicks I began to see the luminous glow of the white hull ahead of me.

TWENTY-THREE

Two hours later I dropped anchor again about a hundred yards off the cliffs beneath Otropoco's house. The soft wet ripples of the waves gave the chill an edge. The moon had not risen yet and in the dark it was hard to estimate accurately, but give or take a stone's throw, I figured I was in the right place.

I launched the dinghy with my equipment in it and slowly and carefully started paddling my way in to the shore. Soon the ghostly form of the cliffs began to rise up before me. The sigh and suck of the waves became louder and a few strokes after that the hull of the dinghy crunched on the sand and shingle. I jumped out and dragged her in onto the beach.

Working quickly I pulled on the Kevlar vest, stuck the Fairbairn and Sykes fighting knife into my boot, slipped the Sig into my waistband, slung the M16 and the crossbow across my back and stuffed everything else, including a large towel from the boat, into the rucksack. Finally, I pulled the night vision goggles down over my eyes, turning the world into a bizarre, black and green nightmare, and set off at a run across the luminous green sand toward the steep gully that rose up to Otropoco's house.

It was a slow, painful climb and I cursed myself for not thinking to bring gloves. The ground was dry, with loose sand

and stones that slipped under my feet, forcing me to cling to shrubs and bushes which tore the skin from my fingers. It was slow, painful, and worst of all it was noisy. And the higher I climbed, every time I slipped or was forced to scrabble to safety, the rocks and stones cascading down the gully echoed more like a landslide in the green blackness. I only prayed the neighbors were all safely behind triple-glazed windows listening to loud TVs.

It took me a full twenty minutes to cover a distance of little more than a hundred yards from the base of the cliff to the base of the perimeter wall of the house. Albeit a hundred yards that were practically vertical, with loose sand and gravel, and undergrowth that was virtually a jungle.

When I finally got to the top I consulted my watch. It was just after nine PM. My hands were bleeding and I was shaking from the strain. I gave myself five minutes to recoup, and turned my mind to climbing the wall.

It was sheer redbrick and about eight foot tall. However, over time small trees had seeded and grown on the cliff, and sturdy vines had started to climb across the porous brick surface. So, using the trees and bushes as support for my feet, and gripping the vines for leverage, I managed to pull myself up the two feet necessary to be able to reach the top of the wall.

Once up there I felt carefully along the edge and found, as I had expected, broken bottles cemented into the surface of the wall. It had been a foregone conclusion. It was going to be either broken bottles or barbed wire, and barbed wire would have been deeply unaesthetic in a neighborhood like this.

Plus, the fact was, the risk of anyone but a complete lunatic attempting to enter from the cliff side of the house was practically zero. So broken bottles did the job.

Practically.

I folded the towel and slung it across the top of the wall, placed the rucksack beside it and pulled myself up, laying my belly across the towel. It was very uncomfortable, but the Kevlar and the towel made it bearable; and I needed a few seconds to scan the area before I went over.

I took a moment to make sense of the eerie green and black imagery. I found I was above an orchard. There were what looked like rows of cabbages, lettuces and tomatoes and other vegetables; and there were also a dozen or so fruit trees that partially obscured my view of the house. Presumably it obscured their view of me, too.

I scanned the wall, left and right and found no cameras or motion detectors. That is not unusual in the homes of drug barons and cartel bosses, just as they never have alarm systems connected to the local precinct. They don't want what goes on in their houses recorded on camera, and they don't want the cops descending on them every time an alarm goes off. They deal with their problems in house and unrecorded. And if you break into their house, they sure as hell don't want what they do to you recorded on camera.

So I swung my leg over and lay flat, letting the Kevlar protect my chest while the towel protected possible future generations of Bauers. Looking through the black silhouettes of the fruit trees I could see the bright green glow of the floodlit lawn.

I eased myself over and lowered myself slowly into the orchard, dropping the last foot or two into soft earth. There I hunkered down, pulled on a pair of latex gloves and took the crossbow from my back. I loaded it and crawled silently on my belly through the garden produce and through the fruit trees, until I came to a winding path separating the orchard from a large lawn, maybe thirty or forty yards across, fringed with dense trees, cypress or poplars. It was probably fifty or sixty yards long, leading to a large, paved terrace at the back of the house.

There were six strategically placed spotlights that floodlit the area, and I could see, up on the paved patio, two guys in suits sitting and smoking. Two more were pacing the perimeter of the lawn, at the edge of the light, with that look guards get when nothing ever happens. One of them was walking away from me on the far side of the grass. The other was approaching along the path, thirty or forty feet away.

I silently pushed the goggles up on my head, took careful aim through the night scope, placed the red laser dot on his esophagus and, when he was just four paces away I pulled the trigger and, with just a whisper, drove the barb diagonally up through his throat, severing his spinal cord at the base of his skull. Death was instant and silent.

I stepped out quickly to catch him and pulled him in among the trees. There I laid him to rest under an apple tree. It was more than he deserved.

It would not be long before his absence was noticed. So I needed to act fast. Staying in the cover of the fruit trees, I crawled ten feet to my right, through the mulch to where I could see the two guards on the terrace, sixty paces away, and the third walking toward me. I rested the M16 on its bipod and sighted the two guards without engaging the laser. Then I loaded the crossbow, took aim at the approaching guard's forehead and waited.

He was maybe thirty yards from me. He wasn't walking fast, roughly a yard every second or so. I held my breath. When I had counted twenty I knew I couldn't miss, and at any second he was going to see me. I pulled the trigger. There was a whisper, and then a hard, sickening *thwack!* as the barb smacked through his skull. He stood very still. By the time his eyes had rolled up I had fixed the laser sight on one of the two guys on the terrace.

I fired. They were sixty yards away, the sound was suppressed and they were subsonic rounds. The report was more of a muffled thud than a bang. By the time the gorilla was bending his knees to lie down, I had the dot on his pal's temple. I squeezed and saw the spray of blood and gore erupt from the exit wound.

I didn't waste time. I slung the crossbow over my shoulder, picked up the assault rifle and ran, unscrewing the suppressor as I went.

I avoided the floodlit lawn, keeping to the shadows of the trees until the last minute, when I ran up the steps onto the terrace. It was fifty yards across at its widest point, and twenty yards from where I stood at the top of the steps to two large, sliding-glass doors. There was no light inside, but I could see that one of the glass doors stood open to about six inches. I moved to it and slipped inside.

There was absolute silence. By the filtered light from the lawn I could see an Art Deco marble fireplace, a couple of large, modern paintings on the walls, a couple of huge, modern sofas with matching armchairs, and a big, rustic coffee table.

I counted thirty seconds and still heard nothing. So I moved to the double doors, turned the handle and eased it open just an inch. It gave onto an entrance hall which was bigger than most people's houses. It had a fountain in the center and a couple of potted palms at the foot of a winding staircase. Opposite that was a heavy, arched oak door which stood firmly closed. Pacing the hall, clasping his hands behind his back and jerking his knees like a dancing chicken, was a crew cut in a suit.

He reached the nearest potted palm, flexed his knees, stared at the ceiling and started his chicken-dance walk back toward the door. Perhaps he was a towering intellect, trapped in an unfulfilling chicken-walk job.

I slipped through the door and moved up behind him. When he felt the muzzle of the Sig in the small of his back he froze. I clamped my left hand over his mouth and whispered in his ear.

"If I shoot you right here, it won't kill you straight away. The pain will be excruciating, and if you do live, you will never walk again. You have to ask yourself, is it worth it?" All he did was swallow. So I said, "Into the living room, quickly and quietly."

I pushed him through the door, closed it behind me and hit him hard in the kidneys. He went down gasping. I rolled him on his back and placed the crossbow over a place no man should ever have a crossbow placed.

"I pull the trigger," I said, "and this son of a bitch will pin you to the floor. It will hurt like nothing you can imagine. So get wise and cooperate with me. Maybe you'll get to see your girlfriend tomorrow. I am not interested in you. You understand that?"

He nodded. His eyes were huge and pleading.

"You tell me where Otropoco is, and when I am done asking you questions, you get the hell out of here. You understand me? What's your name?"

"Oscar."

"OK, Oscar, well tonight is Oscar night, and you get the prize. Where is Otropoco right now?"

"He is in the dining room. He is eatin' dinner."

I nodded and smiled, and repeated, "Where?"

"Pass the fountain, on the other side of the hall, the big white door. Please don't shoot me. Please."

I shot the bolt through his heart and stapled him to the floor. Death came instantly. I reloaded the crossbow and stepped back out into the hall. I wondered how many guards were left. I had done no recon at all, and just a minimum of preparation. I smiled to myself with little humor. It was exactly the kind of thing the colonel was always complaining about. At least I hadn't blown anything up.

Yet.

I crossed the broad, white marble hall, passed the fountain and the potted palms, and came to the big, double white doors. I didn't kick them in, or charge through them in a hail of bullets. I just opened them and stepped inside.

There was a long, highly polished, oval mahogany table. It had no tablecloth. There was an elaborate candelabra in the center, shaped like a medieval juggler dressed in red and orange patch-work. He was laughing and had one candle on his head, one in each hand and another on the sole of his upturned foot. It was strangely exquisite.

At the farthest end of the table, staring at me with absolutely no expression, was Otropoco. The light from the candelabra was reflected on his bald head, and in his large, black eyes. He had his fork halfway to his mouth, and on the willow pattern plate in front of him he had a steak, sautéed vegetables and Vichy carrots. Beside his plate was a glass of red wine.

On his right was a slight man in a suit. He was holding his wineglass and frowning at me, like he was trying to understand me. He had heavy glasses and investment broker written all over him.

Standing behind Otropoco was the hair, who was gaping slightly, and either side of the door were two monsters who would have dwarfed a wardrobe. The one on my right had a long black ponytail and a nose like a can opener. He was scowling down at me with an expression of outrage like I had just pissed on his favorite shoes.

The guy on my left had the same expression, but he was bald and his nose looked like it had been stepped on by an elephant when it was small. I ignored them both, pointed the M16 at Otropoco and said, quietly, "Freeze."

The guy with the ponytail stepped in front of me. The action surprised me and made me hesitate for that all-important second. During that second he snatched the barrel, levered it up and drove a fist like a ton of concrete into my face. I managed to weave back and to the side, but the massive force drove me into the door and left me dazed and in pain.

Next thing the world rushed at me. The bald guy had grabbed me by my collar, dragged me off the wall and was pulling back his right fist in what looked like an attempt to tear off my head. It was slow and telegraphic, and though I felt like I'd just been hit by a small mountain, I also knew my life depended on what I did in the next tenth of a second. So I hugged his wrist tight with both arms and smashed my right heel into his knee.

The pain surprised him, so I did it again. His eyes bulged and I put my whole body into twisting his wrist and putting him between me and the ponytail. The whole thing took maybe one and a half seconds.

Ponytail was trying to get at me and Joaquin the Hair was shouting furiously in Spanish. The bald one was bent double, dancing around trying to avoid his shoulder being dislocated. So I kicked him hard in the face a couple of times and as he went down I lunged at the ponytail and landed two beautiful straight leads on his jaw followed by a massive left hook.

I might as well have hit the wall. He slapped me backhanded and sent me sprawling across the room with my head reeling and my ears ringing. As I hit the floor I knew that if he hit me again I wouldn't be able to get up and he would kill me.

I was halfway to my feet when he rushed me and got my head in a front lock, and started pounding my kidneys with his fist. The pain was draining away my strength and I knew I had only seconds left.

That was when I remembered something some guy had told me once. When somebody is choking you, if you think about their hands or their arms, you will die. You have to think only about your own hands and weapons. So I reached down and clawed the fighting knife from my boot and rammed it with all the savagery I felt burning my gut, deep into his chest. I felt him go into spasm and wrenched my head free from his grip. I roared, pulled the blade from between his ribs, charged him and rammed it again, with both hands through his sternum.

The room was spinning from the lack of oxygen and my body was numb with pain. I could see Joaquin the Hair, just ten or fifteen feet away from me, leaning out the door, searching for the guards. I was on him in two strides and my third turned into a savage kick into his liver. As he doubled up I pulled him away from the door and slammed it shut. I kicked his legs from under him and when he hit the ground I stamped on the back of his neck, snapping his vertebrae.

Then I turned toward Otropoco and his guest.

TWENTY-FOUR

OTROPOCO AND HIS GUEST WERE SITTING VERY STILL. I pulled the P226 from my waistband and walked to the table. I was aware that my hands and my breathing were shaking and unsteady. I jerked my head at the guy with the glasses.

"Who is he?"

"My chief accountant."

"Good. How much cash have you got in the house?"

He shook his head. "Negligible."

"OK. How many guards have you got in the house?"

He thought about it. "I don't know. Seven, eight. Joaquin used to take care of that."

"OK, we are going to go to your study now. For every guard we meet, I am going to shoot you in one of your joints, both of you."

The accountant spoke for the first time. "Why me? I'm just the accountant. I don't know anything."

"Why?" I asked him. "Why? For the same reason Ash Cooper is dead, for the same reason his daughter Sonia is dead, *for the same reason a nameless child in Al-Landy is dead!*" My voice had been rising as the rage welled inside me. I stopped, took control and rasped, "Because life sucks, and then you die. If you have any useful information, pal, you had better start sharing. Get up!"

They both stood. I stepped behind Otropoco and grabbed the scruff of his neck. I held him at arm's length with the Sig aimed at his head.

"I am going to tell you both right now that at this time I am extremely dangerous. What you need to do is humor me and do absolutely everything I say."

Otropoco spoke and his voice was as calm and expressionless as it had been on the yacht.

"What do you want, Mr. Bauer?"

"I told you, we are going up to your study. Lead the way. And you," I snarled at the accountant, "stay where I can shoot you."

We went out into the white marble entrance hall and crossed toward the bottom of the stairs. There I snapped at the accountant, "You go ahead, nice and steady."

He led the way to the landing on the next floor. It stretched from right to left. The accountant turned to the right, then looked back at his boss for confirmation. Otropoco nodded and we moved down the corridor, past a dogleg and finally to a large door on the right. It was the kind of door a European would put at the entrance to a castle, but in California they put them at the entrance to their dens.

Otropoco reached in his pocket. I shoved the Sig hard into his spine. "Easy," I said.

He pulled out his key and showed it to me. He fitted it to the lock, turned and pushed the door gently inward.

It was not what I had expected. I'd expected lots of mahogany, Castilian antiques, suits of armor and leather chesterfields. But I was wrong. The walls were covered, floor to ceiling in blond wood bookcases. The books were a mixture of hardback and paperback, and they all looked well used. There were also books on the desk, on the occasional tables and stacked on the windowsill.

The desk itself was modern, made of plain, blonde oak. The chairs and the sofa looked Scandinavian, heavy and well padded.

On the walls were paintings that looked original, and to my uneducated eye, they looked good too.

We went inside and I closed the door with my foot.

"You," I jerked my head at the accountant, "what's your name?"

"Ernesto, sir."

"Ernesto, you get to go home today. Your crime is laundering money. Maybe one day the Feds will catch up with you. But today, unless you do something really stupid, you get to live." He made an incoherent noise. I said, "Get behind the computer and switch it on."

He did it and said, "The password..."

"Now," I said, "what happens next depends on you. In a few seconds I am going to start blowing off bits off Mr. Otropoco's body. I'll start with fingers and toes, and move up to elbows, ankles and knees. Death will be slow and extremely painful. If you are both smart, we can avoid that."

I kicked Otropoco hard in the back of his legs and he went down on his knees. Before I could push him down on his belly he half yelled, "ZQG, oh seven oh five eight seven, hash."

As Ernesto rattled at the keys I pulled Otropoco to his feet and dragged him over behind his accountant, where I could see the screen. He was in.

"OK, Otropoco, here is the sixty-four-million-dollar question. How much are you prepared to pay for your life?"

His breathing was becoming a little ragged but his voice was steady and calm.

"That's the wrong question, Mr. Bauer. There is no limit to how much I am prepared to pay for my life. I'll pay everything I have, and steal more besides. But the real question you need to ask is, how much *can* I pay? Most of my fortune is tied up in—"

He didn't get any further. I kicked him to the floor, knelt on his back, put away the P226, forced open his left hand and placed the blade of the fighting knife on the joint of his baby finger. He was as close to frantic as he had ever been in his life and kept saying, "*No, no, no!*"

I snarled at him, "I don't think you are taking me seriously." And I trod with my heel on the blade. It made a sickening crunch. Otropoco made a high-pitched keening noise and began to sob silently, with closed eyes. I picked up the finger and tossed it onto the desk. The accountant turned away, covering his mouth.

"Now how about we get serious? You, Ernesto," I pointed at him with the knife, "from this moment on, you are responsible for every digit and every limb your boss loses. Are we on the same page?"

"Yes sir."

"So how much can this son of a bitch afford to save his life?"

He buried his face in his hands. "Oh, my god! Is not that easy!"

I put the blade on the knuckle of his ring finger and snarled, "*Give me a number!*"

Otropoco screamed, "*Ernesto!*"

And Ernesto started waving his hands at me frantically, screaming, "*No, no, no!* I am just thinking aloud! Please! Please wait!"

I figured I had their attention and waited. "Give me a goddamn number, and you better pray it's the right number."

Ernesto held up his hands like he was trying to frame my face for a movie. "Just, please, just give me a minute. Is not the kind of information you have at, at, at..." He was going to say fingertips, but stopped and glanced at the thing on the desk.

"Ernesto," I said, staring hard at him. "Make it happen."

He rattled at the keyboard, muttering to himself. I heard the occasional, "...transfer from here..." and, "So, if I..."

I looked down at Otropoco. He had gone into shock. He was a waxy yellow color, he was trembling with cold, but he had sweat beading his forehead. There was a large pool of blood around his hand. I knelt on the small of his back and unlaced his nearest shoe and made a tourniquet around the stump, pulled it tight to stop the bleeding. I wasn't ready for him to die yet.

Ernesto looked at me and joined his hands like he was about to say namaste.

"Mr..... Mr. Bauer, Mr.....please, I am doing my best. This is what I have been able to gather together in a very short time and without warning. It is thirty million dollars. It is a very handsome sum, please."

I stared at him a long time. I believed him. He was too terrified to try and screw me. But I also knew it was a fraction of Otropoco's fortune. Thirty million wouldn't buy you the house we were in.

"OK, Ernesto, here is what I am going to do for you."

I stood and walked to the desk. I knew that Otropoco was too weak to stand. "You are going to transfer that money to this account in Panama."

I typed the account number in and he made the transfer. When it had gone through I pulled over a pad and I wrote a note and showed it to him.

"Do that for me," I said, "and you walk out of here. Trick me, set me up, try and be smart, and I will find you, and what Mr. Otropoco has gone through tonight will seem to you like a fond memory. You understand what I am saying to you?"

He nodded. After a moment he scrawled something on the same pad. I read it and said, "Show me."

He showed me and I nodded. "OK, get the hell out of here, and Ernesto?" He stopped, halfway to his feet. I said, "Apply for a job with the Bureau. They need men with your expertise. They don't pay as much, but you get to live longer. I never want to see you again, understood?"

He nodded. "Can I go?"

"Go. But never, never talk about what happened here tonight."

He opened the door and ran. I heard his feet down the hall, clattering on the stairs. Then the front door opened and slammed.

I wondered if he had guards out the front and if they would come looking for me. I felt suddenly very tired and everything hurt.

I went and hunkered down beside Otropoco. He was sweating profusely now and his breathing was shaking. His eyes, which had been closed, fluttered open. I tried to feel compassion for him, but instead I was transported back to the woods by Fremont Lake, looking down at Slick. I felt my lip curl and tried to squeeze back the tears. I was about to kill him, within seconds he would be dead, but that gaping emptiness in my gut was still there. And I knew that as he died, it would still be there. And no matter what I did, no matter how many of them I killed, the emptiness could never be filled. There was no restitution, there could never be restitution, because death is final. It is irreversible. All the Ash Coopers, the Sonias and the children of Al-Landy were irretrievable. There is no turning back.

I stood and moved around the study, knowing that I was wasting time, knowing that with every moment the chance of the cops storming in increased. I collected his hard drive and his laptop and every flash drive I could find, and stuffed them in my rucksack. I went through his drawers and his files, grabbing at anything that might be remotely useful, putting off the moment when I would have nothing left with which to try and close the ugly, gaping hole inside me.

Finally I went and stood over him.

"Get up," I said. "Get on your feet."

He struggled, propped himself against the sofa and climbed unsteadily to stand swaying in front of me. I stared into his hooded eyes and wondered how I should do it. How would it be most satisfying? With my bare hands? Clean and clinical with a knife to the heart? A shot in the head like an animal…?

"How weak…?" he said suddenly, looking at me from under his long, thick eyelashes. "How weak do you think I am?"

I frowned and he smashed his forehead into the bridge of my nose. White-hot pain filled my head and I staggered back. Twice I felt his foot lash out and kick savagely at my thigh. The pain was meaningless compared to the agony in my head. I stepped back, trying to orient myself and knowing if I did not respond he would kill me.

Instead the door opened and he stumbled out onto the landing. I tried to go after him but stumbled and fell, retching onto the carpet. I dragged myself to my feet and made the door. At the end of the corridor I saw him leaning against the corner and weeping. I pulled the crossbow from my back and with trembling fingers, trying to see through the sickening pain in my head, I loaded it, aimed and pulled the trigger. But he was gone and the barb thudded into the wall.

When I got to the bend in the corridor he was staggering and sliding down the stairs. I managed to run the few paces to the head of the banisters, but by the time I got there he was slamming the door of the living room behind him. I staggered, half-falling, to the bottom of the stairs and ran to the living room, feeling I had a blunt axe wedged in my skull. I searched for my Sig and then for the M16, but realized I had left both upstairs, along with my knife.

I loaded the crossbow and pushed my way into the living room. It was still dark, but the sliding glass door was fully open, a large moon hung over the ocean and through the door I could make out the figure of Otropoco hobbling across the lawn toward the orchard.

I burst out onto the terrace. Aimed at his hobbling silhouette and shot. The barb disappeared harmlessly into the trees. I ran after him, loading the crossbow again as I went, and suddenly he lurched to the right and disappeared among the trees.

I followed, expecting him at any moment to rush at me, shoot me or swing at me with a weapon. But he didn't. Instead I heard him panting and whimpering a short way ahead of me. Then there was the sound of a heavy iron deadbolt on wood, and the squeak of rusty hinges.

I hurried on among the clawing branches, becoming dimly aware of the aching pain in my left leg, where Otropoco had kicked me. And the pain in my head, now turning to nausea, was draining all the strength from my limbs.

Suddenly I was in a small clearing created by the converging of three gravel paths, and exactly on that intersection there was an arched, wooden door in the wall, with a large deadbolt pulled back. The door stood open onto the blackness beyond.

I poked my head out and saw that the door led to the steep gully up which I had climbed. There was a narrow, overgrown path and, thirty or forty yards away, Otropoco was disappearing along that path into the morass of black undergrowth. Recklessly I ran along the path, struggling to catch up with him. But where he was obviously familiar with it, to me it was invisible in the limpid, dappled light of the moon. I slipped, stumbled and fell at every turn, grasping at the branches and bushes, tearing the fabric of the latex gloves. Twice I nearly lost my rucksack and had to go scrambling after it. And inevitably, relentlessly, Otropoco pulled ahead of me, speeding down the gully toward the beach.

I tried to think. One thing was clear to me. He was making for his yacht. And that was because he had seen that it was inevitable now that his house would be raided by the cops. There were bodies everywhere that would be impossible to get rid of or explain. And then there was his accountant, whom I had instructed to go to the Feds. So what Otropoco needed desperately to do was to get the hell out of the USA—and fast.

And then there was the question of his Panamanian accounts. He needed to get to them fast too.

Suddenly I was at the bottom of the track. The sand looked luminous white under the moon, and the ocean was rich with liquid silver on impenetrable black among ripples, sighs and whispers. Silhouetted against it I could see his small, black form, wading into the water; he had his cell in his hand and he was waving his arms. He had called somebody from the *Espíritu Santo* to come and get him, and across the bay there was the high buzz of an outboard.

I sat suddenly in the sand, with my back against the cliff, and felt the deep exhaustion and nausea wash through me. I watched as the launch pulled up onto the sand. I heard the exchange of low, urgent voices as the sailors helped him aboard. Next thing they were pushing the launch back out, rising and dropping over the waves; and a few seconds after that the small boat, now an inky stencil on the moonlit path, was speeding, smacking across the water toward the schooner, the unreachable ghost ship.

I walked to the shore and pulled off my boots and socks and sat with my feet in the cold water. The small boat was eventually swallowed up by the greater form of the schooner, and after just five minutes or so the high whine of the outboard was replaced by the deeper roar and thud of the big diesel. Then came the rattle and clatter of the anchor chain as they desperately made their escape.

Then the beautiful tall ship began to move, stately and sedate, out toward the open sea, toward international waters where they would be safe. That was when I climbed into my dinghy, now that they could no longer see me. I slowly and painfully paddled my way back toward my own, small yacht. And as the larger ship was slowly engulfed by the darkness, I clambered aboard and sat in the cockpit watching the last wraithlike vestiges of the pale hull meld with the night.

I gave it a couple more minutes, allowing strange tides of grief, exhaustion, rage and physical pain to wash through me. Then, finally, I pulled my cell from my pocket and turned to my address book. I found Doc Erickson, stared at her number for a while and moved on to Sheriff Seth Levi, then Maria and Les Divine, until finally I came to a number with no name. I sat staring at it for a moment until, wiping tears I did not understand from my face, I told Sonia and Ash goodbye, and begged them to forgive me for not having been there when they had most needed help.

I committed their souls to a heaven in which I did not believe, and to eternal peace. Then I dialed the number. It rang just once and on the second ring the line went dead. A moment later there was a violent flash that lit up the sea brighter than the moon.

Against it, for just a few seconds, there was the spindly stencil of a fragmenting tall ship being engulfed by flames.

I had set the twenty pounds of C4 under the fuel tanks, and under the large propane bottles they used for the kitchen and for the hot water system. I had taken care to keep them wrapped in plastic bags with a cell phone detonator buried deep inside, and water-resistant duct tape to fix it to the hull.

I had hoped I would be able to kill him, but I had known also there was a chance he would try to get away. So I had taken out my small package of insurance.

Now he was dead, and now it was over.

TWENTY-FIVE

The small sloop and I limped back through the dark wetness. I had managed to hoist the spinnaker before shock set in. Then I had lain on the floor of the cockpit shivering, semi-delirious, occupying a world of pain. Physical pain because of the beating I had received at the hands of the two gorillas, but a much deeper, more frightening pain at realizing what I had become, at realizing that the black wound I had received at Al-Landy, by that small child's dark, terrified eyes, had not been diminished by my murders, but had yawned to a vaster ugliness.

As I approached Mission Bay I forced myself to my feet, lowered the sail and motored in to the berth. There was practically nobody there and the place was dark, but for the few tall, spindly lamps. They drizzled a misty, orange light over the place that made it somehow desolate. I thought about sleeping on the yacht, but I knew I couldn't. I knew I had to leave, and I had to leave now.

I loaded my stuff into the Mustang and, as I closed the trunk a voice behind me spoke.

"You OK, pal?"

I turned and was blinded by a flashlight. The shadow behind it said, "Man, you been in the wars."

I shielded my eyes with my hand.

"I'd feel better if you shone that flashlight somewhere that wasn't my eyes." He shifted it down and I saw he was in a brown uniform. A security guard. "Thanks. I guess I'm not used to boats." I smiled on the ironic side of my face. "I used to sail when I was a kid, but that was a long time ago. I caught a swell and fell down the stairs."

"You need a doctor. You want some help? Maybe you shouldn't drive."

"No, I'm OK. My wife is a doctor. Thanks all the same." With more conviction than I felt, I added, "It looks worse than it is."

As I went round and opened the driver's door he said, "Say, did you see the explosion?"

I showed him a blank face. "What explosion?"

"Were you sailing north or south?"

"Up and down. Then I fell."

"Some kind of yacht exploded out there, sailing north. It was on the radio. Up by Torrey Pines."

"A yacht?" I did my best at an incredulous laugh. "How does a yacht explode?"

"I know, right?"

"Listen, I don't mean to be rude, but I need my wife's tender mercies right now, and a very dry martini."

"Sure." And as I went to climb in he added, "You're not from round here, are you, sir?"

My smile grew strained. "We'll catch up tomorrow. Hang loose."

I slammed the door closed and pulled out of the driving lot before he could answer.

As I turned onto Mission Boulevard I called the hotel. It was answered by a young man who worked hard at being agreeable.

"Hilton la Jolla, how may I help you?"

I told him who I was and added, "Something's come up and I need to go out of the country unexpectedly. I'd like to settle my bill by card now."

"Certainly, sir."

While he worked it out I told him to send my stuff to Les Divine's office in Vegas. By the time I had paid the bill I was turning off the Ted Williams Freeway at the Carmel Mountain Ranch, and accelerating onto the I-15, headed north toward Vegas. I knew it was a five-hour drive and I would not get there till four in the morning at the soonest. I was exhausted, in considerable physical pain and I knew I was going to have to rest sooner or later. But I also knew the later the better. I needed to put space between myself and Torrey Pines.

But the miles passed in the dark, and the dark hours passed in a steady procession through the night as I drove north over the hills. I ached with exhaustion, but any thought of sleep was impossible. I saw the blind houses and the sleeping towns, the lurking gas stations and the secret motels bathed in dead light, all slip by, luminous against the night sky; but the Mustang kept going, pushing forward, driving relentlessly toward Vegas.

Twice I stopped for gas and twice I got coffee. Both times I looked at the red and blue neon signs against the black sky. They told me I should sleep and rest. I told them not yet and climbed back behind the wheel, and moved on, like the hounds of hell were howling at my heels.

I finally rolled past the AMC and the Town Square at four twenty AM. It was dark as night but the glow from the city ahead killed the light of the stars. I followed the black ribbon of asphalt through the concrete desert, under one bridge after another until I came to exit thirty-eight for Flamingo Road. There I swooped over Frank Sinatra Drive and descended into Caesar's Palace, where I parked, grabbed my rucksack and staggered to the reception desk.

The concierge looked at me with eyebrows arched higher than I would have thought physically possible. I slipped him my Panamanian credit card and, though he didn't lower his eyebrows, he did echo them with a big smile.

"I had a suite here a few days ago," I told him. "The Augustus

Premium Suite. I want it again. Have a kid deal with my car and take my bags up." I put a hundred bucks down and found my way to the bar. It was open and busy. Maybe in Sinatra's day New York was the city that didn't sleep. Now it was Vegas.

At the bar I slipped the barman fifty bucks and told him, "I need a double Bushmills straight up, and I need a hamburger. Can you do that for me?"

He looked at my bruised face, my ragged clothes and the fifty bucks and nodded.

"Sure. I can do that for you, sir. Did you have some trouble? Do you need to call a doctor, or...?"

He trailed off. I leered at him, overwhelmed suddenly with exhaustion. "Nah," I told him. "We're well past that."

I took my drink to a corner table and dialed Les Divine's home number. It rang four or five times before a very sleepy voice asked me, "Yeah, who is this?"

"Listen to me. You're going to have plenty of time to sleep when you're dead. Right now I need you in the cocktail bar at Caesar's Palace."

"Do you realize what time it is? It's nearly five in the morning!"

"Yeah, that's why you get so well paid. I'll see you in twenty minutes."

He sighed and the line went dead. I took a pull on the whiskey, leaned my head back and closed my eyes while I savored it.

Next thing there was a voice telling me, "Sir? Sir, I have your burger."

I opened my eyes and saw the barman standing watching me with a frown. In his hand was a plate with a burger and fries.

"Are you sure you're OK?"

"Yeah, I just need a beer to go with this. And bring me another large Bushmills. I'll be fine. How long was I out?"

"About fifteen or twenty minutes. I thought I'd best let you sleep."

I'd taken another pull on the whiskey and bitten into the burger when Les walked in. He scanned the bar, I raised my hand and he found me. He weaved his way through the tables to where I was sitting and paused before sitting down.

"Jesus!" he said, and pulled out the chair. "You look awful. You need to get cleaned up. What happened to you?"

"That can wait." I handed him the rucksack. "In there you have everything you could possibly need to bring down the Gulf Cartel and Otropoco with it, if he were still alive."

He stared at me. "If he were... What are you telling me, Harry?"

"Otropoco died last night. He suffered a house invasion in which all his men were killed. His chief accountant escaped with his life and is going to cut a deal with the Feds. All of that there," I pointed to the rucksack, "will be corroborative. I want you to make copies of everything and let me have the originals."

"Jesus," he said softly.

"It should make your friends in Sinaloa very happy."

"What did you do?"

"I hope I never have to tell you."

He was still frowning, shaking his head. "I mean, how many men... He must have had security..."

"Eight men."

He stared at me a long time. "You're very dangerous."

"That's what the midwife said to my mother when I was born. You want to change our agreement?"

"No!" He laughed. "No, I would rather have you on my side. I don't ever want to have you as an enemy."

I nodded. "I'm glad to hear you say that." I slid the sheet of paper Ernesto had given me across the table. "These are Otropoco's accounts in Panama and in Belize. They are mine now. Close them down, transfer their contents into my accounts, take one percent for yourself. One percent is good and your kids will never have to work if you don't want them to."

He took the paper and nodded. "I will send you proof of

every step of the transactions. Once everything is clean, I'll get you a legitimate accountant to oversee these transactions."

"That's fine, but there won't be any more of these transactions. I'm done. I want you to set up the Ash and Sonia Cooper Foundation with that money. But we'll talk about that when I have stopped hurting."

"I'm very glad to hear that. So will..." He trailed off and studied my face a moment. "What about Maria?"

"What about her?"

"Come on, Harry. Don't be a brute. She's a nice girl. She is pretty serious about you."

"She tell you that?"

"No, but you don't go far in this business if you don't know how to read people. She talks a lot about you, and I see the expression on her face whenever you're mentioned."

"You sure that's not just curiosity?"

"I'm sure it's not curiosity. In all the time she has worked for me I have never seen her go on a date with a client, much less stay in the same hotel. She may look like a million bucks, Harry, but believe me, she is a good Catholic girl. I know her father and her family. And I have known her a good few years."

The waiter brought my beer and my second whiskey. Les told him he'd have a large coffee. When he'd gone I said, "Her father owns the restaurant you took me to lunch at. He's Sinaloa, and she is the daughter of Sinaloa."

He didn't answer, so I went on.

"When I was in Panama, Otropoco's men showed up. They knew where I was. I didn't know if they were simply good operatives, or if they had received information. So I set a trap for you. I apologize, but I had to be sure." He frowned. I said, "I told you I was going to Escondido, and where I was going to be. You were the only person aside from me who knew. And that afternoon four men turned up, posing as federal agents.

"At first I was satisfied that you were the leak, but the more I thought about it the less sense it made. For a start, when I spoke to you after the attack, you didn't sound surprised to hear from me. Then, the trip you arranged for me to go to Panama was unnecessarily careful and complicated if you planned to have me killed once I got there, and when I was in California, you made no effort at all to know where I was. Finally, if your market was Sinaloa, what the hell were you doing working with the Gulf Cartel? You are too smart and too careful to make a stupid mistake like that.

"So, I am going to ask you, but I already know the answer: did you tell Maria that I was going to Escondido?"

"I have always told her everything. She has my absolute trust. Everything you have just said about me applies to her. There must be another explanation. Harry, you can't..."

"I am not going to, Les. I draw the line at women and children."

"But her whole family are Sinaloa. She would never betray a client of mine to the Gulf Cartel."

"I know. I keep telling myself that. But if it wasn't her, who the hell told Otropoco where I was?"

"I don't know, Harry, but have you any idea what her family would do to her if they found out? Have you any idea of the risk she would be taking? And for what? What possible benefit would she be getting?"

"Les..." He stared at me. "You were the only person who knew where I was. So either you have a very sophisticated bug, or Maria was informing for Otropoco."

He shook his head. "I can't believe that. You can't hurt her, Harry. I won't allow it."

"No, Les, I won't hurt her. On the contrary. You need to tell her Otropoco is finished. You have to make her cut her ties with the Gulf Cartel, and you have to make damn sure her family never finds out."

He nodded. "Don't worry about it. There are no ties with the Gulf Cartel. You'll see." He paused and smiled. "You fell for her too, huh? It was mutual."

"In another world, in another life, it might have been."

"Will you see her? She wants to see you."

I frowned. "She knows I'm here?"

He shook his head. "I only just found out myself. I wasn't going to phone her at five AM. But she has been expecting you daily, and she asks about you every day."

I thought about it for a couple of minutes, staring across the bar full of early morning drunks, life's gamblers and losers having one last one for the road. I shook my head.

"No. It would never work. You have to be able to trust, don't you. Besides, I'm going back to Pinedale. I might take over Ash's ranch, buy some horses, think about retiring. I don't know." I shrugged and sighed heavily. "I'm tired, Les. Maria is a Vegas girl, she'd go crazy in Pinedale."

"You might be surprised, Harry. I think you're wrong about her. I am certain you are. Let me make some inquiries."

"Don't do anything to put her at risk, Les."

"I won't. My God! She's like a niece to me. Her father is one of my closest friends. I simply can't believe she would betray me or my office, much less you."

"Well, maybe you're right. If you are, you need to sweep for bugs. Either way, it's over. He's dead and any record of me is erased."

A great weariness settled on my mind. I frowned, trying to make sense of my own words, "She is aware of how dangerous I can be for her, and, if she knows we have a truce, she will take great care not to upset that truce. We'll leave it at that."

He studied me a moment, frowning. "I really think you should talk to her. Get some sleep, you're not making a lot of sense right now. Talk to her after you've slept, before you leave for Pinedale."

I drained my whiskey and stood.

"I have no idea what I am going to do in the next few hours, Les. But sleep sounds like a good idea. I am going to sleep like the dead. Then I will collect the originals from your office, and after that I am going to go back home. Pinedale? New York? Who knows? But try to rebuild my life. Aside from that, I am too tired and too bruised to even think."

He stood and we shook hands, and we walked together to the foyer. There he patted me on the back and I watched him walk out into the early dawn. When he'd gone I made my way up to my suite, where I stripped off my clothes, showered, brushed my teeth and crashed into black oblivion.

TWENTY-SIX

I awoke to the sound of hammering, then the ringing of a bell. The curtains were open and the sun was streaming in through the window, making my head ache. I closed my eyes and tried to find a place in my existence that didn't occupy some space on the ache-agony spectrum. I couldn't find one, and then my phone started ringing.

By the time I had got to my feet, pulled on my pants and failed to locate my phone, it had stopped ringing and the hammering had started again on the door. I crossed the suite and opened it. It was Maria and I scowled at her. She didn't seem to notice. She said, "Oh, thank God!", put her arms around my chest and squeezed.

I backed into the room and closed the door.

"What are you doing here?"

After a moment she released her grip and looked up at me. Her cheeks were wet and she was searching my face.

"You don't seem very pleased to see me."

I repeated, "What are you doing here, Maria?"

"Les told me you'd arrived last night. I came to see you. I was so worried."

I turned away and walked into the living room. I opened

the balcony, stepped out and took a couple of deep breaths. When I turned back she was standing in the middle of the floor, biting her lip and fiddling with her fingernails, watching me. I felt a stab of pain, pity, and compassion, and hated myself. She said:

"What is it?"

"You know what it is."

She shook her head. "What's happened? Why are you being like this?"

I walked to the hotel phone and ordered coffee for two and a full American breakfast.

She had taken a handkerchief from her purse and was wiping her eyes. They were swollen and her nose was pink, like she had a bad cold. It didn't detract from her looks. It made her look vulnerable and you wanted to look after her and keep her safe. I told her, "Otropoco is dead."

She nodded. "I know, Les told me."

I said, savagely, "Is that why you're crying? Because he's dead?"

She frowned and stared at me like I was crazy. "*What?*"

"What? You're shocked? You're scandalized?" My voice was rising. "Why don't you go ahead and explain it to me, Maria? What was your *relationship* with Otropoco?"

"Are you out of your *mind?*"

"*Maybe!*" I shouted and glared at her. "*Maybe I am!*" I took a step toward her and pointed. "Because it seems to me that what I am seeing and what I am hearing *makes no damned sense at all! So maybe I am! Maybe I'm out of my fucking mind!*"

She took a deep breath and closed her eyes. She spoke slowly, like she was laying down one word after another. "I-had-no-relationship-whatever-with-Mr. Otropoco." She opened her eyes. I stared at her. My belly was on fire and my heart was pounding. She shook her head, her eyes narrowed. "Where did you get such a *stupid* idea?"

I shook my head and my mouth was foul with bitterness. "I

don't know why you did it, Maria. God knows it makes no sense to me. But the fact is you did it."

"Did *what?*"

"I can even make sense of you betraying me and selling me down the line—"

"Harry, *stop!*"

"But your father, your family, what they would do to you if they knew that you were in *bed* with the Gulf Cartel!"

"What are you talking about? Harry, for God's sake stop it!" She took a step toward me, her arms reaching. "I am not in bed with the Gulf. This is crazy! It's like a nightmare. Last time I saw you… I thought…" She trailed off.

There was a knock at the door. I went and opened it and a waiter wheeled in a trolley with coffee and breakfast. I gave him ten bucks and he left.

The anger and the madness seemed suddenly to drain from the room. In silence I poured two cups and gave one to her. She sat in the armchair by the open balcony watching me. She seemed to examine my face. She looked real sad and her cheeks were still damp. Then she shifted her gaze a moment to the cup I was holding before she took it.

"Harry," she said. "You're talking and talking, like you're crazy, but you're not listening. This is what happens to men who live in that world of killing. You're accusing me of this awful thing, but you're not showing me any evidence, you're not telling me why you believe it, and you are not allowing me to defend myself. I am *telling* you, I have no connection or relationship with the Gulf Cartel, and I certainly had no relationship with Mr. Otropoco. You *know* that! You said yourself it was not possible." She gestured at me with her open hand. "I thought we…" Her bottom lip curled in and her eyes flooded with tears again. "I'm sorry," she said, "I thought we had something. I thought we trusted each other." She appealed to me, shaking her head. "I think all this stuff you have been doing is making you crazy."

I stood on the balcony looking down at her, aware that some

part of my mind was longing to believe her, praying for her to prove me wrong. Maybe she was right after all. Maybe I was driving myself crazy. I said:

"Two people knew that I was going to Escondido. Les and me. I did it deliberately, as a test, to see if he was giving information to Otropoco. I stayed at a motel and waited, and by the afternoon Otropoco's men knew I was there and showed up, posing as Feds. At first I thought Les had sold me out. But the more I thought about it, the less sense it made. And the less sense it made, the more obvious it became that you were the only other person who could know. You were the leak."

"That's not true."

"And last night I asked Les if he had told you I was going to Escondido. He told me he had. So that means three people knew. Him, me—and you. You are the only person who could have told Otropoco."

She was looking down at her cup, crying quietly. She said simply, "I didn't," and looked up at me. "I wouldn't. What possible reason would I have?"

"I wish you would tell me."

"There is no reason, Harry. You said yourself, my father is Sinaloa. If I helped the Gulf Cartel they would kill me. They might even kill him. Much worse than that. They would torture him in ways you cannot imagine. They are monsters, Harry. They are not human. I would have to be crazy to work for the Gulf." She shook her head, tears spilling from her eyes again. "Please, Harry. You have suffered so much, losing your friends, everything you told me, you are afraid, you suspect everybody. But I would not betray you, Harry..."

"How did they know I was in Escondido?"

"*I don't know!*" She stared at me in silence. "Maybe they followed you? They are rich, they have lots of resources, the latest technology. Maybe they bugged your car, or used the GPS on your telephone. Sometimes they use five men to follow one car!"

"How do you know?"

Her face flushed red with anger. "Because I grew up in Sinaloa! Because my father was a hit man for Sinaloa. I know *all* about their methods. Sinaloa, Gulf, Zeta, they are all the same! I want *nothing* to do with *any* of them!"

A bug in my cell was out of the question. A bug in the rental car... I went cold with a sudden wave of shame. That was feasible —just. Using my GPS, either my phone or the car, that was feasible. Did it make more sense than Maria selling me out to the Gulf?

I went and sat opposite her. I couldn't find any resentment in her eyes, or anger against me. She said:

"Harry, this is what they do to you. They suck you in to their darkness. First they destroy your family, then, slowly, a little piece at a time, they destroy your humanity. All the time you think you are doing what you *have* to do to fight them and resist them, that you are not one of them, that you are doing it because they are threatening you, blackmailing you, threatening your family. But in the end you are doing it because you have become the same as them. I have seen it so many times."

"Your father."

"And my brothers, cousins, friends. And now you." She touched my face with her fingers. "I could ask you, how could you do this to me? But I know, they are sucking out your soul."

My mind went back to an old Zen saying I had been taught when I was young, by my first Jeet Kune Do teacher. I heard my voice like it was somebody else's: "Do not look into your enemy's eyes, lest you become your enemy. By that reckoning, I am as much a monster as Otropoco."

A tear spilled from her eye, carrying my reflection down her cheek. "Stop," she said, "Harry, please stop. That doesn't make any sense and you know it." She shook her head again. "Your friends' deaths, they were killed by a kid who was crazy. You said yourself, he was out of his mind from too much weed and coke and then peyote."

"I looked into his eyes," I said, staring at the floor. "He was so scared. He was just a kid." I looked up at her. "All he needed was a father and a mother who cared enough to put him straight. And I put a knife in his heart."

"He killed your friend's daughter, he was pushing drugs to schoolkids. Any father would have done the same. Don't lose it now, Harry. You went crazy. Who wouldn't? You did some crazy things, but you killed some very bad people. Who knows?" She reached for my hands. "Maybe you *saved* some lives. But now it's over. Now it's time to look for peace, and to heal."

We sat in silence for a long while. Gradually her fingers laced in with mine and I had to either detach or put down my glass. I put down my glass and stroked her face with my fingers.

"What happened to your mother, Maria?"

She became very still. "She's dead. She was killed by the Gulf Cartel."

"What about brothers and sisters?"

"Dead. They killed them all. It's just me and my dad now."

"Like Ash and Sonia. But Sinaloa take care of you."

"They take care of my dad. I told him, I told them. I don't want nothing to do with them."

"He's retired—or semi-retired, right?"

"Yes. Things got very hot for him—for us—in Mexico. There was a raid on our house."

"Cops?"

"No, Gulf and Zeta, they worked together back then. They killed my brothers, my mother and my sisters. My dad escaped with me and a couple of his men. They were fighting over the routes through Texas. So they killed women and children, each side competing to prove they had less humanity than the other."

"So your dad asked to be retired here."

"He had become a target for the Gulf Cartel. So they gave him the restaurant. He has some boys who protect him. Sometimes he helps with some papers, or some information, some mediation with clients." She sighed. "Once you have been touched, you can never escape completely."

"I'm sorry."

She took my hands in hers again. "Otropoco is dead."

I nodded. "Yes."

"That will not destroy the cartel, but it will be much weaker." I drew breath but she kept on talking. "You killed him and his top men. I know how these things work. Their power depends very much on personality, on how crazy, ambitious and ruthless you are. Violence is like a religion for them. And with him and his top men dead, they will begin to collapse. What you have done is very important, you have probably saved a lot of kids, cleaned out a lot of trash. Now you can rest, heal, look for peace."

"Yes."

She squeezed my hands. Her lip curled in again and her eyes flooded with tears.

"Will you let me help you, Harry, please? Please let me help you."

I nodded, looked away at the wall, trying to steady my own breathing. "I'd like that," I said quietly. "I'd like that, Maria."

A while later she waited for me while I showered and dressed. My face was a mess, but once I had shaved and put on fresh clothes I looked almost human. Downstairs at reception I settled my bill and arranged for my car to be collected by the rental company. Then Maria drove me to the office. She parked in the garage, we went up together, and I went in to see Les.

As I closed the door he stood, came round the desk and shook my hand.

"You look a little less terrifying than you did this morning."

"Thanks, I think."

I sat and he handed me a stack of files about six inches thick. "These are the originals. Obviously I haven't had a chance to study them, but what I have seen so far looks pretty incriminating. If the FBI and the DEA got their hands on this, a lot of people—both sides of the border—would go away for a long time."

"Assuming they are still alive."

He nodded. "But I stress, not just in Mexico, Harry. I am going to get a team to go through them with a fine-toothed comb, and then I'll send you a full report so you can decide what action to take."

"That's good, thanks."

"Second, your *new* accounts." He didn't make inverted commas with his fingers, but he implied them with his voice. "It's going to take some looking into, because there is regular money coming in and some money going out. I have stopped the outgoings and I have someone looking into where the credits are coming from. But Harry, on the face of it, you have become a very, very rich man."

"How rich?"

"I can't say exactly yet, but you're looking at nine digits."

I felt an odd stillness. I didn't feel joy, jubilation, excitement—not even sadness. Just a very strange stillness.

"OK, look into setting up the foundation for me, will you? You'll let me know when you have more details."

"Yeah. I'll be meeting with your accountant tomorrow. Will you still be here?"

"No, I'll drive over in a couple of weeks. We can meet up then."

He'd been nodding quietly to himself since I'd failed to react to having nine digits in my bank accounts. Now he said, "You OK? You coping?"

"Just about. I think I need to get home."

"You guys manage to talk?"

"Some."

"Everything OK?"

I gave my head a small, sideways twitch. "Yeah, maybe." I pointed at the files. "You didn't tell her about these?"

"No."

"OK." I sighed. "I think I left my truck in San Francisco."

"We can have it collected. You can book a private jet now if you want. I'll have you driven to the airport."

"Nah, I think I'll drop in on some secondhand car lot, buy myself an old Jeep, or a RAM."

"Feel like getting your feet back on the ground, huh?"

"Something like that."

"You going to be OK when you get there? Have you got someone...?"

I nodded. "Yeah, I got a couple of people."

I stood, grabbed my bundle of files, stuffed them in my rucksack, and reached out for his hand.

"I'll be seeing you, Les. Hang loose."

TWENTY-SEVEN

I found a place on Western Avenue that sold me a twenty-year-old Ford F-150. I passed by Les's office to pick up my rucksack and my cases from Maria's trunk, and after a brief farewell I hit the road.

It was six hundred and fifty miles, through the tail end of Nevada and all of Utah, that should have taken less than ten hours. But I took it easy, allowing the movement, the passing desert and the vast skies to soothe my mind. I didn't think. I didn't plan. I had no idea what I was going to do when I got back to Pinedale, much less New York. In fact, I didn't even know that I didn't know. I was just in the truck, with the world rolling by.

Dusk began to close in as I crossed the border from Utah into Wyoming, just west of Evanston, and as I climbed north for a couple of hours into the night I began to smile. At Fontenelle, on the US-189, I started following the Green River, and on the bridge I stopped and got out to look up at the enormous, icy sky with more glittering stars than any city dweller has ever imagined possible. I wept quietly and laughed out loud at the beauty of it, and leaned against the truck, wiping my eyes at seeing a billion shards of ice dancing in the heavens.

Eventually I climbed back in behind the wheel and continued

my journey north, with the windows down and the cold night air battering my face. At Big Piney I knew I was home, and I felt a strange excitement as I turned right for Pinedale.

I rolled into town, crossed the river and, without really knowing why, I pulled up outside Stockman's. I glanced at my watch and saw it was nine PM, so I swung down, went inside and ordered myself a large Bushmills, a beer and steak. When I was sitting at my table in the corner I pulled out my cell and called Seth.

It rang once and his voice came on. It was good to hear and it made me smile.

"Son of a bitch." He said it slow and quiet, not like he was surprised at all. "I didn't think I was ever going to hear from you again. Where the hell are you?"

"I'm at Stockman's having a bite to eat. You want a beer?"

A moment's silence, then, "Yeah, I could use a beer. You want me to come alone?"

"Yeah, we can take it one thing at a time."

"Give me five minutes."

I hung up and signaled the barman two more beers. As he was pulling the second one the door opened and he looked up to say, "Evenin', Sheriff."

Seth raised a hand to him and came over to pull out a chair at my table. He didn't sit. He stood leaning on the chair and watching me.

"You look like hell."

"Thanks."

"I'm being nice. I could say you look like shit and I wouldn't be lying."

"Why don't you sit down before you start speaking your mind."

He sat down, the barman brought over the beers and returned to the bar. Seth nodded at the steak.

"You're eating that like you need it. What the hell they do to you in San Francisco, hold you down and hit you with their handbags?"

His own humor was too much for him and he sat and wept with laughter for a couple of minutes while I ate in silence. Eventually I said, "I wasn't in San Francisco."

"Y'don't say. Where were you, then?"

"Here and there. I got something for you."

He raised an eyebrow. "Mighty kind of you. What is it?"

"Well," I said with my mouth full. "Just for argument's sake, let's imagine it's enough documents and hard forensic evidence to put away half of the Gulf Cartel, plus a bunch of politicos and judges this side of the border who have been playing house with them."

"Well, that would be nice, but I'm thinking it would be more exiting for them boys down in Texas or Miami."

I shrugged. "OK, but you still get brownie points for handing it over to the Feds, right?"

"Sure, hypothetically."

"So, if I did you that favor, how excited would the DA be?"

"Well, like I say, Harry. It would be more exciting for the DA in Texas or in Florida."

"OK, so suppose this cache of evidence showed that there were plans to distribute coke and heroin up into the Midwest, targeting high schools and the Wind River Reservation?"

"Why didn't you say so from the start?"

"So, in that hypothetical situation, do you think the DA could be persuaded to offer me, in exchange, immunity from prosecution?"

"Prosecution for what, Harry?"

I laid down my knife and fork on the empty plate, drained my beer and held up my thumb.

"One, the murder of Slick Connell. I am not saying I had anything at all to do with his killing, Seth. So don't go getting your panties in a twist. All I am saying is that, if I am going to try to rebuild my life, I don't want to have that hanging over me for the next forty years."

"I think maybe we could swing that, Harry. But what the hell is this 'One' business. How many damned things do you expect to be prosecuted for?"

I held up my index along with my thumb.

"Two, any other crime, up to and including murder, that I might have knowingly or unwittingly committed in acquiring that evidence."

"Holy shit, Harry!"

"Hear me out, Seth. Nobody knows about this except you, me and my lawyer. I have a stack of files six inches high which I took from the Gulf Cartel's top man in California. I took them from his office along with his laptop. My lawyer has looked them over and he figures there is enough to put a lot of very senior people away for a long time, on both sides of the border. It might not finish the Gulf Cartel, but it could seriously damage it—and give the DEA and the Bureau a lot of very useful information. And nobody except you, me and my lawyer knows I had anything to do with it. All I want is the assurance that if I hand this over, I am not going to spend the rest of my life looking over my shoulder in case some woke crusader decides to go after me."

He was quiet for a long time, turning his beer this way and that. "Nobody but you, your lawyer and me. Are you sure 'bout that?"

I nodded. "Everybody else is dead."

He raised a hand. "I don't need to know that." Then he frowned and made a very worried face. "Is this for real? You know if you don't come through, that immunity won't be worth shit."

"I know that, Seth. I have worked with the Feds, remember? It's good. It's as good as it sounds. Hell, I took all his private papers, pen drives and his laptop from his office, Seth. How much is that worth?"

He sighed heavily. "I can't promise you anything, Harry, 'cept that I'll give it my best shot. If I was a betting man, I'd say you had a pretty good chance of pulling it off. The fact that nobody knows about it helps. There won't be no scandal, the press ain't going to be asking questions, all of that is going to work in your favor. What have they got to lose?" He paused a moment and frowned. "My only worry is, can they prosecute you? I mean to say, these crimes you might, hypotetically have committed, can they connect them to you? Because they might just decide to prosecute you instead."

I shook my head. "I doubt anyone could ever connect me with any of this. I just don't want it hanging over me, Seth. All I want is to make a new start."

"OK, leave it with me. Where've you got this stuff?"

"I never said I had, but if I had, don't you think my lawyer would have it?"

He snorted something like a laugh. "Most probably. I guess so." He leaned back in his chair and stretched out his legs, and took a hold of his beer. "So," he said, "speaking of making a fresh start. What *plans* have you got?"

"Plans? Nary a one, until I know whether the Feds and the DA are going to buy my proposal."

"And after that? You going back to New York?"

I thought about it. I had not even called the Brigadier. I thought about the colonel, my large empty house in Manhattan. "I don't know," I said. "I am very tired. Driving up here I thought maybe I could buy Ash's ranch. I might put some money into it, buy some horses."

"That's a nice idea. But that's it? Nothing else?"

I shrugged. "It's too soon to be thinking about that kind of stuff, Seth."

"Yeah." He nodded. "I guess you're right. Trouble is, Harry. I've known you just a couple of weeks, and already I know it's always going to be too soon for you. You're still hurtin' over whatever it was happened to you years back, and you can't let go. You can tell me to go mind my own damned business, but I am just wondering if the right time is ever gonna come for you. Harry, you're alone.

And I have to be honest with you, I don't like the idea of you up in that house, alone, day after day. A man needs company."

"I told you I might buy some horses. Maybe I'll get a cat, too, and call it Seth."

"That ain't funny. God dammit, Harry, a man needs a *woman* in his life. It's natural! It ain't good to be alone like that all the time."

"Well, let's take it one step at a time. For now..."

"She told me about your date."

I stopped dead. "What?"

"She's known me for years. Hell, I'm like an uncle to her. I went to see her and she told me about your date, and you sayin' you'd call."

"I guess we are talking about Dr. Erickson."

"Don't play dumb, Harry. You know that's what I'm talking about. She was real hurt that you stopped calling. Professionally, and as a woman."

I sighed. "I had other things on my mind."

"I can see that, and I can understand it. But what I am telling you is it's about time you stopped having other things on your mind. This is a good town, these are good people, and the Doc likes you."

"I don't know, Seth. I need to think things through. I have a whole life in New York... Either way, I don't see what this has to do with Doc Erickson, but—"

He laughed and interrupted me. "You know damned well *exactly* what this has to do with Doc Erickson." He drained his beer and set the empty glass on the table. "Well, you look about as tired as I have ever seen a man. I'm going to let you get on home and I'll drop by tomorrow so you can show me all that stuff." He stood and as he fitted his hat to his head he said, "Maybe you should drop by the clinic on the way home, have them bruises looked at."

"Yeah," I laughed, "and we can gossip about it over coffee in the morning." I reached down and grabbed my rucksack from the floor and dropped it on the table. "Here's some bedtime reading. It's a sample. You get the rest, and the laptop, when they agree to the deal."

He nodded, took it and left.

I sat a while thinking about what he'd said, thinking also that it was good to be home. Then I paid my check and stepped out into the cold night air. I stood a moment biting my lip and staring at my new old Ford, then I climbed behind the wheel and rolled slowly down Pine Street as far as the intersection at Ridley's. There I slowed to a halt. There was no traffic, and the light from the streetlamps made the road, the mall and the low buildings around look like a strange, dead stage set.

Right would take me down to the Fayette Pole Creek Road, and "home" to Ash Cooper's place. I could see it in my mind: dark, cold and very empty. Left would take me to the clinic. At this time there would be the emergency staff only. There was a fifty-fifty chance Doc Erickson—Claire—would be there.

I told myself I should at least drop in and say hi. I spun the wheel, turned left and covered the half mile at a steady pace. A minute later I pulled up in the parking lot and pushed through the glass doors into the waiting room-cum-reception.

It was bright, very quiet and empty, with rows of blue chairs bolted to the floor, facing a row of doors. On the right there was a reception area, and behind the desk there was a guy in a white coat looking at a clipboard. He looked up as I came in and pointed to the blue mask he had over his mouth and nose. I figured he was in his thirties. He had blond, floppy hair and blue eyes, and probably played quarterback at college.

I shook my head. "I haven't got one. I'm looking for Doctor Erickson."

He opened a drawer, pulled out a pack of masks and slid one across the counter.

"You have to wear a face mask at all times in a medical establishment. I am Doctor Chad Baker. Is there something I can help you with?"

He was looking at the bruises on my face. Something about his tone needled me. I picked up the mask but I didn't put it on.

"Yeah, you could tell Claire that Harry is here."

He stared at me a moment. "You are Harry Bauer?"

"Yeah. Can you tell her I'm here, please?"

"She's gone home, Mr. Bauer. I suggest you call her after ten tomorrow morning."

"After ten..."

"She comes in at nine thirty, and for the first half hour she is very busy."

I nodded for a bit, looking down at my boots.

"Thanks for the advice, Chad."

I tossed his face mask on the counter and walked back out into the cold parking lot with a strange anger in my belly. I climbed behind the wheel of my truck and rolled slowly back toward the intersection at Ridley's. There I stopped again. Left would take me home to the cold, dark, empty house. Right would take me to Doc Erickson's house. I had picked up clearly that I was no longer welcome, that the handsome, floppy-haired Doctor Baker was the new kid on the block and if I wanted anything, I should call. After ten. That's what you get if you don't stay in touch.

"Go home, Harry," I told myself, and spun the wheel right. I turned into North Bridger Avenue and took the first left onto Magnolia Street. After four blocks, no more than five hundred yards, I pulled up outside her house and saw a glimmer of light through the drapes. I killed the engine and sat for thirty seconds unable to move. Finally I took a deep breath, climbed down from the cab and followed the stone path across her lawn to the front door. As I put my finger on the bell I wondered what time it was. It must be ten, maybe later. It was too late. Maybe Doctor Chad Baker was right, and I should call in the morning, after ten.

I pressed the button and heard the bell chime inside.

After a moment the door opened and she was standing there, in jeans and a Snoopy sweatshirt, with no makeup on and her hair in a ponytail, staring at me. First her eyes widened in astonishment, then she frowned, showing concern for the bruises, then she remembered she should be mad because I hadn't called, and then it all kind of fused into confusion and she said, "Harry!"

"I'm sorry, I know it's late. I went to the clinic and Doctor Baker told me to telephone tomorrow, after ten." I shrugged. "I thought I'd take a chance. I figure I owe you an apology, and I didn't think it could wait that long. So I dropped by."

She smiled. It was a tired, serious smile. "I'm glad you did."

"I'm glad you're glad. Floppy Baker made me feel I was not very welcome."

She suppressed a smile. "What happened to your face?"

"I used it to bruise a few knuckles. Listen, I'm sorry I didn't call. It was complicated. But I was wondering..."

She stepped back and pulled the door open. "You'd better come in and wonder inside."

I hesitated, smiled and stepped over the threshold. When I was in, she closed the door and looked up at me. "And, Harry, you are always welcome."

TWENTY-EIGHT

Next morning, even though she insisted it was just a five-minute walk, I insisted on driving her to work and giving her a long, lingering kiss right outside the plate-glass doors. When I was done and I had given it the final touches, she gave me a wise smile with hooded eyes and said, "I think you made your point."

I returned the smile. "I have no idea what you're talking about."

"I'll come and check on you after work."

I watched her walk inside and, finally, took the road home. I had done everything I could to put it off, to try and fill the void, but as I approached the gate beside the creek, the darkness began to close in again.

I stopped, got out of the truck and pushed the gate open, then sat on the grass beside the creek looking at the old house, at the sweep of rolling hills and the peaks of the Wind River Mountains beyond. I sat there for a long time, wondering what it was about Ash Cooper and his daughter, Sonia, that had triggered this reaction in me. What had made it so personal? Why, every time I thought of them, lying cold in the morgue, or him clinging to her dead body under the water as he wept and drowned, why did I remember that small girl in Al-Landy, weeping in fear and desolation?

Because I had not been able to help her, and I had not been able to help them either. It was that simple. They had been in fear and pain and distress, and that was how they had died. They had asked for help, as the child in Al-Landy had begged for help with her eyes, and I had failed them.

By the time I got back in the truck and rolled up to the house it was noon. I unlocked the door and pushed in, and felt an overwhelming desire to crash on the sofa and open a bottle of beer. But I fought it and instead I went around the house opening all the windows, allowing in the light and the cool air. At twelve thirty my cell rang.

"Seth, how's it hanging?"

I could hear he was driving. He said, "I went by your house this morning. You weren't there."

"Yeah. Mind your own business."

"Tell me this, at least. Should I be happy?"

"If it's a boy we'll call him Seth."

He laughed out loud. "Listen, I'm on my way to Cheyenne to talk to the Feds. That was some pretty interesting bedtime reading. If there is more like this, plus his laptop, I can't see them saying no. I'll call you tonight, or tomorrow morning."

"Call me in the morning, Seth. Tonight I am going to be busy."

"Doing what?"

"Cooking dinner for Doc Erickson."

"I am very glad to hear that. She is a damned fine woman. I'll call you in the morning. Not too early."

The line went dead and I sat for a while on the wooden steps of my porch, not thinking much, just remembering, replaying movies in my head, asking myself what would have happened if the Brigadier had sent somebody else.

That made me pull out my cell and call him.

"Harry. Any news?"

"Otropoco is dead. The colonel would have been proud."

"Splendid. Are you all right?

I briefed him on everything. Then told him, "I need a break. I'm not sure if I can carry on. I'm tired, sir."

"We'd be sorry to see you go, Harry."

"Yeah, I'm not sure why I'm doing it anymore, sir. I don't know if I am becoming one of them."

"Take some time, Harry. You're a rich man now. You have been for some time. But stay in touch. Don't go off the radar."

I hung up and after a while I climbed in my new old truck and drove out along the Fayette Pole Creek Road, skirting Half Moon Mountain on the west side down to Half Moon Lake, and after that it was just a couple of miles to where Sonia and the kids had sat looking for UFOs, and taking peyote.

By the time I stood over the cold fire where they had sat, the light in the air had acquired a copper tint, and the shadows of the trees were growing long, stretched out across the grass. I sat on a rock beside the fire. It was close to where I had sat with Slick when I had killed him. The ground in front of me was flat for a way, then dipped sharply toward the woods and the lake. The dark water was visible from where I sat. That was where they said they had seen the green lights suspended.

In that peaceful, quiet space in time, I spoke to her, to the nameless child in Al-Landy. I knew it wasn't possible. I knew she was dead, had been destroyed and did not exist anymore, but somehow that didn't matter. She was there, for me, and I spoke to her.

I apologized for having failed her, for having allowed that terrible thing to happen to her and her parents, and I apologized for not having brought peace to her memory. I told her I wasn't sure what was going to happen in the future, but I was going to try and find some peace for me, and for her.

Dead people don't talk. Dead people don't really exist anymore, except as a part of us. But, even so, I felt that she forgave me, or I knew that in her heart she would not have held me to blame. The guilt was mine, and not hers to give or take away.

The sound of birdsong had changed. I wasn't sure exactly when. But the copper had gone from the light, the shadows had grown denser and the air had grown cooler. And the birds had started chattering, like they were preparing for bed and closing up shop for the night. It occurred to me that I had to get back for the Doc, and as I thought that I heard the hum of an engine. It crunched to a halt a distance away. Kids, perhaps, coming to smoke weed and look for UFOs in the dying light.

I thought about getting to my feet, but managed only a deep sigh. I heard a single pair of boots approaching from behind. It wasn't Seth because he was on his way to Cheyenne, if he hadn't arrived already. And the Doc was probably still at work.

A shadow fell across the cold circle of stones where the fire had been, back when the kids were alive. I turned and saw Maria, smiling from behind her eyes. She was wearing jeans, a sweatshirt and a leather jacket. It seemed uncharacteristic. I didn't know what to say, so I just frowned.

"I followed you," she said. "I thought about it. Harry, we can't just leave things as we did." She looked down at the cinders and the stones. Her left foot was on the stain left by Slick's blood. She looked down at the canopy of the trees, and at the lake. The wind trailed her hair across her face and she fingered it away.

"Is this where it happened?"

I nodded. "How did you know I was here?"

"The GPS on your phone."

"You followed me all this way?"

"I stopped for a few hours in Utah."

She sat on a rock beside me and leaned against me for a moment. I asked her, "Is it your mother?"

She nodded. "And my sister."

"How old were you?"

"Just twelve years old. I don't remember much. They burst into the house in trucks. They murdered everyone, even the old ladies that cooked and cleaned for us. Papa was fighting with them. We had uncles and cousins fighting with them too. Otropoco was there. He was younger then, of course. He came up to me, in the middle of all the screaming and shooting, and he hunkered down. I remember thinking that the devil had very beautiful eyes. He put his two fingers under my chin and made me look into his face.

"I was crying, but he smiled. 'Do you think I am cruel?' He asked me that, smiling. I just told him I was scared. Then he showed me his right hand, and it was covered in blood. 'I want you to remember,' he said, and he called me by my name. 'I want you to remember, Maria, that I am the cruelest man in the world. *No tengo alma.*' That means, I have no soul. 'This blood,' he told me, 'is from your grandmother's heart, which I have ripped out with my own hand. Do you understand?' I was crying too much to answer, but he told me he was taking my mother, and my sister Olga Lucia, and that if I did not want him to be cruel to them, I must do everything he said. He told me he would contact me in a few years, and when he did that, from that moment on, I would belong to him."

I nodded. "When we last talked, and you were telling me about your family, I wondered if this was what you were trying to tell me."

"I want you to know, I want you to remember always, whatever happens, that I love you, and I always will. I am sorry that I betrayed you."

I looked at her beautiful face. It was peaceful. I shook my head. "Don't talk like that, Maria."

"I'm tired. I don't even know if they are still alive. I don't know if he killed them that night. In the beginning I received some recorded messages from them. They sounded afraid, broken. He said they were recent, but I had no way of knowing. So I had to betray my father, my family, everybody, in case. In case my mother was alive, in case Olga was alive, knowing that I could never trust what he was telling me, but knowing also that I could never take that step of saying, 'I believe they are already dead.' He knew that too. He knew I could never do that."

I nodded. "I understand that, Maria."

"Do you? Do you really?"

"You know I do."

"Can you forgive me, Harry, for what I did?"

I thought of all the people I had betrayed because I had no choice, and smiled. "There is nothing to forgive."

She reached in the pocket of her leather jacket and brought out a snub-nosed .38 Police Special.

"Otropoco is not dead, Harry."

"I saw his boat explode. He could not possibly have survived."

"Did you see his body? Did you feel his pulse?"

"No."

"Did you drive a stake through his heart, or cut off his head?"

"Maria, stop. He's dead."

"He called me."

"No," I shook my head, "that's not—"

"He called me. His voice is imprinted in my brain. It was him. He called me and he told me that if I found you and killed you, I would be reunited with my mother and my sister, and we would be free forever of the cartel."

I looked down at the weapon, then up into her eyes. "Do you believe him?"

She shook her head. "No, I am sure they have both been dead for many years. And I am tired of hoping, tired of forcing myself to believe, tired of suffering day after day, night after night, wondering what happened to them."

"Maria, I am so sorry..."

"I just wanted to tell you. It was important that I told you, that I put it into words, so that you knew. I am sorry, and I love you. I will always love you."

She did it quickly, without pause or hesitation. She bit hard on the barrel and pulled the trigger. The powder and the gasses scorched her beautiful mouth and her cheeks. Her head whiplashed and the slug exited the back of her neck, shattering her vertebrae and bringing death ebbing in instantly.

I was very, very cold inside. I knelt down next to where she had fallen, with her eyes squeezed shut. I took hold of her left hand in both of mine and made her a promise.

"I will find your mother and your sister, Maria. And whether they are dead or alive, I will tell them what you did for them." I faltered a moment. "And I will find Otropoco, and I will make him pay. I promise you, I will make him pay."

Then I pulled my cell from my pocket and called the Brigadier.

"Sir," I said, "I need your help..."

DON'T MISS ANYTHING!

If you want to stay up to date on all new releases in this series, with this author, or with any of our new deals, you can do so by joining our newsletters below.

In addition, you will immediately gain access to our entire *Right House VIP Library,* which includes many riveting Mystery and Thriller novels for your enjoyment!

righthouse.com/email

(Easy to unsubscribe. No spam. Ever.)

ALSO BY BLAKE BANNER

Up to date books can be found at:
www.righthouse.com/blake-banner

ROGUE THRILLERS
Gates of Hell (Book 1)
Hell's Fury (Book 2)

ALEX MASON THRILLERS
Odin (Book 1)
Ice Cold Spy (Book 2)
Mason's Law (Book 3)
Assets and Liabilities (Book 4)
Russian Roulette (Book 5)
Executive Order (Book 6)
Dead Man Talking (Book 7)
All The King's Men (Book 8)
Flashpoint (Book 9)
Brotherhood of the Goat (Book 10)
Dead Hot (Book 11)
Blood on Megiddo (Book 12)
Son of Hell (Book 13)

HARRY BAUER THRILLER SERIES
Dead of Night (Book 1)
Dying Breath (Book 2)
The Einstaat Brief (Book 3)
Quantum Kill (Book 4)
Immortal Hate (Book 5)
The Silent Blade (Book 6)
LA: Wild Justice (Book 7)

A Christmas Killing (Book 21)
Mommy's Little Killer (Book 22)
Bleed Out (Book 23)
Dead and Buried (Book 24)
In Hot Blood (Book 25)
Fallen Angels (Book 26)
Knife Edge (Book 27)
Along Came A Spider (Book 28)
Cold Blood (Book 29)
Curtain Call (Book 30)

THE OMEGA SERIES
Dawn of the Hunter (Book 1)
Double Edged Blade (Book 2)
The Storm (Book 3)
The Hand of War (Book 4)
A Harvest of Blood (Book 5)
To Rule in Hell (Book 6)
Kill: One (Book 7)
Powder Burn (Book 8)
Kill: Two (Book 9)
Unleashed (Book 10)
The Omicron Kill (Book 11)
9mm Justice (Book 12)
Kill: Four (Book 13)
Death In Freedom (Book 14)
Endgame (Book 15)

ABOUT US

Right House is an independent publisher created by authors for readers. We specialize in Action, Thriller, Mystery, and Crime novels.

If you enjoyed this novel, then there is a good chance you will like what else we have to offer! Please stay up to date by using any of the links below.

Join our mailing lists to stay up to date -->
righthouse.com/email
Visit our website --> righthouse.com
Contact us --> contact@righthouse.com

 facebook.com/righthousebooks

 x.com/righthousebooks

 instagram.com/righthousebooks

EXCLUSIVE SNEAK PEAK OF...

THE UNAVENGED

PROLOGUE

They came with the cold, gray dawn. They came from the north on the Shali road, and from the east on the road from Avtury: two long columns moving slow and lazy through the dim light toward the town of Novye-Yurt.

As they arrived they slowed and fanned out with care and precision. The armored cars took up positions on the main streets, the Jeeps and Land Rovers in the smaller side streets. In the remaining alleyways, footpaths and side roads, foot soldiers took up their positions.

The townspeople peered at them from their windows, from their shops and from the early-morning cafés where the farmers and workmen were having breakfast.

At eight AM, Timur Edilov, the mayor, Salambek Zaytseva, his secretary, and Zaur Bazurkaev, the chief of police, approached the armored car on Ulitsa Kadyrova, the main street of the town. Unlike the armored cars on the other streets, this one was flanked by a Land Rover and a Jeep. The three men were surprised to discover, as they approached the vehicles, that the colonel standing in front of the armored car with his arms crossed over his chest, and the soldiers surrounding him, were not Russians. They were Chechens like themselves. The surprise was replaced by a sick, hollow feeling of helplessness and dread when they realized that this was Colonel Abbas Magomadov, and these were soldiers from the 141st Special Motorized Regiment, otherwise known as the Kadyrovitsy, the private army of the Kadyrov family, used amongst other things to do the dirty work not even the Russians would touch.

Mayor Timur Edilov tried hard, and failed, to keep the tremor from his voice.

"Colonel Magomadov, what is the meaning of this blockade? Why are your men and your tanks blocking the entrance and exit to the town?"

Magomadov was tall, lean and fair for a Chechen. He had always liked to believe that he was from Cossack descent. He held a cigarette in the fingers of his right hand. He examined the burning tip for a moment, spat elaborately at his feet and squinted through the smoke at the mayor as he took a deep drag.

"We have information, Mayor Edilov, that you harbor separatist rebels in this town."

"No!" The mayor shook his head violently, with terror hot in his chest. "No, we have never harbored rebels. We are just old men! Women! Young children and their mothers! Please, we have no rebels here! Have mercy! Have pity!"

"Pity? Mercy?" He looked at the men around him and they started to laugh. "What are you saying, Mayor Edilov? Are you accusing the Kadarovitsy of being criminals? That sounds to me like the seditious talk of a rebel."

The mayor's face seemed to fold in on itself and he began to sob. Zaur Bazurkaev, the chief of police, stood beside his friend. They were cousins, they had been to school together, played and fished in the river together as children. He appealed to the colonel, "I am the chief of police, Colonel. I can vouch for the mayor, he is a good and loyal man, we have never had rebels in this town. We are all loyal, please, we are a harmless village. Just women and children and a few old men..."

The colonel smiled as he sucked the last of the smoke from his cigarette and dropped it on the road. There he crushed it with his boot.

"Are you telling me, Sergeant, that a Chechen woman cannot fire a gun?"

Chief Bazurkaev spread his hands. "The women in this village..." He trailed off, raising his shoulders. "They cook, they clean, they look after their husbands and their children."

The colonel turned then to the secretary and jerked his chin at him. "And you, Mr. Secretary Zaytseva, what do you say? I have information from reliable sources that you are harboring criminals, traitors and rebels in this town. Do you think my informant is a liar, like these two?" He pointed at the mayor and the police chief.

The secretary shook his head. "I am sure your informant is not a liar, Colonel."

"He is telling the truth, then!"

"But equally, sir, I promise you that we have no rebels here. We are a simple town, we work, we obey... I don't know how your informant got his information—"

"What are you trying to do, Mr. Secretary Zaytseva?"

The secretary shook his head, not understanding the question. "Trying to do, sir...?"

"Are you trying to confuse me? Do you think I am stupid?" The colonel stared at the secretary. The morning was still, cold and silent. The mayor, the police chief and the secretary stared back at the colonel. Somewhere distant, among the trees, a bird chattered. The secretary said quietly, "No..."

The colonel turned to his captain and gestured at the secretary with his open hand. "Here is the evidence we needed. He is trying to confuse and bewilder me. My informant is not lying, he says, but there are no rebels here. Yet, clearly, if my informant is not lying, then there are rebels here!"

Again the secretary shook his head. "No..."

It was a denial, but more than that it was a plea for mercy. But Colonel Abbas Magomadov was not there to dispense mercy. He was there to bring death. He pulled his MP-443 Grach from its holster and shot the secretary in the head. The man swayed and folded to the ground. The mayor and the police chief began to sob, holding their hands out as though their fragile palms could ward off bullets. The colonel shot the mayor first, through his palm and between the eyes, and the police chief last, in the back, as he turned to run.

He lay groaning, coughing and dribbling blood from his perforated lungs. The colonel stepped up to him, placed his foot on the man's back and pressed. He took aim at the back of his head and fired once.

And that was the beginning. He climbed up into his Land Rover, picked up his radio and as it crackled in his hand he said, "OK! Advance, let's find these rebels!"

The advance was not rapid, it moved deliberately, in stages, house by house. The boots ran, tramping on the hardtop. Fists and boots hammered on doors, and soon the screaming started, women and crying children. But the weeping and the begging did not elicit compassion. When you put men into uniforms, they leave their humanity in the changing rooms. The weeping and the begging elicited shouts, aggressive and bullying as the soldiers invaded one home after another, dragging the families out into the streets, herding them and pushing them, with their hands held high, toward the town square.

Then there was a shot. It was a single, heartless, pitiless, irreversible crack. It had a small echo which trailed among the facades of the houses. It was followed by a cold stillness. A moment of abject terror, a shared moment of awful realization among the soldiers and the people they were going to kill. A line had been crossed, and now there was no way back. Then the killing started.

It started with the soldiers opening up on the gathered crowd. It didn't last long, twenty or thirty seconds of rattling and crackling; a lot of screams soon replaced by quiet sobbing, and sporadic single shots.

A moment of silence followed as the soldiers looked down on

what they had done. It was broken by the bellowing voice of an officer, and the soldiers launched into a rampage, driven by some half-articulated sense that if they did not stop, if they sank deeper into the carnage and pitiless madness, somehow guilt and remorse would be crushed, smothered, drowned in blood. So that the terrified eyes of the children and the aged, and the twisted, heart-broken faces of the wailing mothers and fathers would cease to have meaning, cease to torture their minds and hearts.

Minds and hearts that in most cases had been those of school-children barely two or three years earlier.

They ran, swarming over the gates and walls, ever present in Chechen villages and towns, shooting out locks, kicking in doors and smashing windows, not bothering now to drag people out of their houses, but shooting them where they found them. Those who managed to flee from their houses were shot down in the roads by the armored cars.

Not all the females were killed. The younger ones, some as young as eleven and twelve, were raped or taken as sex slaves to be gifted to the commanders. By eleven o'clock that morning, Colonel Magomadov had accumulated six young girls to serve him.

The massacre did not end that day, nor did the pillaging. It continued for a week longer. The colonel set up a base in the town, effectively turning it into a concentration camp, and the inhumanity continued at a leisurely pace for the next six days. Public executions were preceded by public mass rapes and followed by sessions of public torture whose purported purpose was to obtain information about the whereabouts of the men of the town, but whose real purpose was to instil terror and bring the population of Chechnya as a whole into submission. There was no information, no answer those interrogated could have given, that would have changed their fate.

After a week the population of Novye-Yurt, which had stood at slightly less than ten thousand inhabitants, had been reduced to slightly less more than six hundred girls between the ages of eleven and twenty-two. Some would be given to commanders and officials, others they would sell into Europe, America and the Middle East, through Poland.

On the seventh day Colonel Magomadov ordered the retreat from the town. The columns left as they had come, with the cold, gray dawn, into the north along the Shali road, and into the east along the road to Avtury: two long columns moving slow and lazy through the dim light toward the next village reported to harbor anti-Russian rebels.

However, by the time his column had reached Agishty, just three and a half miles south of Novye-Yurt, Colonel Magomadov had called a halt. He instructed his second in command, Captain Vakha Umarov, to camp outside the town and leave the townsfolk in peace. He took a Jeep and drove back, retracing his steps from the town, but he did not stop when he got there. Instead, he continued on, climbing ever higher into the forests among the peaks of the Caucasus Mountains.

Much later his Jeep was found abandoned among the trees outside Agavi, just a few miles from the border with Georgia and the wilderness of the Tusheti National Park. There was no sign of the colonel. Nobody had seen him, there was no blood, no sign of a firefight, no sign of struggle. He had simply vanished without a trace.

There were those who knew him who said that he had been ambushed and killed by Chechen separatist rebels. Others said that the weight of the atrocities of the Kadarovitsy had become too much for him and he had become a hermit in a cave on the border. Still others said he had been abducted by aliens who had punished him for his cruelty by sending him to a galactic prison camp on Ganymede. A very few, a small handful, said he feared Russia could not guarantee him safety from prosecution by the International Court of Human Rights, and he had run and changed his identity, taking stolen loot with him, to the one place in the world he believed nobody would ever look for him.

That had been just after the turn of the millennium.

CHAPTER 1

I was in Bolinas Altas looking for Abe McGore because the brigadier and the colonel had identified him as Colonel Abbas Magomadov, who had led the massacre of three towns in Chechnya at the turn of the millennium, and then disappeared with twenty million bucks' worth of stolen art treasures and cash. Over the years various agencies had tried to track him down in Chile, Brazil, Mexico and Colombia, with not much success. Africa and the Indian Ocean had proved equally unfruitful, and finally the trail had gone cold. Until 2020, when an anonymous tip-off had placed him in Northern California.

Then a little known agency attached to the Five Eyes treaty, that went by various misleading names, had found a trail that went from Chechnya through Georgia to Turkey and then went cold. It went cold until a guy in the Passport Office in Ankara, who could arrange you a genuine Turkish passport for a fee, even if you weren't entitled to it, was persuaded to remember that in 2005 he had issued a special, green passport to a man who might have been Chechen. It had been issued in the very un-Turkish name of Abraham Major, as the man claimed to be naturalized Turkish of British origin.

That trail had eventually led the operative from the so-called

Office of the Democratic Intelligence Network, based in Arlington, Virginia, to New Zealand. From New Zealand he had moved on to Australia, and there his trail had gone cold again. Until the operative, who clearly knew how to do his homework, found Abraham Major's death certificate. The British-born naturalized Turk had, apparently, died while exploring the Australian outback. Most of him had been consumed by various inhabitants of the wilderness, but his right hand and one leg, and his rucksack, had been found intact. The rucksack contained his papers and ID, and that had apparently been enough to ID him.

But the operative, not one to be easily satisfied, had dug deeper, and a search through passports granted in the two months following the discovery of Abraham Major's body had thrown up one Abe McGore, who had requested an Australian passport and, shortly afterwards, a United States visa. This had in turn yielded a passport photograph, a request for a resident's permit and a work permit in California; and finally a Social Security Number.

A few final checks, including the use of facial recognition software, had made it incontrovertible. Abe McGore, the guy living at 17 Manzanilla Avenue in Bolinas Altas, overlooking the Bolinas Altas golf course and the Gulf of the Farallones, just twenty miles north of San Francisco as the crow flies was, beyond any kind of doubt, Abbas Magomadov.

He was apparently a man of private means who lived off the interest from foreign investments; probably trusts set up in British dependencies nurtured by the City of London. According to his file, part of his money he had invested in some kind of quasi-religious cult with a charitable status. Whether he had set it up himself or simply bought into it was not clear. Neither did it really matter. I wasn't there to write his biography. I was there to kill him.

Bolinas Altas was a leafy, residential area where people who could afford it came to retire and play golf, or families who could afford it came to protect their kids from the modern world they had conspired to create. From there they commuted to the hive for work every day, to help consolidate the world they wanted to protect their kids from. It was quiet. Every house had its plot of land with a pool and gardens, a high wall and a big gate. Each cell was almost identical to the next.

Manzanilla Avenue was situated high up, near the heart of Bolinas Altas Village, near Main Street and the Farmers' Market. From there it curled down in a big sweep, past the golf course, toward the coast and Palomarin Beach.

Magomadov's place was a two-story villa with a swimming pool. It was set among palm trees, and had a Spanish-style orange-tiled roof which was turning pink in the dying sun. There was an iron gate with a wooden name plate beside it that read "Eden." The gate was open and there was nothing telling me to beware of the dog. So I stepped through, closed the gate behind me and climbed the steps through the exotic garden to the front door.

It was a sultry evening. The heat hung humid in the still air, though the light was turning a grainy blue-gray, with a few pastel pink tinges only nature could get away with. I could make out the smell of barbequing meat from neighboring gardens, and some-where people were laughing. You could almost hear the tinkle of ice in their tall glasses, and see the warm glow spilling from their French windows onto their patios.

Only there was no light spilling from Magomadov's front door or windows, and the only sounds were the lapping of the water in his swimming pool and the high-pitched grinding of the *cicadas* on the warm air. I rang the bell and hammered on the door, but there was no reply. So I took a walk round back and explored his shrubs and flower beds, his patio and the French doors. Then I stood a moment staring into his pool, thinking about the fact that, like his gate, the French doors onto the patio were not quite closed. They had been left half an inch open. Whoever had left the gate open had pulled the French doors too, without closing them.

Finally I went, slid them opened and stepped inside. It was dark, silent and oppressively warm. I didn't put the lights on. I waited for my eyes to adjust and then had a look around. I was in a big dining-room-cum-sitting-room affair which extended into an open-plan kitchen. There was no one there and everything looked clean, tidy and well ordered. There were no family pictures and no photo albums.

Over on the right there was a staircase that ascended to the top floor. I climbed it. The stairs creaked, but the creaks got no response. No voices called to see who I was.

I got to the landing and stopped. It was darker upstairs and I had a prickling feeling in the back of my neck. There was a banister on my left overlooking the stairs, and on my right I could make out two doors, with a third right ahead of me. The two on my right were closed, but the one ahead of me was open.

Dark blue moonlight reflected off the ocean gave the room an eerie luminescence. I could see plate-glass doors that stood open, and the moonlight was making silhouettes out of a balustrade, a round table and a chair.

And an unsettling pile on the floor.

I walked quietly into the room and stood in the doorway. I could now see the moon setting over the Pacific far below. I looked at the dim stars in the turquoise sky, I looked at the swaying palms, and finally I forced myself to look down at the mess, the remains of the man lying in the pool of blood; blood which outrageously reflected the peaceful light of the moon.

He had been dismembered. His legs lay at grotesque angles to his body. His left arm lay with the hand pointing to his hip and the shoulder toward the balustrade. His right hand was by his feet and his head, on the table, sat grinning savagely out at the sparkling, silver path the moon had laid across the black depth of the ocean. His thin, sandy hair moved in the evening breeze.

I pulled my cell from my pocket, took a short video of the scene and then photographs of the dead man's face from several angles. I sent them to the brigadier with a short message:

"Looks like somebody got here before me. Is this our guy?"

Then I stepped back into the dark house and took my

pencil torch from my inside pocket. I played the beam around the room and found it was some kind of an office or study. There was a computer on the desk to my left, and there were low bookcases against all the walls. To my right there were a couple of filing cabinets, a small sofa and a lamp on a small, heavy, marble-topped table. Some other time I might have nosed around some more to find out what he was about. Maybe I should have done that, but with a dismembered body lying out on the balcony I didn't feel like hanging around all that much. All I wanted was some clue as to who had beat me to the punch.

I sat behind his desk and pulled open the drawers, and let the circle of torchlight rest on the contents. There was nothing there but paper and ink, a stapler and some boxes of staples. There was also a passport in the name of Abe McGore. I picked it up and opened it. The picture looked like the head on the table. The few stamps there were seemed to be entering and leaving Mexico. No surprises there. I stood up and crossed the room to the filing cabinets. They weren't locked so I was pretty sure what I was going to find—nothing much.

I was wrong. The drawers were full of files, and each file was about a person. A quick flick through showed that these people had practically nothing in common. They were of all ages, from young children to people in their eighties; and they were of extremely varied backgrounds: from builders and tradesmen to academics, businessmen and women and professionals. In fact the only thing I could find that they shared in common was that they all belonged to his cult, the United Church of Nergal.

I went down to the kitchen, found a couple of plastic refuse sacks, returned to the terrace and collected his right hand. I also took one of the files. I used a cloth to remove my prints from anything I had touched and made my way back down the stairs and out into the balmy evening. The pool was still lapping and you could still hear the laughter and the music from the nearby barbeque. A chorus of frogs had added their voices to the revelries, but managed somehow to make it all sound peaceful and still under the moon.

I made my way out to the street and climbed into my rental car. The slam of the door insulated me inside the cab and I called the brigadier. As usual he made it sound like I was calling about an invitation to a cocktail party.

"Harry, good to hear from you."

"You got my pictures and the video?"

"Indeed. Very interesting. Any ideas?"

"No, but I think we need to get somebody in there before the cops or the Feds find him."

"Really? Why's that?"

"Call it a hunch, but I found a couple of filing cabinets full of files. There must have been a couple of thousand at least, on members of that cult he was involved with, the Church of..."

"The United Church of Nergal—"

"That one. I couldn't put it into words right now, but I know those files, and the state his body was in, add up to something that ain't mom's apple pie. Aside from anything else, I'd like to know how it was done. There was a hell of a lot of blood, which suggests it was done while he was alive, or in the process of dying. I didn't have time to inspect the wounds, but I'd like to know if his limbs were hacked, sliced or surgically removed."

"I'm inclined to agree. I'll call the Director of Intelligence. They've had the case since Georgia. Did you recover anything?"

"Yeah..." I looked down the empty street, dimly lit by replicas of nineteenth-century gas lamps, and glanced in the mirror. There was nothing there but more empty street and more gas lamps. "I thought it was the Office of the Democratic Intelligence Network."

"Yes, well, as the Bard said, what's in a name? They're attached to the Five Eyes, as are we, so we cooperate."

"Right. In other news, I have a couple of presents for our forensic team."

"I thought you might. Is it his right hand?"

"Yes, sir, and a sample of the files."

"Good, Harry. Good work. I'll have someone collect them. Meanwhile, the job seems to have been done for us. So book yourself into a hotel in San Francisco and I'll be in touch in the next few hours."

I hung up and cruised down the Shoreline Highway, watching the smirking moon sink ever lower toward the horizon. At Manzanita I joined Highway 101 and let it carry me through the majestic trees that fringe the recreation area, and across the Golden Gate to the Presidio. There I called the Four Seasons and booked a room.

There was something playing on my mind as I cruised down Van Ness and turned into California Street at Nob Hill. I kept going over the dark living room, the dining room and the kitchen, the creaking stairs and the tidy, well-ordered den. I couldn't see anything in my mind, but my gut told me it was there; not upstairs, but somewhere between the living room and the kitchen.

Something that was wrong.

I could smell it. The voice in my head repeated it a couple of times, and I realized there had been a smell. I turned into Sansome Street, parked illegally outside the hotel, checked in and handed my keys to the valet parking valet along with twenty bucks. In the elevator I called Cobra and left a message for the brigadier, telling him where I was.

I had a long, hot shower, fantasizing that the scalding, soapy water could seep into my brain and wash away what I had seen.

When I climbed out of the shower my cell was ringing. I answered it with wet hands and water running down my face from my hair.

"Yeah."

"Harry, it's me, Jane..."

I went very still, ignoring the slow burn in my gut. "Hi, I was expecting the brigadier."

"Yes, I told him I'd call. I hope that's OK." She didn't sound ironic or sarcastic. "After..." She paused. "After Cabinda, we seemed to lose touch."

"That probably had something to do with my terrible timing. Every time I called you, you were out."

"I'm sorry about that, Harry."

"And when we did meet it was either in a briefing or a debriefing, and you always had to run afterwards."

"I'm sorry."

I shrugged. She couldn't see me, so I guess the gesture was for myself. "It's work. It's the way it goes. So who's coming for the package?"

"Don't be like that, Harry. I have apologized twice."

I took a deep breath and trailed water to the window overlooking the sparkling city. "I don't know what to say. Hell, I don't even know what to call you. It's always a helter-skelter ride with you. I never know from one turn to the next what to expect. One minute it's Marilyn Monroe, the next it's the girl next door and then it's the ice queen in a US Air Force uniform."

"That's unkind, but I guess I deserve it."

Her voice, the tone of her voice, made me soften and I couldn't stop a smile from entering mine. "I had my leg bitten off by a crocodile while rescuing you. Did you know that?"

"Yes, I know, Harry. It didn't actually bite it off..."

"It almost bit it off. A couple of inches higher and it could have been serious. Not a lot of guys would do that for a girl."

"Can you forgive me, or do I have to keep apologizing?"

"I shouldn't. But yeah, I guess I have to."

"I heard you met somebody. A doctor, in Wyoming."

I floundered a moment. "Yeah, I...we...yeah..."

"Buddy says you're thinking of resigning, and setting up a ranch out there."

"The brigadier has a big mouth."

"I almost hope you do, Harry; resign, I mean. Is she good for you?"

"I—I don't, I'm not ready for this—I'm not sure I'm r\
for this conversation."

I heard her sigh at the other end of the line. "I hope she ca\
help you escape from Al-Landy, from all the daemons."

"Yeah, well, I don't see it that way, Jane. Because the other possibility, the more likely possibility, is that I'll drag her down into hell with me. That's why guys like me live alone. Because women who are foolish enough to get involved end up getting burned, and the smart ones steer clear and don't answer their phones."

She took so long to answer I began to wonder if she'd hung up. Finally she said, "That's not what happened. This isn't the time or the place—"

"No, with you it never is, Jane."

"This job looks like it's done. I seem to recall we have an appointment in New York that's well overdue. Maybe, when you return home..."

She trailed off, leaving her meaning hanging in the air.

"Sure, but when I get there, are you going to disappear again, and hide behind the brigadier and the job?"

"No. I'm here in San Francisco. I am going to collect the package from you in half an hour. When the job is done, we'll meet in New York, I promise."

"That's two promises you owe me."

There was a long silence. Then, "I know, Harry. I haven't forgotten."

Scan the QR code below to purchase THE UNAVENGED.
Or go to: righthouse.com/the-unavenged

Made in the USA
Monee, IL
23 July 2025

21718323R00166